STRUGGLING TOWARD HOPE

A novel

BY ALLI CARTER CLOSE

COLORADO

Red Barn Publishing House
Monument, Colorado

Library of Congress Cataloging-In-Publication Data
Name: Carter Close, Alli, 1965- author.
Title: Struggling Toward Hope / A Novel, Alli Carter Close
Description: First Edition. | Colorado, 2021
Identifiers: ISBN 9798506142553 (e-book), 978-1-7372779-1-0 (paperback)
Subjects: Native Americans, 1860-1881—United States—Fiction |
Colorado—Fiction |
Meeker Massacre—Fiction.
Historical Fiction.

First Edition: December 2021

Printed in the United States of America
Jacket Photo: Denver Library Digital Collection, detail of the full image, The Denver Public Library, Western History Collection, [Call #].
Jacket Design by Alli Carter Close
Book Design by Alli Carter Close
Author photo by Casey BradleyGent, Snowshoe Studios

This is a work of fiction and is a product of the author's imagination.
This book has been printed in Book Antiqua font.

Table of Contents

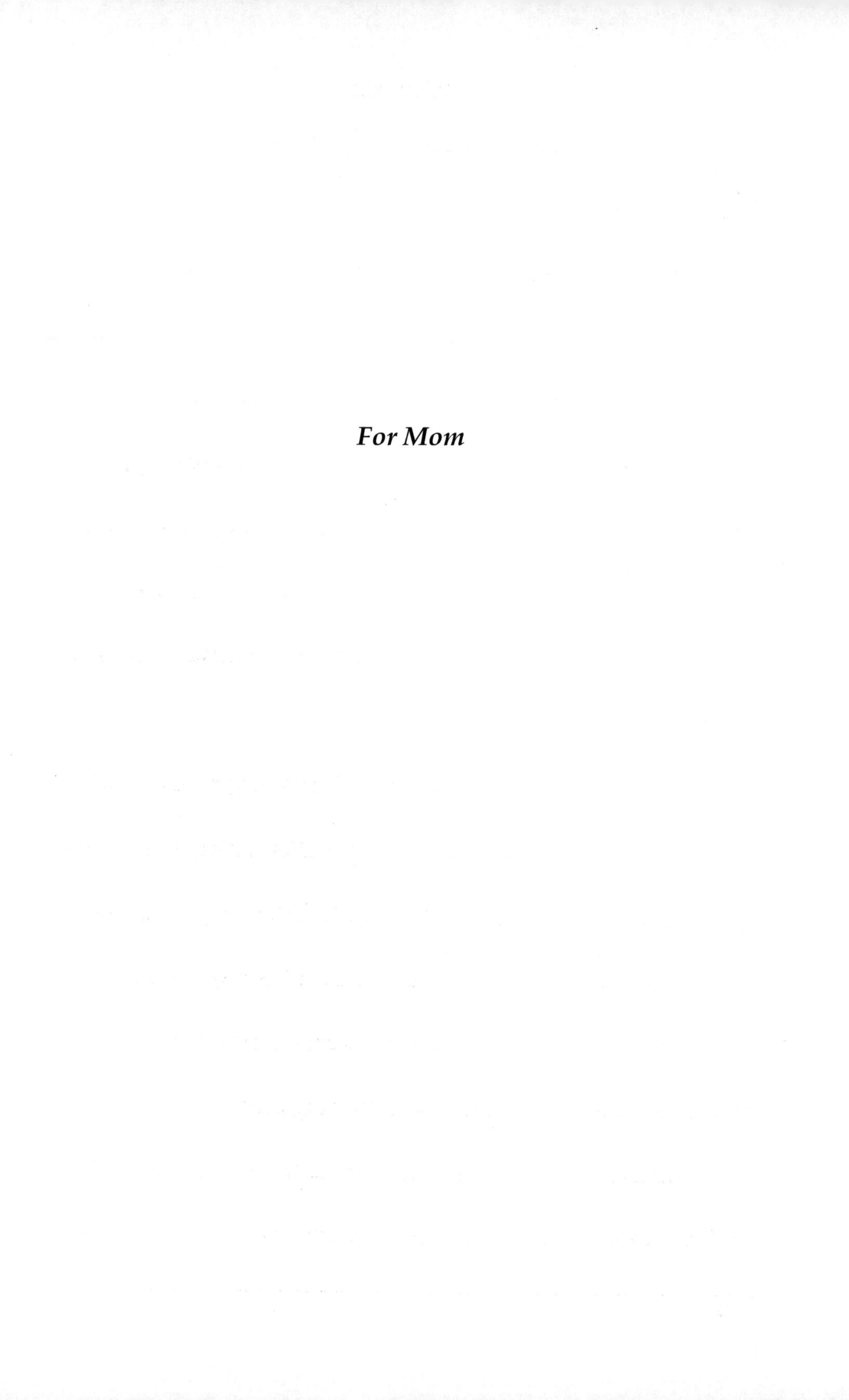

For Mom

Preface

This book started as an homage to my beautiful mother Geraldine Bernadette Battista, née Close. It was also my way for me to process her death after her six-year battle with dementia. This disease takes everything from the person who suffers under its terrible hold. It isn't just about losing memories, but about changes to and loss of personality, history, understanding, and personal knowledge. Any person with dementia must suffer incomprehensibly, but those watching and caring for them battle with understanding and sadness too.

That was where I found myself in the spring of 2018 after my mother's death. I took long walks through local parks including Fox Run Regional Park in Colorado Springs. Here I found what I thought to be numerous culturally modified trees that symbolized Native American's connection to the land. The trees, explained as wayfinding signs, are controversial—some people claim these trees were created by the Ute tribes to point to the best campsites and to identify gravesites of the deceased. If these were modified as wayfinding tools, there is no one here today to care for these trees. I wondered why. Thus began the journey that culminates in this book.

To my horror, I discovered that these people, the true natives of this land, were unceremoniously removed from the area after years of trying to find peace with the Americans. And with their removal, so went much of their culture. A number of Native American cultures lived near one another in the Pikes Peak region, including Ute and Arapaho, to name a few. Although today these Nations exist in different regions of the United States, none remain in the Pikes Peak region to care for the land. Indeed, many of us who live in the region thought our homes had been built on "virgin" land—land where no homes had ever been erected and no people had ever lived. That isn't the case. Indigenous people lived and worked in the region for centuries before European settlers arrived. This is just to say it is important for us to know a little bit about those people who came before us. In my case, in the shadow of Pike's Peak, the Ute tribes lived all along the front range.

*

The character of Kit Carson as presented in this book has largely been created within the confines of my imagination as representative of several concepts: adventure, manifest destiny, dementia.... A special note to the reader here: Although Kit Carson lived from 1809 to 1868, this book "tweaks" this timeline. I've done this deliberately for several reasons. The main reason is that many have heard of Kit Carson: an explorer who held the ideals of the American West. I needed someone well known who readers could identify with, while putting the pieces together as to how many Native American tribes were removed from their land. For those who are familiar with Kit Carson's autobiography, some events will be similar to those about which he has had written, albeit not the same time frame. The character presented within these pages takes actions that ensure the Utes are removed from their land, stripped of their heritage and their identity, just as dementia strips its victims of their memory and identity.

Dementia is opportunistic: researchers believe dementia might result from deposits of a protein called tau on the brain's neuropathways leaving the affected nerves inoperable. In his time, Kit Carson, as well as all the miners, trappers, and traders who flooded west, opportunistically took advantage of the lands they mistakenly believed were theirs for the taking. Those trails, by the way, were used to create many of the roadways upon which we travel today.

The disease takes every chance it can to negatively influence its victim. It causes people to lose their sense of knowledge, their memory, their identity, until all that is left is a shell of the person they once were. Similarly, the Ute—indeed many indigenous people of America—lost all they had.

I was asked why the Ute characters are fictional and Kit Carson is based upon a historical person. Although hardly any autobiographical, first-person accounts of the Ute Nation in the 1800s exist, Chaska's character isn't entirely fictional. She is based upon the great Chief Ouray, who worked for peace until his passing. Chaska conveys the hope for peace and the anguish the Natives felt as their culture and land were being removed from them. If Chaska is the peaceful one, working hard to keep her tribe safe, Ahwatt represents those who disagreed with Ouray's ways. There were those who wanted to fight the Americans intruding onto their lands. When they tried peaceful negotiations, such as treaties, Americans ignored the promises. When the Indians fought back, they were considered too dangerous to be around any of the Americans trespassing upon their territories. By the way, there is only one book written about Ouray in the Pikes Peak Library system that isn't a children's book. It can be viewed in my favorite part of the Penrose Library, in the Carnegie-Special Collections. Jack Luther Benham's Ouray is available for viewing by special request. Chaska's husband, Kaib, is also based on a historical person. The Americans called him Jack, though his name was Kaib, and he too worked tirelessly for peace.

I've written most of the Ute characters in a voice that might be one we recognize today. That is to say, these characters speak as if talking with me or you. Perhaps they truly spoke in this manner, but the reasoning for their voice is this: I want those who read the book to know that these people of history are just like us. They are mothers and fathers, sisters and brothers, who are searching for a peaceful happy life. Just like us.

In writing this book, my goal has been simply to educate people living today about those who came before us. I don't think it's enough to consider generally that Native Americans lived on this land before Europeans came here. Instead, we should know a little bit more about them, to humanize our understanding of them.

Struggling Toward Hope is not intended to make anyone feel guilty for the lives they live or the places upon which they live and work. Instead, my aim in writing the book is this: to provide educational material for all who wish to learn.

The genocide of the Ute Nation—indeed, of all Native Americans—and the disease of dementia might not be linked in your mind, but they are in mine. Both are insidious, evil, and should have been stopped far sooner. For that reason, a portion of the proceeds from the sale of this book will go to the Ute Indian Tribe Education Department, Ute Tribe Education | UITED Home, and the Alzheimer's Foundation (http://www.alz.org).

Book 1

Chapter 1

Our Walking Story (Autumn, 1860)

Mawic suddenly makes a fist with her right hand and holds it to the sky—the sign to stop. We're traveling to our winter camp, single file behind her. Mawic's horse Kyra, a dark brown pony, flicks her normally long and flowing tail back and forth. Her ears stand up straight, pointing forward. Snorting, she paws at the ground and shakes her head so that I can see the splash of white on her nose.

A loud, drawn-out whinny from a far-away horse resonates up from the valley. It's asking, *where are you?* Kyra makes a low nicker in her throat. Hooves are pounding the dirt trail coming from the basin where our group is headed.

"Who is it?" I ask Mawic, sitting atop my own pony.

Auntie—we call her Mawic—looks over at me but stays silent.

The others in our group sidle up next to auntie and me, spreading out so the rider won't be able to pass through. The ponies we ride are packed down with all our belongings. They drag dismantled teepees and poles behind them, so it would be difficult to move everyone off the trail to hide in the forest.

Our tribe's men left early this morning and would be too far away to help. Though our winter camp has always been situated in the same low valleys where the hills meet the plains, the men go ahead to make sure there is still a good food source, and the place is safe. My brother worries we won't have food. But my brother has a habit of making up stories to suit his needs, so I don't trust him.

"Cahvah," says Mawic. It's an Indian pony coming toward us. The short gait gives it away. The problem is this: Mountain men who come to our land and trap beaver have become accustomed to riding our horses, so we can't be sure if the rider is friendly or not.

Still urging his mount forward, the horse and rider come around the bend. When he looks up and realizes our presence, he stops short, leaning way back on the horse, pulling the reins tight.

"Aha," I shout involuntarily when I see them. I'm not sure if it is from apprehension or comfort.

I breathe a sigh of relief. It's a boy, one of ours.

He looks to be maybe thirteen years old and is riding bareback. Must have had to get onto the horse quickly. *This won't be good,* I think. He can barely catch his breath and is shaking from excitement. "They sent me," he says on an exhale.

The horse is lathered with white sweat on her chest and neck. The boy scrubs at his face. I recognize him. His name is Po, the young man who won so many of our pony races last summer.

Just as Mawic moves forward to talk with the boy, flakes of snow gently fall around us, but now that seems to be a secondary concern.

"What do you mean, boy? Who sent you?" auntie asks.

The men, he tells us.

A look of fear flashes across Mawic's face, but she quickly composes herself. She's scared but won't show it.

The boy takes one big inhale and seems to have found his breath. "Our winter camp…it's gone," he sputters. "Get off this trail now and go through the woods. Otherwise, the trespassers will find you."

This has never happened to us—not being able to walk freely. The trail is a welcoming reminder of who we are, the Ute people. I've walked it and many others since I was a little girl and so has Mawic. Our footprints are mingled with those of our ancestors on dirt paths that zigzag from the mountains to the plains. Tree markers made long ago show us the way to camps or to fresh water.

The teenager continues telling us, "Trappers followed our trails into the valleys. Loads of them. They set up their winter camps where ours is usually."

Took our winter camp? I think. I'm surprised the trappers would come that far into the mountains. Winter winds skim over the valleys where we camp, howling down from the mountains and onto the plains. They would have to leave the streams where the beaver are plentiful and trek into the mountains to find verdant valleys.

Mawic is quiet, but I ask, "Why didn't our men fight them?"

"There are too many," the boy responds. "They're maybe two hundred merikac" — our word for Americans.

I can tell auntie is trying to remain calm and figure this out, but she must be terrified.

I'm worried, biting at my bottom lip. The forest around us is dense with tall pines and lots of low brush. It's a safe place to be in a time of trouble like this. But it may not be possible to get through it with the animals packed down with so much.

Mawic looks to the elders, who meet her eyes but don't have a satisfactory answer to this predicament. Then she turns to me.

A smile curls around her lips. "You're thinking about how we get out of this mess, aren't you?" she asks.

I smile too though I'm not sure why. Maybe it will calm my children if I look outwardly confident.

"We'll be all right," she says in a calm voice. Her answer is more comforting than she will ever know.

What would Pia—my mother—have done at such a time?

While we've been contemplating our next move, the snow has picked up. It lands and sticks to me. *Best to be in the woods at a time like this anyway.*

We're trying to make the best of a bad situation: The tree canopy will protect us from the snow.

"Let's find a camp for the night in the woods," she says decisively. "It'll give us time to think and make a plan for tomorrow."

Chapter 2

Leaving Missouri
(Autumn, 1860)

Kit pretends not to notice the man eyeing him. After walking through a cold drizzle Kit is finally meeting up with the crew that will make their way west. The men stand along a dirt road in Franklin's sleepy downtown. All of them look to Kit like they haven't seen a bathtub in a while. The trail leader, his name is Virgil—a broad-shouldered man with a shock of red hair—has already agreed to bring him along.

This man Bridger hasn't taken his eyes off Kit since he met up with the group. He circles Kit once, then again, looking him up and down. The man smells of campfire smoke and sweat. Kit tugs on his right ear, a nervous tick he hopes to break on this trip.

Bridger stops pacing, and stands still, his boots caked with mud. He points his thumb toward Kit. "This scrawny kid comin' with us?" he asks.

Kit squints into the last rays of summer sunshine, raising his hands to his eyebrows to see the elderly trapper better. The man is either really old or just seen too much for one lifetime. Horizontal lines run across his forehead. Deep, reddish-colored bags lie under his eyes. His deerskin breeches are dark brown and stained with dirt; they are also ripped at the knees and cracked open in spots. One leg has a length of fringe down the side, but the other has only a few strings intact.

Virgil heaves his broad shoulders up, then lets them drop. He looms over Kit, though most people do, then pinches the bridge of his nose and claps a paw-sized hand on Kit's shoulder. "Yes, he's signed on with us—and he'll pull his weight. Right, boy?"

Kit nods once, not meeting either man's eyes.

Satisfied with Kit's answer, Virgil sidles up close to Bridger. They stand toe to toe. "Bridger, mind your business. Don't start problems before we've even left town." Bridger snickers then picks up his bag and slinks off. Kit can hear him talking out loud to no one: "Somethin' ain't right with that boy. I can feel it in my bones."

Kit's seven burly companions wear matching unkempt beards; they've stuffed scraggly hair into fraying beaver caps. Kit can't guess their ages, but he considers them all much older than himself. *I got just as much right to be here as the others.*

Determined to prove himself, Kit plans to work harder and outpace all the others. All he's got is a shotgun thieved from his older brother and a meager bag of possessions. *These won't slow me down none.*

One of the seven, the men call him Doc, tells Kit to pay no mind to Bridger. He takes a quick hop onto his saddle then nods his head for Kit to follow. Kit grabs his gear and starts walking. A few of the other men mount horses, and several sit atop wagon seats driving oxen, but Kit can't afford such luxuries. He'll be walking the entire trail. Kit notices a few of the others will be walking too. Unfortunately, one of those is Bridger.

***

For the first five days, all Kit can see to the horizon are golden grasses waving with the breeze. No animals, no people, save those in the caravan. The dry desert trail and relentless dusty breeze have parched and enlarged Kit's throat. It's been hours since Kit tried to take a swig of water. The last time, Kit took a big drink from his sack, but it just came right back up and left him coughing.

Each man carries his own water.

Virgil rides up to Kit. "Once we see the Arkansas, we'll be all right," he promises. He looks down from his mount but doesn't say more. Kit can feel Bridger's eyes on his back. The old trapper walks up behind him and sneers. "I heard men has been so thirsty on this trail, they cut off the ears of their mules and sucked out the blood."

Kit ignores him.

A suspicious-looking man named Joseph Doyle sniggers. He and Bridger seem to always be up to something. Doyle's gaze never quite seems to focus. It could be because his eyes look out in two different directions, like a lizard.

The trail leader shakes his head, clucking for his horse to move.

***

Tonight, Kit comes off the trail dusty and hot. Normally, he sets up next to the fire; but there's no need for that this evening. Instead, he flops down on his dingy bedroll—a heavy, wool blanket pilfered from his mother's closet. He's lain the blanket near the chuck wagon: far enough away from the others to discourage conversation. But he looks up just in time to see Bridger sauntering his way. "I's gonna sleep right here, boy," he smirks, then drops his bag on Kit's bedroll. Leaning down to where Kit sits on the ground, he commands: "Tell me your story, Kitty." Ever the faithful follower, Doyle stands right behind Bridger, all smiles and with at least one eye on Kit.

Kit doesn't say a word, just pulls the blanket out from under Bridger's pack then walks to the far side of the fire. Doyle nudges Bridger, saying, "Rumor has it, the kid's a runaway. He gots a bounty on his head."

"Do tell," says Bridger. "Thought he looked familiar. That kid's in trouble up to his eyeballs."

Kit pretends not to hear them. No use explaining that his no-good stepfather bound him to a saddle maker. After two years of forced slavery, and brothers constantly needling him, Kit had had enough. The only good thing about that job? It was where he learned about the treks headed west.

***

Men used to come into the saddlery all the time, telling stories of western adventures. It takes time to fix a saddle, and that time was well spent spinning tall tales. They had Kit hankering to pull up roots and leave town. *Ain't nothin' keepin' me here anyhow,* he had thought. It would be good to get out from under his brothers' constant brawls and teasing—they called him the *token child* or *marginal boy*—nicknames conjured when Kit never grew taller than the unforgivable height he had achieved when he was barely fifteen. One trapper, a tall guy named Beckwourth, used to come in claiming he was the chief of the Crow Nation. Said he'd been on his own since he was a teenager. He told bold tales, probably a bunch of hogwash, but the man had an honest-to-goodness Wyeth saddle. Tooled leather softer than any Kit had felt. Wide fenders. Real stirrups and saddle strings. *Them's hard to come by for a trapper who ain't successful,* Kit had thought. The lure of the West was even stronger after hearing the man talk. Like the time he saved his captain from going over a waterfall on the Gunnison. Or the one about keeping a bear at bay while the others in his party snuck away to safety. Beckwourth's stories were awfully exciting.

A month ago, Kit signed on to this caravan and never looked back. He figured it was best to just work hard, keep to himself, and stay out of trouble until the bounty expired. Heck, most of the men heading west had bounties on their heads. The odds of one of the men in the group turning him in weren't great—unless he crossed them. *Just three more years,* Kit reminded himself daily. *Then I'll be free*. Maybe Bridger would forget about the warrant once he got moving down the trail.

***

Walking that trail there wasn't anything to do but think. The footpath, wide enough for wagons to travel single file, stretches all the way to the horizon, giving his mind time to wander. Low lying scrub grows along browning grasses. Deep, purple-colored thistles stand above it all. Now and then, Kit distractedly bends to feel the softness of wooly lamb's ears that grow here and there.

Would have been the same if he was riding a horse. Since he couldn't afford one, he puts one boot in front of the other, trying to keep up with those on horseback as best he can.

Kit thought of his ma. It broke his heart to think he might never see her again. Nobody knew he'd left Franklin. When he didn't show up for dinner that first night, she'd no doubt been worried sick. Anytime Ma got to worrying she'd sit in the rocking chair out on the little wooden porch.

Probably there still. Once she got herself into town and saw the posters for his arrest, she'd be worried sick. *Gosh darn. Wish things could 'a been different*. She has loads more children, but Kit is her youngest.

"How old are you, son?"

Kit hasn't heard Bridger at first. Too busy looking out at the scenery and dreaming of Ma's cooking—oh, those fruit pies!

But Bridger being Bridger, he walks up close to Kit, knocking him off balance. The old geezer hovers above Kit as he picks himself back up, reaching for his ear, tugging it to calm himself.

"Ever been away from your mama before?" the man asks, laughing a bit. Doyle stands just off to the side of Bridger, possibly looking Kit's way. From where he stands, Doyle's eyes are both pointing away from Kit.

George Simpson, another seasoned trapper who keeps in step with Bridger, is glaring at Kit, both of his eyes firmly planted on him. The man's jaw is clenched tight. Both of

Bridger's chums stand on either side of Kit, who works hard to keep his eyes forward. The trail leader is too far in front to save him this time. When Kit starts walking, Doyle stumbles forward, blocking his route. Bridger runs into Kit's path. "I said, when did you start drawing breath?"

Kit has no choice but to stop dead in his tracks.

"I'm fifteen."

"Fifteen? Why, you're just a babe!" Bridger jeers while the other two trappers chuckle. "From now on, you need to stay close to us"—grabbing at Kit's arm to bring him closer to him. The man is too strong for Kit, no matter how much Kit tries to wriggle free.

"Don't struggle now, boy. We ain't gonna hurt ya. Not too much anyways," says Simpson, his hand held high, readied for a good solid punch to Kit's middle. All Kit can do is close his eyes and let out a low, slow moan in anticipation of the pain. But none comes.

When Kit opens his eyes, he sees a horse's head hanging quietly at Simpson's shoulder with the arm that Kit had anticipated delivering a frightful blow wrapped gingerly around the horse's neck. Bridger is trying his darndest to look innocent. Simpson has a look of fear on his face. Doyle has his face pointed up to the sky. The horse is connected to Doc, who had been riding unseen behind the men and had witnessed the entire scuffle.

"Move along," is all he says, eyeing the trappers. Bridger starts to walk away, but not before he's scolded by the doctor. "Not you. Bridger, you and your buddies can walk along with me. Get movin', boy."

Kit stalks away quickly, thankful for this man's intervention. It seems Bridger has a few enemies amongst the trappers.

***

One night as the group finishes dinner, it must be Doyle's turn to stir the pot: He sidles up next to Kit and urges him to drink. "Sit down and have a swig! This here's the finest Taos Lightning this side a' the Mississippi River."

Kit merely shakes his head: No.

When Virgil makes eye contact with Doyle, Kit takes the opportunity to stand and head toward his bedroll. He can't risk landing on the man's bad side.

"Leave him be," says Simpson, who then uses the opportunity to head into one of his stories.

Simpson stays close to Bridger and Doyle but can obviously think for himself too. The seasoned trapper tells a good yarn around the fire. Even Kit chuckles at the man's stories.

***

The morning of the fifth day, Kit is walking along the trail and dreaming of his ma's cookin' when he hears, "You missin' your mama, boy?"

Kit looks over to see the camp cook driving the chuck wagon. If he thought Bridger looked old, this man is an antique. The wagon's slow-moving oxen amble quietly along. He hadn't realized the chuck wagon was so close. Normally, he can hear that rickety-looking kitchen-on-wheels rattling, but he had been dreaming about the creek in back of his house. Sometimes after dinner, he and his brothers would jump into the cool water. A rope tied many years ago swung them out into the middle, where the current carried them downstream. They'd float on their backs until dark, then climb out to the bank and walk home barefoot.

"Nah," Kit lies.

"How old are ya?" Cookie asks.

Everybody calls the man Cookie; Kit never caught his name. He's an old codger, rough around the edges, with a snarly look in his eyes.

"Old enough."

"Come on, boy. Just making conversation. I been out here for years, and these ox ain't talkers." A smile curls up at the sides of Cookie's lips. He sits in the driver's seat behind the slow-moving oxen. Kit easily keeps pace with them, walking even slower than normal.

"I'm sixteen," Kit says, hoping he sounds manly. "Left home to get in on the adventure."

Cookie nods.

Kit had noticed early on Bridger and Cookie don't like one another. At chowtime, they eye one another and move in wide circles around each other. Having a friend like Cookie, Kit suddenly realizes, might be a good thing on the trail.

Kit must have slowed himself because he has to trot to keep up with the wagon. Could be the constant wind that tries to push the group back toward home, blowing the sandy gravel into Kit's face, planting itself in every nook and crevice. Is the wind warning him to turn around? In spite of the gusts, the hot, Kansas summer sun has blistered his bare head. It's burned so bad flecks of his scalp come off in his fingernails whenever he scratches too hard.

"Hop on up here, boy," Cookie says. "What's your name again? Kit? What kind 'a name is that?"

Kit grabs for the wooden frame then easily swings his legs up onto the wagon. Once he's seated next to Cookie he says, "It's short for Christopher."

Cookie nods. "You know how to cook, Kit?"

Kit mumbles a faint yes, fearing he'll be made fun of yet again. Men aren't supposed to cook, except on camps like this. Back home, Kit loved to be in the kitchen watching his mama cook. He would bring in kindling then stoke the oven's fire. While it got hot, his mama mixed flour, a little sugar and salt. She'd let Kit cut in the lard. Then mix in a little buttermilk left over from making butter. Ma would set out a kitchen towel, flour it and pat the biscuit dough atop it. She'd use an old tin can, pushing it into the soft dough to cut the biscuits before baking them. While they cooked, she and he would take turns cranking the butter maker until the cream fluffed into butter. Meanwhile, he felt safe sharing his stories and dreams with her. If he was the only one in the kitchen with her, she'd give him a hot biscuit straight from the oven and slather fresh butter on it before his brothers took them all.

"I need some help," the old cook says.

Kit rolls his eyes instinctively. Another apprenticeship where he'd get treated like a slave.

Seeming to read his mind, Cookie shakes his head. "Not no damn servant boy. I need help fixing the fire and getting the grub out in the evenin'. I'll pay ya." Kit grows excited at the prospect of being paid cold hard cash in exchange for serving a few measly dinners. Not sure how to act, Kit nods his head thoughtfully. He'd like to bargain for his wages but doesn't know where to start. Too nervous to make a fool of himself, he settles for just knowing he'll have pocket money at the end of the trail.

***

At day seven Andrew Broadus removes his rifle from the wagon and accidentally discharges it, shooting himself in the arm. Broadus is a strong, reliable trapper, but when his arm begins to blacken, the wagon train halts for the day.

Kit finally gets to see what's in the long wooden box Doc's been conveying tied to his saddle all this time. The wooden case, as it turns out, is a surgical box. Doc opens it to display a set of knives and a long metal saw, all stacked neatly in blood red velvet casing. Doc pinches along the length of

Broadus' arm as the injured man grimaces in pain. Doc confirms the bones have been shattered and verifies the arm must be removed.

Broadus is carried down to a trickle of a stream and propped up against one of the nearby cottonwoods. No easy task because the man must weigh two hundred and fifty pounds. Kit gets stuck holding onto his middle, which is squishy and fleshy. There aren't any good handholds, so Kit is forced to put his hands and forearms under the man's back. Broadus' stomach wobbles back and forth like jelly as the group makes their way down to the streambed. The wind has gone still. Kit smells the drying grasses all around—musky, like yeasty bread. The men lay Broadus in a crook of the tree—the cottonwood's roots meander and extend above ground, creating a nook that can hold his head like a hard pillow.

Kit is asked to make a fire along the sandy beach of the stream. He collects sticks and pieces of the cotton dropped by the tree earlier in the season.

It is decided the arm should be cut off at the elbow. Broadus sucks down a good quantity of Taos Lightning given to him by old nosy body, Bridger.

"Ready?" asks the man doctoring the arm. Virgil and Doc seem to be the only ones ready. A length of what looks like a belt is secured just above the elbow. Virgil begins turning a screw that tightens the belt, squeezing Broadus' arm. The men have surrounded their ailing colleague, all holding different body parts, preparing for the inevitable kicks and thrusts as the saw bears down.

Bridger stuffs a rolled towel fast between Broadus' teeth. Kit takes in a deep breath and holds tight to Broadus' good arm. Doc reaches for a scalpel to cut away the flesh just above the elbow. The flap of skin hangs down alongside blood pouring from the cut. Kit has to look away as his vision goes fuzzy. Doc reaches for a Caitlin knife and begins to cut away the muscle on Broadus' underarm. The curved knife is so sharp that Doc removes most of it in one swipe. The bloody muscle falls to the ground; several of the men groan. It reminds Kit of the infrequent portions of beef his ma cooked. All this time, Broadus has been howling in pain; it takes all they have to hold him in place. Kit is practically laying on Broadus' good arm.

Doc grabs the saw from his surgical box and begins to hack at the elbow until the arm is severed. Then he holds on to the bloody, sinewy mass of Broadus' upper arm while sawing back and forth across the bone until the stump falls to the ground. The sound of bone breaking makes Kit's stomach flip, but he retains his composure. A quick peek at the elbow, where Broadus' flesh hangs off white bone, causes him to yak once. He swallows it down before any of the others notice.

Virgil removes a metal wagon wheel bolt and stuffs it into the fire. When the bolt is red hot, the doctor uses his fingers to scoop tar from inside a spare wagon wheel then smears it over the wound. Broadus howls in pain. "Easy, easy," Bridger says, and all the men hold on tight. *Maybe Bridger has a good side?* Kit thinks…For some reason, he can't look away. But the next moment, he hears, "Hold him, men…" Cookie passes a pair of old tongs to the trail leader, who extracts the heated bolt from the fire. Then the leader turns and presses the hot bolt to the tar covering the wound. The heat quickly binds the tar to the open flesh, and Broadus shrieks in pain. The towel between his teeth falls to the ground.

Then, suddenly, he falls quiet.

"Must 'a passed out," Kit hears.

While Broadus is carefully laid to the ground, the stump arm is secured with an old shirt that has been ripped into rags.

***

The men settle in for a few days to see if Broadus will pull through. Cookie sets up the chuck wagon just on the bluff of the overhang where Broadus had surgery. He remains in the same spot although the men collected dried branches from the tree to make a lean-to. Some of the men make lean-tos of their own, spreading out between where Broadus has been set up and the wagon. There are enough dead branches from the trees to make a few shelters. Kit couldn't be bothered making a shelter. That is until the rain comes. Although the days had been hot and dusty up to this point, once the men settled in for a few days, the rain decided to visit. Every afternoon, he watched the clouds gather toward the west and move their way. At first, it just came in a mist, but then picked up so that the drops were so fat and so many that he couldn't stay dry. He tries to stand as close to the cottonwoods as possible to find a bit of relief.

At the same time, he is so thirsty that he often tries to stick his head out, lean back and open his mouth to get as much water as possible. The rain dribbled onto his face, but he didn't care. He was so parched that what little water got into his mouth, he thought he might not be able to swallow it as his throat is so dry.

Some of the men, including Doc, dance in the rain with their mouths hanging open too. Cookie scurries around the wagon, grabbing pots and pans to set out and collect the water.

Kit learned the hard way the rain will go wherever is easiest for it. He'd had to seek cover under the wagon where he got absolutely soaking wet when rivulets of water, big thick trails of it, meandered through cracks in the parched ground running down to the nearly extinct stream.

But, when the hail started, he was bombarded regardless of his protection. It flew from the sky nearly sideways, as if someone up above was pelting him as hard as they could. It hit him everywhere—his ears, his eyes—and it even went down his shirt.

The storms lasted only about fifteen minutes at the most each day, so there was little chance the nearby stream could gain any strength.

Kit is tasked with collecting large rocks from along the near dry stream to build a sturdier fire pit. It is staged next to the wagon so that Cookie can use it, and the men can sleep nearby in the evenings. He collects the cotton that blows off the trees at this time of year to store and use as fire starter.

Cookie keeps Kit busy cleaning cooking tools, organizing—and reorganizing—the wagon's many tin cans. He finds more bits and bobs, tiny cupboards and stolen-away items than he can believe. Kit already had known the back portion of the wagon folded down to make a flat work surface for him and Cookie to work. When it was folded down, it revealed cupboards that held most of the cook's everyday tools of the trade—spatulas, spoons, forks, and of course his set of knives. But then he found so much more. Climbing into the box of the wagon, Kit found even more cupboards. These held tins of peaches, pears and a few of corn. Although Cookie liked to hang his Dutch oven and skillets over the side of the wagon, Kit found even more of them in a variety of sizes, all darkened black from use.

"You cleanin' or leanin' up there, boy?" Cookie yelled up to him one day. Kit swung a leg over the wagon and hopped down holding one of the cans of peaches he'd found. "Hey, Cookie, why ain't we never had none a' these for dinner?" he asked.

Cookie just chuckled and shook his head. “I been savin’ them for a special occasion. Grab a few more a’ them cans and I’ll show you how I make my peach cobbler.” Kit just smiled at the thought of a sumptuous dessert.

True to his word, Cookie had Kit mix up some biscuit batter, but let him put in more sugar than usual. They hung the Dutch oven over the fire, emptied the cans of peaches in and let them get bubbly and gooey. Kit spooned the sweet biscuit batter over the fruit and covered the pan. By dinner time, when he lifted the lid, the biscuit mixture had browned nicely. Some of the peach juices had run up over the dough in pink and orange streaks. When he and Cookie served it up to the others, there wasn’t any talking, just happy mouths chewing and enjoying the cobbler.

While Kit and Cookie cleaned the dishes and put all the utensils away, Kit couldn’t help but smile. This was one of the best nights he could remember on this trip. Even better, Bridger had left him alone.

***

Kit's mouth is full of dust. Again. No matter where he walks in the pack, the man or horse in front of him kicks up enough dust to make him want to cry. Sometimes Cookie lets him ride in the wagon. "We gonna make it?" Kit asks when he gets one of these wonderful rides. The accident with Broadhus set the caravan back a few days; like everyone else, Kit is anxious to get to the Arkansas.

The hills roll endlessly to the horizon, never changing even though the group is traveling twenty miles each day. In Missouri, the trail started in the lush green banks of the Mississippi River. When Kit began this walk, his boots stepped around puddles of freshly fallen rain that created a slimy muddy walkway. The heavy oxen didn't have a problem, their giant hooves dug through the mud, but the wheels of the wagon they pulled weren't so lucky, sliding sideways on the downhills and threatening to slide the wagon sideways. Farther from Kit's hometown, the trail became less damp. The tamped-down earth felt almost soft to walk on. The farther west the caravan has traveled the drier the conditions have become. The trail is dry and cracked and stony gray. The small particulates dust up at the least breeze.

Cookie nods in answer to Kit's question, but he won't meet Kit's eyes. "Why don't ya get out and walk a bit?" Before Kit could register Cookie's request he was unceremoniously made to walk. Kit can't figure out what's bothering the generally easygoing cook. He'd seen too much in his days on earth to be bothered by too much.

As Kit walks, he's soon mesmerized by the green and gold grasses waltzing in the wind, slow, like Ma and Pa used to do. Before. Heat shimmers on the horizon and blurs his vision. Yet far off he can make out what looks to be a large billow of cotton floating in midair. Of course, he can recognize clouds. But that's not what he sees exactly. These are closer to the ground, appearing dull colored, not reflecting the sun like a cloud might. Kit stops walking altogether when he realizes what he sees. Yes! Apparently, Bridger has made the connection too because he starts yelling, "Saved! We're saved!"

Dropping his rucksack, the busybody dances a jig, leaping and smiling through yellowed teeth. Twirling around first Simpson and then Kit, the man looks mad.

Kit can feel the other men's apprehension melt into the sky. There are five cottony billows, all willing to share a bit of water. Enough to allow them to get them to the river alive.

"Another two days and you'll be there," the wagon driver says. "Look for them trees."

Sure enough, after another two days of travel, Kit sees them: big cottonwoods that he was told will flank the river. Leaves that still hold on to their green color fluttering from the dark branches off in the distance.

As the caravan approaches the stand of trees and the river, Kit sees lush green in a strip that cuts up the gray dry ground all around like a zipper. Tall cottonwoods with trunks so big around it would take three of the trappers holding hands to reach all the way around them. The thick trunks are furrowed into ridges and gray as the trail he's been walking. High above him, maybe eighty feet up, branches sway in the unending breeze, sending long slender leaves aflutter. The sprawling branches provide what seemed like unending shade from the brutal sunshine.

“This is my fifth trip along the Santa Fe. Each time I get to these trees my heart finds happiness,” said Virgil, who has ridden up next to where Kit stands.

“How old do you think these trees are?” Kit asks.

“Oh boy,” he says, scratching at his scraggly beard and rubbing his chin back and forth while he thinks. “Must be upwards to a hundred years,” Virgil says finally.

Farther along the river Indians are making camp. The first Kit has ever seen. The caravan keeps its distance, choosing to camp upstream of the Indians.

Kit can imagine the fresh, cold water of the river. Just like the creek back home. He drops his bag and walks waist deep into that flow, shoes and all. He lies back into the cool water and floats along with dapples of sunshine intermingling with shade. Some of the others have waded into the water, pant legs hitched up as far as tanned hide can go. Their legs and feet are so white, like the color of clouds. Others lead their horses down the bank for a drink. Oh, that water makes his sunburned skin and head feel so much better. Heck, it seems to make everything better.

***

For a few weeks, the trail follows the river with spots of roaring rapids then clear water lightly flowing over smooth pebbles. On either side of the river is parched earth, but right here along that waterway, Kit feels like he's back home. The ground is muddy and the plants along the shore are green. Shade from the big old cottonwoods keeps them enormously cooler than walking along through the open prairie.

Doc and Virgil take their horses to the river each night and watch as the animals go in up to their knees in the cool water, drinking their fill. Cookie and Kit unhitch the oxen every day.

"Take Matilda down for a drink, would'ya?"

Kit groans as the thought of directing the ox who was named after Cookie's ma. She's so ornery and stubborn. If she gets the better of Kit, the men will laugh at him. So instead, he quickly grabs the other two around the halters. "I've already got Louise and Sarah," Kit yells to Cookie. Neither of them likes to walk Matilda, but the other two are docile as puppies. Kit learned that Louise was his sister's name, God rest her soul. The old man said Sarah was "the best darned painted lady this side of the Rockies." Kit couldn't imagine why some gal would want to paint herself. What color would she use anyhow?

All along the route to the river, the oxen ate the dry golden grasses without complaint. But now that there are cool, water-filled green stalks everywhere, Matilda would try to make a beeline for the grass. Kit looks back to see Cookie scowling, but he just smiles.

Most nights, the wagon train stops before all the others. Once the oxen are watered and fed, Kit pickets them together then gets to work on dinner. He's in charge of collecting kindling and splitting wood for the evening fire. Cookie calls out the night's menu: "Makin' beans and corn bread tonight!"

That is Kit's signal to start hunting through the cupboards of the chuck wagon for the ingredients. "Get them taters in water," Cookie commands. "Didn't hear nothing about taters," Kit grumbles under his breath. "What?" the old man asks. Kit doesn't answer, just grabs the potatoes. After fetching a pot of river water, he does a quick scrub and then settles the lid on tightly over the pot. He sets up the three-legged contraption, hooks the pot to the chain just near enough to the flames for it to heat up. Kit can hear the water boiling in the big pot—no need to peek inside.

When Cookie realized Kit could bake, he shows him how to use the Dutch oven to make biscuits. Kit dips a cup into flour just like Ma, mixes in soda, then cuts rounds that he lines on the bottom of the blackened cast iron pot. He nestles the pot in the coals, then pulls it out just as the tops of the biscuits get browned and crunchy. He enjoys the work; it keeps him away from Bridger, who has gotten to calling him Little Mary, mocking him for helping the cook.

***

A month into the walk, Kit sees the brown adobe walls of the fort. The building isn't like anything he has seen before. Squared off on all four sides, the walls look like somebody made a thick, flat mud pie and stuck it upright in the grass. As he approaches, anxious thoughts swirl in his mind. Would men be awaiting his arrival, wanting to arrest him and bring him home? Maybe Bridger will collect the ransom money by letting on he knows the runaway. Brief waves of fear nauseate his stomach. Sweat trickles down his forehead.

The fort occupies the crown of a low hill overlooking the Arkansas River. Wildflowers and grasses grow knee high and wave along with the tall grasses in the flat fields that surround the building. Far off toward the west, Kit can see the Rocky Mountains, but here the land is mostly flat. Here and there, Indians have set up teepees to trade with the men who frequent this place. Kit walks toward the fort and decides to stay in the shadows of the place—collect his pay for the trip, trade a few of his meager belongings and head out to Santa Fe alone. The fort sits two stories high. All the windows and doors are in the interior of the structure so that no one sneaks in through an outward-facing opening. The only way in or out is through a gate. An assortment of rooms—the trade room, the wagon wheel mender—all connect inside. Around back are the stables and the farrier's fire. Upstairs are rooms to rent.

Entering the fort, however, is no small task. Barely enough room for one man to fit through the entrance after the gate is opened. Kit watches as the others dismount and tie up their horses outside the walls of the building. A hitching post is set up parallel to the building with a wooden trough of water just below the wooden bar. At this time of day, the sun is in the western sky, so this side of the building has plenty of shade. Cookie hops off the wagon, tying Matilda, Louise and Sarah to the hitching post, still attached to the wagon. He hurries with unexpected exuberance, ducking quickly into the entrance. Kit follows the cook, then watches while a man rushes through the dust of the old square, scurrying toward the old geezer. The two men exchange pleasantries as if they have known each other a long time. "Hello there, Mr. Bent!" the cook says, bowing in jest over his large stomach.

William Bent laughs at the shenanigans. "Benjamin," he says, "what a treat to see you. Why, wasn't it just last month you came through?"

The two stalk off shaking hands, leaving Kit alone. He runs ahead, trying to follow them into a shop built into one of the long arcades that lines the interior walls of the fort. William stops short in the doorway then turns to scrutinize Kit, blocking his way into the building.

"Boy, your name?" William Bent says.

"Christopher."

Kit stares him down, but he can see the knowing in the older man's eyes.

Rubbing his scruffy beard William Bent asks, "You Christopher Carson, the runaway?" Kit's palms go sweaty, and he realizes his mouth is hanging open. Puzzled how to handle this, he stands there frozen. Has Bridger already told him?

Again, the trail leader saves him. He has walked across the dusty plaza, following the other men. Pushing past the fort owner, he leads Kit by the shoulder, guiding him into the shop. "Horse feathers!" he says. "Bill, leave him be. Most of the men you have here are on the dodge from the law. This here boy just wants what the rest of us want. To be left alone."

William Bent follows them into the shop, not bothering to close the door behind him. "He's free when I say he's free."

Cookie makes himself scarce. Kit sees his back end moving quickly into an adjoining room.

"If he intends to spend another minute in these here walls, he'll do as I say," William continues.

Kit looks to the trail leader for further help, but Virgil shrugs his shoulders. Kit stands as close to the small window that looks out to the square as possible. If he could melt into the walls he would. As William ducks his head under the wooden counter at the back wall he demands, "He'll cavvy on the caravan to Santa Fe."

“What? No!” Kit says, reacting before he can think clearly. The fort periodically sends provisions down to Santa Fe to trade with the Spanish. Usually, there are more horses than riders, so a cavvy accompanies the traders, wrangling the unridden horses, walking them behind his own horse until a rider calls for a mount.

“Son, you work for me, or I’ll turn you in,” William says matter-of-factly.

Cavvy boy? Kit thinks. *Enslaved again!* At least this time he’ll have a horse to ride.

***

Kit will only spend one day at the fort as the next caravan is heading out in the early morning hours after his arrival. He knows he’s lucky. William Bent could have turned him in and sent him right back to Ma. And his dead-end life.

The others, including Cookie, will hang around a few days, selling their wares. Then, they’ll join up with another caravan heading back toward Missouri and farther west. As

Kit ponders his fate, he hears someone calling to him from a doorway.

"I seen you before," a voice asks. Kit stops short. "You Kit Carson the outlaw?"

Turning around Kit sees the boy about his age, standing in the doorway to the stable.

"Huh?" Kit asks, playing dumb.

The boy walks toward Kit. His feet are bare and nearly black from dirt. His breeches are rolled up just below his knees. The boy's hands and face are nearly as dirty as his feet.

"Nearly everybody passes by the Bent brothers' fort at some point," the boy again tells Kit. Thinking he could outsmart the boy, Kit tries to throw him off the scent by asking, "Why did the brothers build the fort in the first place?" The boy seems eager to talk and sits down cross-legged in the dirt and starts his story.

"I'll tell ya, but don't think I forgot about you and the warrant for your arrest." Kit shakes his head and sits down across from the boy. "The Bent brothers and their friend Ceran

St. Vrain started this fort years ago. They's trappers too. Seein' a need for a tradin' post, they set up here."

"You seen a lot here?" asks Kit.

"Sure. I seen loads 'a mountain men come through here," says the boy. Then, he leans in close. "I might' a met a few outlaws too. None as young as you," he says then winks at Kit.

Kit heaves a sigh and reaches for his ear but stops short. "Look, I'm just trying to find some adventure. Why are you here?"

The boy looks down at the ground and sniffles. He takes so long to answer, Kit wonders if he even heard the question. All of a sudden, the boy stands up and turns to go. He mumbles, "I ain't gotta tell you nothin'." And that was the last Kit would see of the boy, who ducked back into the stable. For the rest of the night, Kit makes himself scarce choosing to sleep outside the fort. Sleep didn't come easy. Mostly because his stomach grumbled somethin' fierce. He propped himself up against the outer wall until daybreak.

***

"Gimme the roan," says one of the eighteen men on the caravan.

Kit hasn't bothered to learn anyone's name. Best to just do his job and avoid arrest. The trek from the Bent fort to Santa Fe will take just over a fortnight.

Kit grabs a blanket and saddle then rustles up the horse from the herd that has been corralled between wagons all night. This is how it always is, at the end of each day, the men hand over the reins. Kit removes the tack from each horse, then lets the horses loose to graze. When the wagons are circled, Kit leads each horse to safety for the night. First, however, he has to catch them. The buggers like to run away from him every damn night. It seems the horses play keep-away, because as soon as they see him coming, they trot just far enough away from him. Kit has to run to catch them before they bolt. By the time Kit gets back to his sleep mat, he's exhausted.

One evening, as Kit finally leads the last of the horses in for the night, a buckaroo stands guard at the entrance to the wagon circle. "You ain't too smart, is ya?"

Kit stares at the cowboy, too tired to complain. When the buckaroo asks, "Can I give you a piece of advice?" Kit nods.

"These horses is scared of being eaten," the buckaroo explains. "They's prey out in the wild. 'Stead a sneakin' up on 'em, come right in front so's they can see ya. Shake a bit of grain in yur hand and you'll nab 'em every time."

"They're so dang stubborn," Kit complains.

"Look, these horses, they's thinkin' all the time. Jus' watch 'em. If he don't want to go one way, you probably don't either. They can see a snake in the grass before you. They'll teach you and keep ya safe," he concludes, clapping Kit on the back.

***

Once everyone gets their mount for the day, Kit ropes the unridden horses and walks at the back of the pack. He's been riding a gelding he selected because the horse is pretty: the color of buckskin with a black mane and tail. Nobody's noticed that Kit has been saving the best, in Kit's mind, saddle for himself. Each morning, he swings a striped saddle blanket that's in better shape than his bedroll over the gelding's back. Once he's secured the saddle, he drapes a length of elk fur over the seat, letting it hang past the high wooden cantle. The horn is positioned way up high; soft leather covers the pommel. The seat jockey fits his small stature just fine. Thick wooden stirrups keep his worn-out boots in place.

Most of the horses are smaller than what he'd seen back in Missouri, where Easterners rode tall horses with long legs. These were horses that stood maybe fourteen hands at their withers. Rather than walking straight on, their back hooves splay out. Their eyes are deep set with strong, heavy bones over each eye socket.

Kit has learned the hard way that none of the mounts will withstand a beating. Before this trek to Santa Fe, he had little experience with horses other than fitting saddles to their backs. These ponies will nip at him if he shoves them into the corral at night. A sharp nip in the shoulder also tells him he's secured the saddle wrong. He's also noticed they love affection. If he strokes the neck of one of the ponies, the others will nuzzle his neck and draw close for cuddles.

A few afternoons back, on a particularly hot day along the trail, one of the horses just wouldn't move. The animal had stopped in the middle of the trail, not moving no matter how much Kit dug in, standing in the middle of the trail and pulling at the reins.

The horse looked ill. His head hung down, nearly touching his lips to the ground. Then the horse looked back to his barrel, as though he'd lost something. Then he stretched out his whole body.

Kit didn't know what to do. If he got one of the horses sick, he'd pay a hefty price. To the entire caravan yes, but especially from the buckaroo who owns the horse. Kit was learning the horses meant everything to these men.

Just as Kit had begun worrying about what to do, the horse promptly got down on his front knees, rolled over on his back and swung his legs back and forth.

"Aw!" Kit said. "Is you just needin' a back scratch then? You old bulldog!"

Kit knew the horses could be moody and would be stubborn until they got what they wanted. But then the horse just stopped moving and slowly collapsed to one side. The other horses nickered and moved away from the animal.

Oh no, Kit thought. *I've killed him!*

Kit stood frozen in place, but a buckaroo ran to the animal, yelling, "Help me, boy! Get this horse up to standin'." He had jumped out of his saddle so fast…Kit had never seen anything like it. The man appeared to be running in midair. "Hey, fellas," he yelled, waving down his companions, "we got a colicky one!"

What's colicky? If it meant stubborn and lazy, the man was right.

Kit helped the man to get the horse back up on four feet. But the horse looked just as sick as before.

"You hold him here," the man demanded of Kit.

Kit did as he was told, watching the man intently. The man looked to be about forty-five years old, and as rough-looking as they come. A no-nonsense kind of guy. First thing he did was open the horse's mouth and look inside. "Gums are blackened. This ain't good."

Kit nodded his agreement as if he knew exactly what the man was saying. *I wonder what the inside of a horse's mouth should look like.* Before Kit can ask, the man put his ear up to the horse's belly. "Don't hear nothing," the man said.

Kit nodded again.

The man felt the horse's neck. "Pulse ain't too strong."

"Well, that's the trouble," Kit whined. "He's been lazy, itchin' his back. Been doin' it all morning."

Kit believed the man was about to give it to the horse; but to his surprise, the man shook Kit by the shoulders as if he was mad. "You nuts, boy! Why didn't you holler for us sooner? This horse is sickly. If he don't stay upright, he'll twist his insides all to pieces."

Kit was surprised at the man's outburst. *Should I have known?* But he was downright astonished by what the man did next. Removing his coat and rolling his shirt sleeves up to his shoulders, the man lifted the horse's tail and, as Kit watched in horror, plunged his bare hand into the horse's rectum. The horse didn't like that one bit: He started to walk sideways. "Hold him!" was all the old man said, still elbow deep in the horse's backside. When his arm finally came out, it was covered in a liquid brown substance. White mucus coated the brown liquid like raw egg.

Kit started to gag, trying everything possible to stop the reflex. The man held feces in his hand and yet bent his head forward to look at it more closely. Kit's eyes were wide as saucers. *What's happening?*

"Poop looks dry," the man said, not looking too bothered by what he had just experienced. "Take him down to the water. Let him drink his fill. We'll walk him until the rest comes out."

Kit wondered if the man would come down to the river too. A wash up the arm wouldn't hurt.

After the horse had drank his fill from the cool water of the river, Kit took a quick peek inside the horse's mouth—pink. If the horse died, Kit would hang.

***

The caravan halts for two days to nurse the horse back to health. Kit has been trying to look important the whole time, as if he had been the first to discover the issue then notified the men as quickly as possible; but he and the buckaroo know better. There isn't much to do except laze about in the shade unless Cookie finds him. "There's always work to be done, boy," he'll tell Kit as he drags him back to the chuck wagon.

Kit had just fallen asleep when he felt somebody kick his boot. "Cookie, just let me sleep!" he begs.

"It ain't Cook," says the deep voice that hovers just above where Kit lay. Kit startles awake to see the buckaroo who helped him with the sick horse. "Do you mind?" the man asks pointing to the ground next to where Kit has sat up straight. Kit nods and the man stretches his long legs out straight and lays back onto his back. The silence is deafening. *Should I say something?* Kit wonders to himself. Maybe he should apologize. As he moves to speak, the older man says, "I know you ain't got a lot of experience with horses. It wasn't right of Bill to put you in charge 'a their health with no knowledge," the man says. Kit has no idea what to say. "I'm Kit," he says, knowing the man only knows him as *cavvy*. "I'm Jim," the man says with a chuckle. Jim and Kit sat and talked for much of the afternoon. Jim gave him a few pointers in caring for horses. When Kit was asked why he was out here at such a young age, he just stared at the ground. "Don't worry, boy. You're lookin' at me like I'm gonna arrest you or somethin'," says Jim. Kit just stares at him. "I understand. This is the most adventure any kid or man could ever have. Don't worry none," Jim says as he stands. He claps Kit on the shoulder and walks away.

***

Occasionally, the caravan stops in the small towns along the trail: Chimayo, Española, Las Vegas, Pecos. Most of the men hand over their horses to Kit and quickly make their way toward trouble. Some find the houses of ill repute. It's as if them soiled doves know just where to find the men coming into town. The girls hang around outside the establishment, looking coy. Once they'd locked eyes with a man, he walk up to her, big ol' grin on his face. They head indoors—not to be seen again for some time.

Other men get their fill of rotgut, slugging it down at the local saloon. Sometimes a man springs for a cold bath. Already-used water and a towel cost less than fifty cents. Kit stays to himself though—and out of trouble. He chooses to sleep in a barn with the horses or find a quiet doorstep to lie down on each night. In the mornings, with the wages he earned helping Cookie, Kit buys a tin cup of coffee mixed with a small bit of sowbelly. He dips a small piece of bread. It isn't good to taste but keeps his stomach from grumbling most of the day.

Once he reaches Santa Fe, Kit doesn't stick around long. He takes time to buy himself his first John B Stetson. Then, while the others trade or drink away their money, Kit gets paid and heads north, sneaking out of town on a horse named Cedar. The horse isn't his to keep, but he figures by the time anyone finds it missing, he'll be long gone. The horse already knows him, and folks have said he's pretty to look at. Kit renames him Taos, after the town he hopes to see one day. A new beaver trap is secured to his saddle too. It was pilfered from the Bents' as well.

He plans to head north and then turn west along the Arkansas River, where beaver are plentiful. Finally, after almost two months, he is free.

Chapter 3

To Winter Camp
(Autumn, 1860)

Auntie is clucking to Kyra, pulling reins, trying to turn around. But the pony refuses to budge.

I lightly dig my heels into my pony's barrel and swing the reins around to head into the woods, but she's not moving either.

It's safe here on the trail, they try to tell us.

"I know," I say, patting Nublada's shoulder. "But we don't have any other choice." I soothe her, rubbing her neck and talking quietly. The next time I dig a heel into her sides she starts to go in the direction of the woods.

Po has stayed to help us move off the trail. We lift the horses' packs over low-lying scrub oak branches and fallen tree trunks. It's slow going. After only a short time, my arms ache from too much lifting. My back is strong though, so I'm sure I can continue this way for hours as long as I don't think about the pain. From my left, I hear Mapia crying.

Oh, no! What now? I wonder, irritated.

My oldest daughter comes up to me, dragging her cradleboard. A hand-made doll of horsehair is perched inside.

"I'm not a good pia to dolly," Mapia confesses. "She is getting hit with branches. It hurts her! Why do we have to walk all this way?"

Mawic and I exchange glances. Leave it to my oldest daughter to complain.

Kneeling down to look her in the eyes I say, "Mapia, look around. Everyone is making the best of this situation. We won't walk too much farther tonight."

Undeterred, Mapia whines, "Why are we walking through the woods?" Then she sits down on the ground, staring at me.

Mawic walks her pony to my daughter and says, "You can sit with me on Kyra for a while."

Mawic climbs into her big wooden saddle using the deep wooden stirrups as a foothold. Mapia climbs up onto Kyra using Mawic's foot.

With my daughter contented for now, I go back to lifting packs.

It isn't long until I hear, "You've had enough." Mawic has Mapia under the armpit and is gently swinging her down to the ground.

As we come up over a hill though, there is a slight opening on the forest floor.

"We'll stay here the night," Mawic informs us. The tree canopy still covers the ground enough that we won't wake under snow cover in the morning. Ponies are relieved of their packs.

"There you go," I say to my youngest. Chipara's chubby face and body have been surrounded by warm rabbit fur in the cradleboard I've carried all day. At only two months old she coos happily from her little mobile home.

Such a contrast, I think—danger in front of me and sweet safety behind.

***

Even before morning light, I rise from where I slept—propped up against the trunk of a pine tree—and walk to the cold ashes of the fire the tribe built last night, rubbing my hands together over them. The morning is cold and crisp, but the snow has stopped.

Mawic is up too. I can make out her figure in the pale light. Other elders are stirring nearby. We all slept relatively close together, huddled close to the fire. The ponies are tied to trees nearby. Just in case.

Chava, my five-year-old, wriggles awake. Noiselessly, she unwraps herself from the elk hide she and Mapia have slept under.

"Ready to go, Pia?" she asks me.

Efficient and hardworking, Chava is always willing to do what's necessary for the tribe to survive. I send her off to collect wood for the fire. Mawic nods her approval, then walks over to me and snatches Chipara from my arms, cooing and smiling as if our situation isn't as dire as I imagine.

"Nuka-vi," Mawic says, pulling on her own ears then gently touching Chipara's tiny ears and repeating the word. Chipara coos, nuzzling her cheek into Mawic's hand.

Mawic blinks at Chipara.

"Pu'i-vi."

Chipara blinks then leans forward to poke Mawic in the eye with her chubby fingers. This little interaction gives me a chance to breathe. In and out, I stretch and wonder at the day ahead of us.

Maybe we should have stayed in our fall camp, I consider to myself. *Down in a valley, safely surrounded by a thick forest of pine trees to the north and west, groves of aspen to the south and east.* I recall the pond where we fish back at that camp, longing to be there at this moment. Yesterday as we got on our way, I had turned back to take one last look at our camp. *See you next year*, I said to myself. Now, I wonder if we will ever see that camp again.

Nublada breaks my thought process, pawing at the ground, and shifting her weight from side to side. Looking into her dark eyes, I rub under her long neck, saying, "I know, girl. It's not what I expected either."

Her tail swishes, then she snorts in disappointment.

Once the packs are situated onto the ponies and Chipara is strapped in, we resume our journey toward our winter camp, wherever that might be. I'm nervous to see the camp the men selected, though I know they did their best.

The morning goes by slowly. Just like yesterday afternoon, we have all picked up packs so the ponies can pull them through the dense underbrush and around trees. The day is cloudy and cold with the smell of water in the air. Snow is coming. After a half-day trek, we come out from the pine forest. Low-growing juniper stand scattered like sentinels, leading us downward between the mountains and the foothills. The ground here isn't earth, but solid rock. The horse's packs skitter across the smooth surface so that we have to walk alongside the packs, pushing them from either side toward the middle. These packs are so heavy, if they slide down the side of these rocks, the horses could go with them.

Down, down the rocks we go. The only footholds are the thick, twisting roots of the juniper spread out about enough to grab onto after several uncertain steps in between. Icy spots cause the horses to lose their footing. We do too. The children find it fun to slide down on their bottoms, but I'm failing to see the humor. What's more, it begins to snow.

Whereas the mountain valleys protect us from winter weather, the area around the foothills takes the brunt of the cold winds. Snow clouds glide up, hugging the ground, and then slide over the foothills and down onto the plains, carrying blizzard winds and heavy snow. Winds whip up snow blusters that hit us in the face. It's even slower moving here than it was in the woods. I wonder if we will have to spend another night camping out before we get to our destination.

The boy has stopped.

"Here we are," says the boy singsong, spreading his arms wide as if he had brought us to paradise. Instead, this is a barren hill of low, golden grasses, rocks, and two large cottonwoods.

This is it? I think. *Would the men truly put us out here in danger of freezing to death with the Colorado winter?*

Though there is a creek that runs alongside the camp, there is no protection from the weather save the two trees. Yes, they are both large around and would make a great place to stop if they were full of summertime leaves. They have almost fully dropped their golden leaves, creating a musty smell as the dead foliage mixes with the sandy soil of the creek. As it is, only one or two teepees will fit behind them. They will have to be enough.

Though it's early afternoon, I'm tired and hungry and just want to be done with the day. But this place is making my blood boil. I can feel my heart beating in my ears. I let out a big sigh and put my hands to my face, shaking my head back and forth. "Why? Why?" I say aloud until I feel a tug at my dress. My two older girls are looking up at me. They wear tanned deer skins and leggings to keep them warm with long moccasins, but their uncovered heads are obscured by snow. Mapia's teeth are chattering uncontrollably. Chava studies me wide-eyed.

"Will we be alright, Mama?" she asks me.

Chapter 4

Lost in the Woods
(Early Spring, 1861)

"Trade for your buckskin?"

Turning, Kit sees an old mountain man looking his way. He tries to ignore the short, scruffy man. *Make yourself look important,* he thinks.

He stands taller and stares straight ahead, trying to make a face of concentration by pulling his facial features together toward his nose. Kit is at the Bents' fort again. Only for a few hours this time. He doesn't know where else to get tins before heading west.

The man speaks up again: "Sell 'im and you can get whatever you need."

Doesn't look like the man intends to leave Kit alone. *Hopefully, this ain't another one like Bridger,* he thinks, remembering the man who gave him grief. If anybody recognizes the stolen horse, Kit will have to deal with that too.

"Nope," Kit says, walking his horse around to the back to stable him up. His empty stomach growls just like the last time he was here. Confidence slipping, he hitches Taos to a post then turns, hunching his shoulders down, and heads for the shop.

Kit removes his hat although he wishes he could pull it farther down to meet up with his eyebrows. *Best thing I ever bought,* he thinks, remembering his sunburned head the last time he showed up here. With the salary he made managing horses during the last caravan, Kit can use a few of the coins he's stashed to buy food. *I'll trade this dinky, good-for-nothin' blanket too,* he thinks, holding onto a two-point blanket he received as a gift from William Bent who must have received it in a trade. The Hudson Bay Company had created the point system to indicate a blanket's size even when the item was folded. Kit would need at least a five-point blanket to keep sufficiently warm. The thing won't even wrap around Kit's body—either his front or his backside is exposed to the elements. Though he hasn't got much, there's enough to trade and buy some tins. He carries three pilfered carrots of tobacco, but only intends to trade one this time. No one would believe he could have purchased all three.

Striding through the open-air yard, Kit heads to the trade shop. He nearly swoons as the delicious smells of the meat stews and corn flour breads hit his nose. Women sit on low wooden stools that dig into the hard earth of the plaza while emptying black iron pots that hang over fires or pull tortillas from the horno in the center of the plaza. Kit pushes down his hunger although he wants desperately to sit a spell, eat some of the handmade food and fill his belly….If he didn't have a target on his back, he could've maybe stayed in one of the rooms for the night. Rest his head without having to always keep one eye open for trouble. "*No rest for the weary*" his ma used to say, but he didn't understand her talk until now.

As much as Kit craves the adventure he finds in the West, a small part of him might enjoy the comforts his family knows. Living in a town like Franklin provides security: You always know other folks are looking out for you. *Nah,* Kit thinks, spitting like the other do. *That life ain't for me.* Even if he could go back to Franklin there'd be nothing there but loneliness.

Instead, he'll settle for eating out of tin cans along the trail tonight. *Get in and get out.* He pushes open the solid wooden door of the trade room, but an unseen hand pulls the door open farther, making Kit stumble forward. William Bent looks at Kit as he steps through the opening.

Kit's heart beats out of his chest. *Steady on,* he tells himself. Just like his pappy used to say. Whichever Bent brother is working the trade counter, it won't matter. Neither will surely recognize him after spending ten days hauling to Santa Fe. That's how grizzled he thought he looked. Kit grabs for the wooden counter to steady himself, then turns and leans against it, standing up tall. Thick wooden beams run in rows, horizontal to the floorboards of the room upstairs that makes the ceiling. If Kit didn't know better, he'd think those beams were shrinking in him from fear.

Kit can feel Mr. Bent's eyes on his back. He reminds himself not to tug on his ear. Instead, he keeps the items he intends to trade in one hand and the brim of his John B in the other, willing both to stop shaking.

"I'm surprised to see you, Kit," William Bent says. "Where's the rest of your party?"

The merchant lifts a levered portion of the countertop, walks into the opening, then places the wooden counter back down. He faces Kit, who stands at the window opposite the counter. Behind Bent, the wall is partitioned into square wooden cupboards packed chockfull of necessities: utensils, tins of food, tobacco, pipes, even whiskey. *Taos Lightning*. In the two months that Kit has been on his own he's seen his share of men strung out on the stuff. Colorful blankets are neatly folded on a table behind Bent. Pots and pans hang from hooks. Animal hides, fur still attached, are slung over a rope that attaches unevenly to nails haphazardly tapped into the walls.

Kit keeps his head down, not responding, shoulders rolled forward. He pushes the two-point blanket and a carrot of tobacco onto the counter.

"You here alone, son?" Bent asks the same question in a different way. Kit squirms under Bent's gaze, but just can't meet his eyes. Call it a lack of confidence or extreme shyness, either way it's too overwhelming for him. Back home, Kit's mama or older brothers always did the talking. He didn't bargain for this part of the adventure, having to talk with the likes of Bent.

When the items just sit between the two of them, no action being taken, Kit feels obliged to answer.

"Yessir," is all he says. But his voice comes out in a deep baritone that doesn't match his scrawny body. Even just last year, Kit's brothers, all behemoths compared to Kit, used to pick him up and haul him into the creek fully clothed.

Minutes pass as Bent just stares at Kit a moment, then turns to the cupboards, tidying the tins and straightening blankets on the table before returning to the counter. When

Bent's eyes fall on him again, Kit resists the desire to grab for his ear, but fingers his hat brim restlessly. Finally, Bent pulls the belongings toward him, fingering the blanket but still eyeing the boy intently. "Other men can teach you—they can protect you from what's out there. Skills you can't learn on your own."

Kit keeps his eyes on his items, not responding.

Bent lets out a sigh, then asks, "What do you want for these, Kit?"

Satisfied he can make a trade, Kit points to a few of the tins in the wooden cupboards and one of the larger blankets on the table. He's never actually done this before, just watched other men the last time he came through. He isn't sure whether he can get more or not for the goods he's trading, but when Bent hands him the items, Kit quickly makes to leave. He packs the tins on top of the new blanket and puts his John B back where it belongs. *Wish my brothers could see me now.*

"Where you headed, boy?" Bent asks.

Kit yanks open the door. Bent ain't his father. Besides, he's sick of people getting into his affairs.

***

Kit heads due west, following the Arkansas. Some folks had talked of a trading post that sits in the fork between the Arkansas and Fountain Creek. Since Kit wasn't sure, he'd come all the way out to the Bents' place. Now, he'd head in the direction of the trading post, see if it exists, then follow the Ark to where it flows in Bayou Salade, west of Pikes Peak: Everyone said the finest buffalo hunting was to be had there. Never mind Kit didn't know the first thing about killing a beast that fierce and large.

Most days he shares the trail with an uncountable number of deer and elk sipping the cold water of the Arkansas unafraid of the man and his horse. And, most days, he lugs the butt of the musket up to his shoulder to fire a shot that never hits the mark. If he could just figure out how to hunt! It isn't the equipment; his brother's musket has a new-fangled flintlock mechanism and is supposedly quick to reload. At least that was what his brother had said. He carries his gunpowder dry, just like Bridger and the other men he had come across the country with. He just can't shoot at a moving target. *And I ain't a good shot with the standing-still ones either,* he admits to himself.

Being eleventh of fifteen children, he'd have thought his brothers might have found time to teach him; but they thought he wasn't fit to be a boy and had just pushed him off when they hunted. Kit had tagged along anyway but hadn't thought to watch them. His father was long gone by the time he was old enough to learn, and his son-of-a-gun stepfather was useless. The deer and elk seemed big and slow…*But they aren't,* Kit thinks. *They's laughin' at me.* The animals silently eye him, eating the cool grasses along the waterway. Kit could have learned a lot more from the men along the trails, he realizes.

Kit ruminates on this, but ultimately doesn't think it's his fault. His brothers were all older and should have taken care of him. All those months, he had depended on the chuck wagon without thinking twice. No chance to lean on Cookie for a meal now. The tins won't last long, he knows. Once or twice, he catches a rabbit in a homemade snare, but the meat doesn't last him long either. *I don't have the slightest notion of where my brothers and me went wrong,* Kit thinks, perplexed.

***

The Fountain heads north to Denver. It's a few days' ride from where the two rivers come together. The snow and cold Kit encountered leaving Santa Fe are making way for clear skies and warmer temperatures. One day the sun would beat down on him something fierce. The next day, he'd be hit by a rush of snow so thick he couldn't even see the scrawny creosote bushes and endless, low-growing sagebrush six feet ahead of him.

Now though the nights have gotten frosty, and the heavier blanket he bought makes the evenings much more comfortable. Down by the river, the water runs cold, but it's not frozen over: little shoots of green pop up from the muddy banks. He's also left behind the puzzle-board ground of dry, caked dirt that stretched for miles north of Santa Fe. He and Taos, his horse, follow a well-worn dirt path probably made by natives long ago. He and the horse begin their march at sunup then take a rest near lunchtime. If the sun is shining, Kit enjoys the heat on his face while Taos browses the newly green grasses, brushing his soft lips against them. On about suppertime Kit makes camp. Opening a tin isn't easy. Kit was able to steal a metal can opener from Cookie the last time they were together. It's about the length of Kit's hand and all metal. One end is a loop he holds in his right hand. The other end is like a little bayonet that Kit stabs into the top of the tin. Now the hard part. Kit has to turn the tin in his left hand, always ensuring the bayonet doesn't come lose from the tin to cut a gash that would probably take off a finger. Usually, he's happy to just get an inch-long opening through which he can pour the contents of the tin into a small metal saucepan, also stolen from Cookie. If he could, he'd lick the contents of the tin clean. *Ma used to open these things with ease*. But he just hasn't got the strength yet. He's gotten good at ignoring the hunger pangs.

***

Built similar to the Bents' fort, the mud adobe outer walls of Fort Pueblo surround the fort's arcade and shops. The one-story garrison also has a small dirt courtyard, and one narrow opening that allows travel in an out.

As snow begins falling rapidly, Kit makes his way inside, trades a bit—exchanging his last carrots of tobacco for another blanket—then heads back out to Taos, who is sheltered from the storm by the thick adobe walls. After a week of sunny blue-sky days, Kit has been surprised by the wintery storm. He wishes he could rest in the relative warmth of the fort. *This here is Indian country,* he remembers. Even so, he hasn't passed a single Indian along the trail. He couldn't say whether they'd been watching him; it really hadn't crossed his mind. But once the idea hits his brain, a chill slides down his back. What would happen if he met an Indian? *I'm probably a gonner.*

All Kit knows is that Indians are bad. He's heard they will kill a man on sight. "Nothin' good comes from an Indian," his stepfather had told him. He said they have no culture and just wander aimlessly in the mountains.

Kit swallows down his fear, mounting Taos and leading him away from the fort. "Let's head for them mountains, boy," Kit tells his horse.

The snow begins falling heavy now. Slanting when a gust of wind picks up and hurls it sideways.

***

Kit can barely make out the trees along the river as he tries to steer Taos in that direction. The horse isn't too happy about the weather. Occasionally, after a particularly nasty wind, he'll stop, plant his feet in the ground and let Kit know he is unwilling to move. But Kit isn't taking any chances on being caught. "Onward, boy!" he says encouragingly. "We're at the foot of the mountains. Just what we've wanted all these months."

He digs his heels into Taos' belly and pulls the reins around to the right. When Taos won't budge, Kit tries reasoning with him. "Taos, don'tcha want to eat more of that delicious green grass along the river? Bet we can find some. I'll dig my boot into the snow for ya' and getcha some."

No movement.

Time to get serious.

"Look, you obstinate cuss," Kit demands, "I'm the boss, not you. Sorry if you'd rather not walk in the storm, but I got to get outta here."

Unfazed by the blizzard surrounding him, Kit figures the storm will last a few more minutes; then the sun will push the snow and ungodly chill away. He slides out of the saddle, grabs the horse's reins and gets behind Taos. Then he pushes the horse's rump while pulling the reins, but Taos outsmarts him by walking in a simple circle. Finally, Kit pleads with him: "Look, boy, I got to go. *Please.*"

Taos turns to look into Kit's eyes. Kit could swear the horse shakes his head at him. *If* he swore.

Finally, Kit hops on quickly and they take off into the white of the storm.

***

Just look for the cottonwoods.

Kit calms himself, tugging at the bottom of his ear, which barely sticks out of his hat. The day has turned dark with the storm, but Kit can tell he's losing light. A trickle of sweat runs down his back. *Don't panic.*

Another ear tug.

He'll find a place, low to the ground, where the big cottonwoods will keep him, and Taos, protected.

The snap of a twig and a quiet huff of breath nearby makes him wonder if he's alone. He quickly hops off Taos then pulls the reins over the horse's head. "Stay calm, boy," Kit says. But he might as well be talking to himself.

Something moves. Kit can see it out of the corner of his eye. He jumps to face the sudden rustle and whatever made it, but he slips on an icy patch. He slides, trying to regain his composure, but lands hard on his musket. A deep searing pain throbs at his back. He knows there is only one shot in the musket; but when he turns to face his attacker, he is surprised to find no one is there.

Taos looks over at him as if he's lost his mind. Kit gets up from the snow, grabs the reins, and starts walking again. No sooner has he taken a step than he hears another sound. A distinct *crack!* The snow is blowing sideways, and the wind howls in his ears. He pulls his Stetson over his ears and stamps his feet. Another *crack!* Like a big tree trunk snapping. Suddenly, Kit feels the ground give out below him, and he sinks into icy cold water.

Taos steps back. Kit pulls hard on the reins he's thankfully still holding. The next moment, he feels his feet being pulled by the water: The undercurrent beneath the ice is strong. *Can't get sucked under!* Maybe his brothers were right, he's just a runt with no skills. The thought crosses his mind but only adds to his fear. The wind blows in gusts, carrying bits of bark and grasses that lodge in his mouth and eyes. Kit's heavy boots fill with water but remain intact, pulling his legs away from him. Frantic, he swings his legs as hard as he can to kick toward the surface.

Still pulling hard on the reins, Kit slowly draws himself out of the hole in the ice that formed when he broke through. He slides his body slowly along the surface, inching toward Taos, who stands safely on shore, watching Kit. The cracking continues directly under Kit's body. *It's going to break again!* he thinks. Quickly, he slides up next to Taos and braces himself, about to stand, when a gust of wind carries a broken cottonwood branch square toward him.

The last Kit remembers is Taos' face, drawing close to his.

Chapter 5

Springtime Find
(Winter and Early Spring, 1861)

"Take these," says Mawic as she heaves her camp broom, sleeping mat and backrest through the opening of our teepee.

My heart stops.

"Why? What's happening?"

But I already know. When I was a small girl, I had seen my great-grandparents do the same thing Auntie is doing.

Panicked, I can't hide my fear from my children. The two older girls jump up to stand next to me.

"No! You don't need to go. We'll be fine here."

I try pushing her belongings back outside the flap of the teepee, hoping I can think of a way to make her stay.

Auntie shoves the items inside the teepee again. The girls look from me to Auntie, trying to make sense of the situation.

"Chaska," Auntie says, taking my hand, "I'm leaving, and so is Uncle. It's better that you and the younger members of the tribe survive. We've had our moment on earth; it's time for me to meet up with my sister in the next life." She looks into my eyes. "Kyra and I will go together."

She and her horse are bonded in this life—and into the next. After I crawl out of the teepee, I see her standing by Kyra. She hasn't packed one thing to take with her: All she holds are Kyra's reins. Two other elders, warm buffalo skins draped over their shoulders, stand next to her. Uncle is looking away from me as he stands off to the side as if to say he isn't with them. Like Auntie, none of the three—neither my uncle nor the two elders—carries anything in their hands. They know what they are doing: If all four of them leave, there will be two more teepees for our family members to live in during the winter.

"Please, don't do this," I beg. "I can't lose Mom *and* you. Who will lead camp?"

She clasps my hands in hers. "You will, my dear."

Turning away from me, she mounts Kyra.

"You watched your mother do it when you were young, and you have helped me now that you're older."

She and the others turn to go. I'm doubled over in grief. Many others in the camp are wailing their anguish.

None of the elders look back as they move slowly away from camp. I know they won't survive. So do they.

***

The weather turns miserable, mimicking my mood…It's been several weeks since Mawic left us. Most of us have sought shelter inside our teepees—a good thing. We need the time to mourn the loss of the four elders.

In fact, the winter that just ended was full of snowstorms. Sometimes the winds blew the snow sideways. And the storms have continued right into spring. The snow has fallen so thick the last few days I sometimes haven't been able to see out of the teepee flap. There have been a few scattered sunny days, like today, but winter doesn't want to let go of her grip. Spring is coming in fits and spurts this year.

Still, the water means that many more plants for us to harvest over the summer.

I head out to clear my head and check on the snares I've set along the creek just north of our camp. My horse, Nublada, seems pleased by the sunny weather: She walks along the soft sandy edge of the cold water. The gray mare is just as good as I am at finding snared animals—she senses their fear. When a hare is caught in a trap, she will stop and paw at the ground. We trust each other—I'm cautious whenever she shows fear, so I keep a good eye on her temperament.

She was a present given to me by my parents when I was three years old. Back then, I learned to ride bareback, mostly because the horse would nudge me from side to side, keeping me on her back. It used to be anyone who had a horse was considered to be of higher stature. Now, we all have one.

The first trap we come to has been sprung: The small loop of sinew used to bend the branch of the tree down to the trap lies on the forest floor. *Must have been all that wind,* I think. I hop off Nublada; she bends her head contently…noses at the snow to nip off bits of green grass below. I can't stop thinking about what Auntie and the other elders did for us. Their sacrifice left a hole in my heart: I can feel the pain of it in my chest. The pain grows fiercer each time I see Auntie in my head. But I also know we need to keep moving forward; Mawic's sacrifice shouldn't leave me hollow, devoid of life. So here I am, checking snares.

I loop the sticky sinew of the sprung trap to a nearby twig standing up from the ground. Just as I'm about to hop back onto my horse she begins to nicker.

Not from fear.

Instead, a sweet low sound comes from her throat. Usually, she reserves those sounds for the companions in her herd. Did someone follow me from camp?

"What do you know, girl?"

I draw my face next to hers to see what she sees. Cheek-to-cheek, I look and listen. Suddenly, out from the brush, a buckskin meanders toward us. My stomach leaps. The horse isn't one of ours: It's a low-standing tan mustang, not an eastern charger. The horse's bridle is still wrapped around his head. The reins rest on the well-worn saddle firmly fastened around his barrel. A man's boot—long, brown, and worn out at the toe—is stuck into one of the horse's thick wooden stirrups.

Where there's a random horse, there's a person.

I quickly grab the musket my brother has been teaching me to use. I always have it with me now. It has been secured to the saddle horn and I quickly release it. Though if I had to use it right now, my hands are shaking so badly I probably couldn't hit much.

As wide-eyed and confused as I am, the new horse is calm. He walks out of the small stand of scrub oak. Black mane, sweet eyes.

"Hey there, boy. Tee-ă-poo-åh," I say. *Buckskin* in Ute.

The horse comes right up to me then nuzzles Nublada as if they are old friends. Nublada nuzzles the unfamiliar horse right back, completely at ease.

"Bet you're cold and hungry," I say. "Where'd you come from?"

I ask the question loudly, hoping the horse's owner hears me. Well, whoever it is has only one boot on—I should be able to run faster than a one-booted man.

Grabbing the new horse's reins, I'm intent on heading back to camp quickly. As I stick one foot into my own wooden stirrups, Nublada swings her head back and begins to back up; whatever is scaring her isn't bothering the other horse at all.

Nublada's eyes track to nothing I can see, but I can't doubt her. A small, faint sound rises from the brush, like a rabbit's last urge before impending death. Perhaps I had caught something in my snare after all? But why would that scare Nublada? The bushes around my trap shiver in the spot where I heard the noise. Whatever it is—muskrat, rabbit, squirrel—the animal is still alive.

Nublada continues her retreat with anxious energy, shaking her head. The other horse watches her back away with little interest. I grab the new horse's reins and drag him toward Nublada. Holding both pairs of reins in one hand and my musket in the other, I walk closer to inspect my prey.

"Ah!" I scream, jumping back.

Lying in the snare is—a man. His hair, long and wild, is mashed over his face. A merikac hat lies in the snow nearby, and a thin blanket lies on the ground under the man's body. His leather breeches appear to be intact. Toes of his bootless foot show through his stockings—but they don't look blackened by frostbite.

The man lets out a soft moan and shifts slightly.

My heart beats out of my chest. Opening his eyes, he reaches his hand toward me. I jump back a few steps, just out of his range. Nublada backs away, making space for me to get out.

Usually, I can move around the outskirts of our camp with little fear of strangers. Our men have kept the merikac away all winter; so, it surprises me that our scout did not hear this man approach. He must have come close to camp during yesterday's snowstorm. He didn't know we were here, apparently, and we didn't know he was so close.

The man stares at me with half-open eyes. "Help me…" he begs.

Should I shoot him and take his horse? He's nearly dead anyway.

My brother, Ahwatt, believes all merikac who trespass on our land should be killed. He says it's the only way for us to survive. I don't agree, so we often quarrel about making a peaceful treaty with the newcomers. Now, although I feel unprotected, I wonder if this particular merikac could be a friend. Should I bring him back to camp? I stop myself…What am I thinking? Ahwatt would have a fit of anger if I did that. He would probably kill the man immediately.

"Please, don't shoot me," he begs, as though reading my thoughts.

I'm torn.

Nublada keeps watching me as I pace back and forth, thinking. The gelding seems half asleep. Or half dead.

Maybe I should shoot the both of them.

"Please, no..." the man says again.

I ignore his pleas. Instead, I tie both horses to a tree nearby. Then, I prepare the musket.

***

Almost as quickly as the gun goes off, I hear horses charging toward me. Luksi, my brother's pinto, is headed my way: I recognize his fast, lopsided gait. "I'm here!" I yell, hoping my voice carries over the horse's footsteps. When Ahwatt and the other men come into view I take a few deep breaths to calm myself: What am I going to tell him?

"What's happening?" Ahwatt asks. I watch as he takes in the scene from atop his horse. "I heard the shot...are you all right?"

Like my brother, Luksi doesn't frighten easily. Both have been in enough battles to be nearly fearless, and Ahwatt is a highly skilled hunter and protector.

"I'm fine," I say. "But I found something."

Ahwatt hops off his horse, eyeing the buckskin standing next to Nublada. Both tied securely to a thick aspen. The other men have come with him. They jump off their horses as well.

"It's a man. A white man," I tell my brother. "I didn't kill him yet, because I think we can bring him to camp and heal him. He could be a friend."

Even saying it out loud sounds absurd….Bring a white man into camp and let him live with us? On a few occasions we've had traders sleep just beyond our camp. They brought us knives and guns in exchange for skins or even horses. This, however, would be much different.

Ahwatt stares at me. He probably thinks I'm crazy. *He'll never go for it.* His inability to make decisions is well known by everyone in the tribe. The truth is our father was the tribe's chosen leader. When he died, Ahwatt inherited the title. Father was a good, strong, thoughtful leader, but Ahwatt hasn't followed his traditions. He doesn't know right from wrong—or doesn't care to think about decisions in that way.

Ever since our parents' passing, he's been unsure, allowing others to talk him into deciding one way or the other.

My brother pulls me closer. He bends down so I can hear him better. "Why do you know this, Chaska?" he whispers. "Why do you believe this white man could be a friend?"

Ahwatt has always seemed envious of my ability to render judgments and stick with them. I can't explain the strong feeling I have: This man *will* make a positive difference for us.

"He's young still," I say. "All the others who pass through have already made up their minds about us. We can make him understand our ways."

Ahwatt continues to look at me as if I've gone mad. He says nothing, just keeps staring at me. So, I stare up at him too.

He knows when I have my mind set on something, I will not change it—especially when the matter concerns the safety of the tribe. As our leader, he can disagree with me and kill the man right here. But the truth is, I won't give up. I've already decided: A merikac who knows us—who sees us as people with traditions and laws—could be the answer we need to live in our tribal territories in peace. So, I stand among the men who hover over me like tall trees and wait for my brother to realize my resolve is stronger than his indecisiveness.

The men who surround Ahwatt become restless as he and I talk. Because Ahwatt would normally be in a hurry to kill the man, one of the men pulls out a knife, raises it, then kneels down to the half-conscious merikac to make the final blow.

"No!" Ahwatt says. He reaches for the knife. "Lift this man from the ground and set him over his horse."

His eyes again lock with mine. The men will always follow their leader's requests, but Ahwatt seems to need a reason for his command. "The man will help us in the future," Ahwatt says, looking to the ground and swiping at his mouth. He does this whenever he says something he doesn't quite believe himself. From years of growing up together, I can tell when he's being dishonest. For as long as I can remember, Ahwatt will wipe away the lies that flow so easily from his mouth! I have to wonder whether he is lying to me now – will he kill the man—or if he just doesn't like the decision he's been forced to make.

The tribesmen stand still amid the trees, confused. In the presence of one another, none dares to disagree with their leader. While they stand incredulous, my brother has already hopped atop Luksi. He turns the horse back to camp, not giving the men a second glance.

Before they decide to disobey my brother's order, I untie the buckskin from the tree and walk him to stand next to his owner.

Chapter 6

Making Friends or Enemies?
(Early Spring, 1861)

When he wakes again, another face. A man this time, with his face up close to Kit's. He looks angry, eyes pulled together tight. The smirk on his lips frightens Kit.

Then everything goes dark.

***

Sometime later, Kit awakes to find himself lying on something soft. Raising one hand, he runs his palm along what feels like a stack of buffalo robes...Smooth tanned hide intermingles with the fluffy, thick fur of what used to be a buffalo.

Where am I? he wonders.

Kit opens his eyes a bit farther to find an Indian woman folding a blanket, humming to herself. The flap of the tent he is lying in shakes violently from the rushing wind outside: The Indian woman looks up quickly. A cold wind rushes down the smoke opening at the top of the tent—is it a teepee—nearly extinguishing the fire that burns in the middle of the structure. She rushes over to close the flap…and that's when her eyes move over to Kit. He sees her look of concern; the next moment, he realizes her face is the face of the woman who peered at him during the blizzard. He thought he had dreamt it.

He immediately tries to prop himself up.

Get out of here, he thinks in fear. *Pa said I'd be killed if they found me.*

Raising himself almost to sitting, he's so dizzied he nearly falls over, his head swooning. When he tries to roll over to his knees, his legs won't work. Panicked, he tries to drag himself through the flap of the teepee, but the woman has positioned herself in front of him. On her knees, she looks into his eyes. She smiles gently, only inches from his face.

"No, yagay," she says, putting her hands out in front of her.

"What?" Kit asks.

"Safe," she says.

Kit's head spins so badly he has to lie back down. The woman must see that he is falling: She comes to his side, helping him get situated. She smiles again. Kit notices her hands are empty of weapons. There's no one else here, just Kit and the woman.

If I could just stand up, I can take her.

Then, he realizes he doesn't have his musket.

He looks around the interior of the teepee.

Only old animal skins and the fire.

"Safe," the woman repeats.

From even this little exertion, Kit is exhausted. Trying hard to catch his breath, he thinks, *I can kill her if I have to.*

She's still kneeling close to him, seemingly without any fear. *Must be too dumb to know my power,* Kit thinks, trying hard to convince himself he's capable of keeping himself safe.

Looking into his eyes the woman taps her chest.

"Chaska."

When Kit doesn't respond, she says it again—"Chaska"—tapping her chest.

"Chaska?" Kit says.

The woman reaches out to touch his chest, but Kit bats her hand away.

"No," he says, shrinking away in fear. She is unfazed and simply repeats the word, then puts her hands out, palms up toward Kit. Without touching him, she raises her eyebrows as if asking a question.

"Kit…?" he says weakly.

Chapter 7

What Do We Do with the Merikac? (Early Spring, 1861)

It's snowing outside the teepee. Again. While my baby sleeps, Chava, Mapia and I clean tools and tidy up the sleep area. My husband Kaib is with the other men, in a separate teepee, also cleaning tools, or guns and knives, because there isn't much we can do outside today.

It's difficult for me to focus on the tasks at hand. Instead, I go through the motions, putting on a happy face for the girls.

"Pia, tell us a story."

"All right."

"Tell the story of Coyote!"

My girls scoot over closer to me with their backs to the fire that burns in the middle of the teepee. It smells of dry leaves. Cozy in our home while the winds rage outside, I tell of our Creator.

"Shin-ob gave Coyote a bag of sticks.

"'Be responsible with the bag—and whatever you do, don't open it,' Shin-ob demanded.

"Coyote walked and walked up and over mountains, past creeks and through forests. When he was finally far enough that Shin-ob couldn't see him anymore, Coyote opened the bag and snuck a peek inside.

"On his first look, he saw just a bunch of sticks.

"'Why would Shin-ob demand that I not open this bag?' he wondered.

"But upon taking a second look, Coyote realized the bag was full of people.

"Before Coyote knew what was happening, the people started climbing up and out of the bag. Coyote tried to catch the people, but they were too quick and escaped. He realized he had to go back and tell Shin-ob what happened.

"Shin-ob was furious. 'What have you done?'

"When Shin-ob looked into the bag there were just a few people left inside. They didn't try to jump out. Carefully, he scooped them out, gently placing them on the ground.

"'Those who escaped will always be the Ute enemies thanks to your selfishness, Coyote,' Shin-ob said. 'The people left inside are my chosen people. The Ute.'"

"And coyote was forced to walk on four feet after making such a terrible mistake!" both girls shout gleefully.

"Yes, my dears," I said, smiling at my mouth while my eyes remained sad.

***

Two days ago, just before this latest storm hit, Ahwatt found Mawic and the other elders. They had settled along a creek bed, not far from our camp. They were huddled together, Ahwatt said, frozen to death. Most of the tribe followed behind the men when they gathered our elders. Each body, including that of Kyra, was placed on wooden sledges dragged behind several horses. The horses led the bodies to a large stand of boulders Kaib had found: They must have been carried downstream when the river was flowing much stronger. The snowpack was deep in amongst the boulders, which seemed like sentinels unto whom was given the care of these poor souls. Kaib, Ahwatt, and the other men dug through the snow then lay the bodies down, covering them with snow. Kyra too. Soon enough we will move their bodies from this temporary burial location and give them a proper ceremony.

As our leader, Ahwatt led us to this winter camp out of necessity. There's little food, and shelter from whipping winter winds is nonexistent. When the tribe is suffering, elders sacrifice themselves for the good of everyone. But this was the first time he had been responsible for it. And Ahwatt hates being responsible for anything.

***

When the snow finally stops, I instruct Mapia to look after the other two children, then I venture outside, running quickly, ducking my head into the white man's teepee. It sits at the very edge of camp.

Opening the tent flap, I hear the white man talking with Medicine Man. The smell of peach willow bark tea hits my nostrils.

"No, not the tea again!" the merikac laments. "Please, no. I hate that tea!"

I conceal a smile. The tea smells like fresh peaches but tastes like only the pit had been used. I hate that tea too.

Medicine Man ignores the merikac. Instead, he tips the cup to the man's mouth. The white man puckers at the bitter taste, but he swallows the contents.

The usual fire burns in the middle of the teepee, smelling of smoldering Wa Wachee—Gambel oak leaves.

Smiling, I sit down near the blankets where the man lies. His sign language skills have come a long way since I first tried to teach him my name. Though he shakes his head from the tea's bitterness he gives me a welcome in sign language.

Setting his right palm down at his heart he quickly moves his hand across his body, toward the right: the sign for *good.* Putting both hands out in front of his face, palms down, he flips them over. *Day*. I do the same, signing *good day* then saying his name:

"Kit."

Smiling, I sit down near the blankets where the man lies.

My heart aches for this man. He's a teenager really. Must have been through the worst of the storm because it seems as though he fell into a thicket of prickly wild roses. His face and neck display wounds that ooze pus and blood. Thankfully, his toes exposed to the snow where the boot came off do not seem to have become frostbitten.

Pots of herbs and grasses lie about the floor of the teepee. Medicine Man comes toward me. He hands me *singabe*—cottonwood buds. Squeezing them, I expose the red pitch and apply it to Kit's wounds while we practice Ute and English vocabulary together. Gently, I smear the pitch to the small, shallow wounds on his arms. I leave some buds for Medicine Man to apply to his legs: It might be too intrusive for a married woman to be touching there.

I nod then make a sign for *horse*, holding two fingers astride my hand. "*Cah-Vah*," he says. Then he points at me, and I say, "*Horse*."

We continue for some time, exchanging Ute and English words: *travel, ride, trade, eat, drink, seasons, hunt*. This way, I can explain parts of our culture to him. He's surprised, I think, to learn we have such a balanced relationship and strong understanding of all that is around us—the snow, the rocks and earth, the plants, the animals. I wonder why or even how his culture doesn't have the same relationship with the world that we do. My head swirls with all the possibilities this man might offer us. If we could have even one ally among all the traders and trappers who come through our hills and valleys, it will help our situation, perhaps even bring the peace our family needs. This merikac will be important to our future. He'll see we are peaceful and good, prosperous people. And perhaps, if he speaks our language, he can help us negotiate a treaty, and make the other merikac understand. He could help ensure land is reserved for my tribe or find peace between us and the trespassers.

***

I go and visit Kit most days, and since he can sit up and even stand, we share short walks outside. We practice our Ute and English by pointing out various plants along the way. When he knows the English word, he shares it with me.

"Tivac," I say.

"Piñon nut," he returns.

"Soo Yoop."

"Tree."

"No-quint."

"Creek."

Since we use sign language often, I teach Kit that too. Eventually, between speaking out loud and in sign, we can talk about how he got lost during the blizzard.

"I remember your face," he tells me, though he can't remember anything after climbing from the river. Now, I can laugh about how scared I had been when what I thought was an animal caught in my snare was actually a merikac.

"Why didn't you kill me, Chaska?"

This is my chance. Finally. I can tell him how much we would appreciate his help in convincing the other merikac to live in peace with us. I take a big breath in and then let out a sigh. Then I stop walking and look him in those blue eyes.

"Kit, you can see that we are being surrounded by other merikac. I truly believe the Ute people can live together with the new people as long as we have an understanding about land. They can have some of our land as long as we can keep ourselves fed and safe."

At this point, Kit breaks eye contact with me and turns to stare at the ground.

"I'd like it very much if you could be our interpreter," I continue. "When Ahwatt negotiates with the territorial government in Denver…will you consider going with him? You can tell the merikac that we are good people who cared for you when we could have left you for dead. And you can read the papers they ask us to sign. We will finally know what they've written."

Instead of answering, Kit toes pebbles with his boot, then starts gently kicking at them, all the while staring downward. We haven't ever had such a difficult conversation. The tension between us is thick, but I'm not going to beg. If he doesn't want to help us, we can still negotiate on our own. Just the same, my heart is beating so loud I can hear it in my ears.

"Denver's a big town," Kit says. Again, he toes the pebbles as though there is more. I'm trying to wait patiently, but he must know what I need and want.

Then he glances at me quickly, whispering something I can barely hear: "I can't read." His boot stops moving, and he stands up as tall as he can, looking me in the eyes as though I will be disappointed with him.

"Oh," I say, giving a little chuckle and letting out the breath I must have been holding. "Neither can I."

He lets out a whoosh of air that he must have been holding and shows just the tiniest smile. "I'll help you, Chaska. It's the least I can do for you."

***

Medicine Man comes to Kit's tent every day and even helps with his English lessons. I point to the Po'rat and say, "Tawac." Then, I pat Kit on the shoulder and repeat the Ute word.

"Tawac?" Kit questions, looking confused.

When he points to me and repeats, "Tawac," it makes me giggle. As busy as Po'rat is with healing him, he grabs Kit's arm then points back and forth between himself and Kit.

"Man!" Kit says, understanding the Ute word.

Pointing to myself, I say, "Mamac."

"Woman," he says, shaking his head up and down.

It's my turn to repeat the English words to Kit when a small boy enters the teepee. He often helps Po'rat by collecting plants for him. Today he walks in with willow branches. Kit plunks his hand atop the boy's head and says, "Tawac!"

The medicine man and I laugh, shaking our heads no. The boy though stands up taller, smiling at his newly upgraded status.

"Apac," I say.

Kit understands and speaks the English word. "Boy."

***

Over the next few weeks, Kit tells me how his horse, Taos, is selfish, going where he wants when Kit intends to head in a different direction.

"Even coming here, that dang horse was a bangtail about heading into the snowstorm," Kit describes. It takes a few minutes for Kit to translate his words into more-proper English; once I understand, I chuckle.

"Going out in a snowstorm was a bad choice," I tell him. By the time Kit and I are able to hold conversations like this, his wounds have healed significantly, and his strength has begun to return. Kit has been out walking near his teepee but isn't quite ready to be on his own. I've been sharing our family's share of food with him, reducing my share so he can have more. It seems obvious to me he should have considered how Taos was acting and decided against going out in the storm, but perhaps merikac think differently.

I tell him, "These ponies know this land far better than you, Kit. Listen to Taos, he will keep you safe."

One day during our daily walk, I ask him if he enjoys hunting, but Kit shakes his head no.

"Per-shi? Hunting? Do I have the English word wrong?" I ask him.

"Hunting, yes that's the correct word Chaska," he says quietly. I'm starting to understand his verbal queues and realize he doesn't know how to hunt.

"Is that it Kit? You don't know hunting?" Kit just nods but won't meet my eyes.

I say goodbye and leave his tent, pondering how I'll make this next request of Ahwatt. It will be a difficult one, I know, but it will ensure Kit survives to help us.

A quick breeze blows up quickly and smacks my face and body. I'm sure there is an ancestor telling me not to ask this of Ahwatt. Rather than listen to the perceived warning, I pull my elk hide tight about my shoulders, stumbling along the path of hard, trampled snow underfoot. I hurry to Ahwatt's teepee.

Once he allows me inside, I slip off the elk hide from my shoulders and kneel by the small fire burning within a circle of stones. I hold my hands to the fire, gazing silently at my brother, who sits cross-legged on the other side of the fire, his elk skin draped across his lap. The light of the fire casts flickering shadows on the broad high wall of the teepee. "I have something to ask you," I say.

He sighs deeply. "Why must you bother me all the time?"

I smile.

"Teach Kit to hunt," I beg my brother. "Show him how to climb trees to scout for food or signs of trouble. Tell him to be patient and silent while he hunts. I've already shown him my snares; he can at least eat the smaller catches."

Ahwatt is silent. I know he's heard me, so I wait quietly.

"You want me to teach this white man to hunt?" he finally says. "Are you *that* sure this man should be saved…or is this merely your kindness coming through?"

"I *know*, Ahwatt," I reply. "I just do.

"Ahwatt, he will tell other merikac about our generosity. How we healed him although we had the power to kill him. He'll tell them we are a strong tribe with peaceful and caring traditions," I beg. Ahwatt grabs a stick, angrily poking at the embers of the fire while remaining silent. The sides of the teepee flex and move with the violent wind gusting outside, making me hug my hide around me even as I sit close to the fire. My brother goes between looking into the fire and staring at me while still refusing to provide an answer. When he heaves his shoulders up and down, letting out a sigh, I know he'll give me an answer.

"Chaska," he starts, shaking his head back and forth. My heart leaps into my throat because I'm expecting him to say no. He looks into my eyes as if searching for the right answer. “Now that we’ve healed this man, I’ll allow a younger man to teach him to hunt.”

A rush of breath comes flowing out that I’d evidently been holding, and I feel the tension in my neck melt away. Ahwatt drops the stick and looks down at the fire. I know I shouldn’t push him further, but Kit must be able to find his way by either traveling over our paths or breaking new ones. “Could you—” Ahwatt holds up his hand, not looking me in the eyes.

“Enough,” he says quietly.

He keeps his eyes down as I get up to leave. Wrapping my elk hide tightly around my head and shoulders, I push open the teepee flap and step outside. Immediately, I’m hit by a slap of icy cold wind that slices my face. It’s biting cold, but I’m smiling as I head back to my own teepee.

***

The next day, I introduce Kit to my husband Kaib. Again, I mimic shooting the gun, but Kit just looks from me to Kaib, still resting on his buffalo hides.

"Stand. We're walking," I tell him then lead Kaib through the tent flap, hoping Kit will follow.

Once outside Kit and I walk single file behind Kaib, who carries his musket with him. It occurs to me that Kit probably thinks we are going to kill him. Chuckling to myself, I just keep walking, hearing Kit's footsteps behind me.

Kaib stops at a big cottonwood tree.

"Ser-vup ar-rick poon-å-ka-oom," says Kaib to me. Since Kit and I haven't learned how to translate these words yet, I'll use sign language to tell him what is happening. Kaib hands me his musket, then grabs hold of the far side of the tree trunk. He places a foot on the trunk and then another so that he is wholly off the ground. He slides his right hand up the tree, then slides his left foot up. Left hand, right foot repeating their motions until he has gotten quite far up the tree. We can both see him, but he stays perfectly still.

I point to my ear as if listening. "Ar-rick," I say. I point to my eyes and move my head from side to side, looking. "Poon-å-ka-oom."

"Look and listen," Kit says though I can tell he's still not sure why my husband is up in a tree while I teach him Ute words. Kaib climbs down and motions for us to follow him.

"Tē-äh," he whispers. *Deer.*

My husband walks silently to some brush, bends to a knee then looks to Kit and me, saying, "To-to-un." *Kneel down.* Kit lets out a sigh as if he's bored. Kaib turns quickly without making a sound and glares. Kit makes to stand, but Kaib sets a hand on his shoulder, strongly pushing him back into place and slowly shaking his head. *No.*

"Poon-å-ka-oom," Kaib mouths, then turns to keep his eye on a deer who walks toward us, then turns as if heading to the water. Kaib has the perfect shot. Kit watches while Kaib slowly raises his musket until the barrel is level with his eyes. He makes no sound, and the deer appears to not notice the slow methodical movements he has made.

A shot rings out, and the deer drops.

Kaib jumps up, now, and runs to the kill, pointing to where he shot the animal. Kit follows and upon reaching the animal, kneels to place his hand on the deer's warm skin. I hope he can feel the heat, the life, the sustenance this animal has provided to us. I wish I could explain to Kit how inextricably intertwined we are with this deer.

Again, I say, "Per-shi."

"Hunt." He understands. We'll stay here while Kaib expertly skins the deer, leaving the muscle underneath completely intact.

Chapter 8

Young Kit Grows Up
(Late Spring, 1861)

Kit sits on Taos and watches Chaska and her tribe head west into the mountains. Breathing deeply, he's settling into his new-found confidence. His time with them has been one of enlightenment, not just for the skills he's learned—hunting and scouting—but for the kindness they showed him. All he's ever heard of Indians is how ruthless they are, how uncivilized, willing to kill at all costs.

"I feel confident you'll be a successful trapper, Kit," Chaska said just before leaving. The two looked into each other's eyes, an understanding of friendship, of loyalty to one another, held fast between them.

"Thank you for all you've done for me, Chaska. I know you could have killed me all those months ago when you found me halfdead, but you didn't. You've given me a second chance to be the man I've dreamed I could be, and I won't let you down."

Kaib simply nods as he walks past atop his horse. Kit tips his hat toward the man who has done so much to help nurture the boy he once was into the man he is now. Kaib had taken him out and shown him how to hold the musket Kit had swiped from his brother back in Franklin. Taught him how to sight just below where he intended the bullet to strike an animal. Kaib had shown him how to let a small breath escape his lips as he squeezed the trigger….At his first kill, Kit was stunned by the musket's power. The deer that had been grazing peacefully in the woods the moment before Kit pulled the trigger had fallen with a single shot. Still, it wasn't the weapon's power to kill that stirred Kit. The gun, he realized, could assure its owner life as easily as it bestowed death. As the smoke of the shot drifted away and the pungent odor of gunpowder struck his nostrils, Kit saw himself—his future self—roaming the mountains, the river valleys, the high hills of the West, musket over his shoulder, loyal Taos at his side, holding dominion over the animals, surveying and conquering the land.

For now, Kit pulls the reins to the right and heads Taos toward Santa Fe to meet up with a caravan heading west into the mountains where he'll create the destiny he's dreamed of.

Once he's past the thick cottonwoods where he's lived with the Utes for the spring, he briefly stops in Fort Pueblo at the confluence of the Arkansas and the Fountain to pick up a few provisions. He guides Taos through the gate of a flimsy wooden fence—just skinny scrub oak tree trunks, each hastily nailed up and down to one horizontal beam. A good wind or an out-of-control horse could knock the structure over. "I ain't been in that saddle for quite some time," he tells no one except Taos as he ties the reins to the hitching post. "Gonna take some gettin' used to"—rubbing his rear end after the long ride.

Grabbing at his John B, Kit pushes a rickety wooden door and enters the plaza within the fort walls. Just like Bents' Fort, there's a hard dirt floor with entrances to rooms surrounding the square. As he passes the horno, Kit can feel the heat radiating from the adobe, mud-brick structure and turns in time to see a woman pulling bread out using a long wooden paddle. He takes a big whiff and is rewarded with the yeasty smell of warm bread that fills him with warm memories of home. "Mm," he sighs. He continues past despite his strong desire to reach down and rip off a bit of the crusty outside. The single-story structure is flat on top, so when Kit enters the trading post's main room, the ceiling is only inches above his head.

There will be no ear tugging today. Chaska gave Kit several gray squirrel and fluffy rabbit pelts to trade. He also carries an elk hide Chaska tanned herself and gave to Kit, but he hasn't decided yet if he wants to trade it.

"Been with the Indians, I see," the purveyor says when Kit shows him the pelts. "These ain't the work of any trapper I know." For a moment, Kit considers keeping the items. He'd never thought to learn how Chaska skillfully skinned the animals she had caught in her snares. They talked all the time, and he had been so focused on learning the language that he missed a valuable lesson. Right then and there, Kit vows to learn that skill too; it obviously was important when trading.

"Yep," Kit says sheepishly, wondering if the man will judge him for living amongst the Ute.

"No shame there, son. We all need their support from time to time. 'Specially in the winter months. It's a good time to learn how they survive so we can survive."

"You got any knives back there that I could use to skin like these are done?"

The purveyor smiles, then turns his back to Kit, fishing through a few of the wooden shelves. "Aha," he says, turning and handing Kit a knife. "The handle is made of elk antler. Nice and sharp. Thick too, so you can really leverage it and scrape clean," says the man, taking in Kit's demeanor. "You's purty young to be out here on your own. What's your story?" Kit ignores him, turning the knife over in his hands.

"I'll take it, plus a few tins. What'cha got for me to eat?" Kit asks.

The man seems to ignore Kit's question, setting out five or six tins from which Kit can select. Once he's gotten what he needs, Kit walks back out to the hitching post: He fits the items into the saddle bag, and hops onto Taos. They carefully make their way past the rickety fence and head toward the south.

Walking through the creosote fields that lead to Santa Fe, Kit remembers the last time he came through here. It'd been so dry then. Now just as summer is grabbing hold of the land, all Kit can see is green. The flat scrubland of the high desert is coming alive. Dainty yellow flowers grow at the tip of the now green creosote bushes, thin green leaves of the sagebrush wave gently when a breeze blows in.

One thing hasn't changed since his last appearance in Santa Fe: He's still broke. Thankfully, Kit held onto Chaska's elk hide. He'd decided not to trade it at Fort Pueblo although the proprietor had eyed it something fierce. He's determined to sleep on an actual mattress during his stay.

"Fine, fine piece of work," says the purveyor to Kit.

Kit has tied Taos just outside the first house of trade he has come to upon entering the town. The open-air market has no doors, just large decorative blankets hanging where the door might have been. Dirt and dust from the roadway outside spill onto the shop's wooden floorboards. Whereas the Bent brothers' trade counter was clear of any goods, the counter at this shop is chock-full of items for sale, all in neat piles—canned goods, boxes of dry goods and blankets. Scales were situated along the counter to weigh out flour and sugar. Behind the counter, shelves that stretched from floor to ceiling held even more items to purchase. Tin plates were stacked neatly next to piles of spoons and forks. Large and small cans of fruits and vegetables were lined up in rows, pictures of what was inside facing outward.

Kit had pushed the elk hide toward the purveyor, squeezing it through a small area of open counter between the register and stacked cans of peaches that made a tower, one can standing atop the rest.

"Them Indians *are* good for something. ain't they?" Kit was asked. Thoughts of the Ute kindness he had just experienced gave him a warm feeling inside. Before he thought better of it, he said, "Good people." The man behind the counter stopped suddenly and looked up at Kit, who tilted his head and made his lips curve up slightly.

"Ah, you's still young boy! There'll be time enough for you to come to hate them." Kit doubted that.

***

Kit's finally getting the hang of this trade business. When the purveyor made a low offer, Kit just stayed silent; something he's darn good at anyhow. He'd been able to trade for more ammunition, a knife, a tin pan, and, most importantly, enough money to rent a room with a bed.

"Come on, boy."

Kit unhooks Taos and walks him, reins in hand, to the stable. The horse seems at ease amongst those walking the dirt roadway. A few women bustle by their long skirts flapping back and forth as they walk. Men with colorful blankets over their shoulders and leather boots on their feet walk by. Wagons kick up dust so bad that Kit has to put his face against Taos' neck to avoid it. The stable is just behind the main road, around the corner from a saloon where Kit intends to lay his head for the evening. Just as he and Taos are turning a corner, Kit sees her. A woman of Indian descent stands just across the street at the opposite corner from Kit. She's shorter than Kit. Her long dark hair is in braids that hang over each shoulder. She carries a basket of vegetables. What strikes Kit are her eyes: warm, brown eyes that seem to crinkle when he looks her way. A small smile spreads across her face. Kit is mesmerized by her beauty. She brings one delicate hand up to her mouth as she suppresses a giggle.

"Wow," Kit says to Taos, who lets out a loud snort, stomping his hoof and shaking his head back and forth. Kit comes back to reality and notices that he's stopped in the middle of the roadway. When he realizes he's staring, Kit immediately turns to look at the ground, shuffling off in embarrassment.

***

When he finally lays his down on the bed, Kit's entire body relaxes. He's spent the last few months on wonderfully soft buffalo hides that Chaska and her tribe graciously offered to him as he healed. He'd never forget that kindness. But now, this bed, albeit just a bunch of straw tucked into some fabric, surrounded his body in a gentle, soothing hug.

Drifting off to sleep, he murmurs to himself, "I'm gonna marry that girl…."

Book 2

Chapter 9

It Starts with the Wind
(Summer's End, 1864)

Summers and winters pass. The seasons turn. We move down the mountain before winter sets in, set up camp, try to survive. When spring finally arrives after the snows and winds have died down, we pack up and move to our summer camp.

Mapia and Chipara complain, but Chava always helps take down the teepees and tie them for the ponies to pull. High up in the Rocky Mountains the steep inclines are just as treacherous going up as they are heading down. The ponies struggle to pull their packs along our winding paths that switchback up through forests of evergreens.

"Steady there, Taima," Chava says, battling to keep her pony's pack from sliding out in front of the animal. The packs are much heavier than the ponies that pull them. If the pack gets away from Chava, it would be a disaster—the pony would be pulled straight down the steep slope.

"Push, Chava!" I say, running over to help my daughter. The pack has slid to the edge of the zigzagging trail, leaning precariously close to the drop-off.

"Pia, pick it up from your side and I'll get it here on my side. Then we can align it to the trail again." Try as I might, I can't lift the pack. Grunting, I'm using all my energy and weight, driving my legs into the ground, but the pack doesn't move.

"Keep Taima steady. I'll get help," Chava says then runs up the steep incline. She and I have been out in front of the rest of the tribe. We have to travel single file because there's very little room on the trail. Even the ponies find themselves watching the ground closely, putting their hooves down purposefully to avoid getting too close to the edge.

Taima is the most playful pony in the herd. As soon as anyone goes for a different horse to ride or pull from the rest of the herd, she will poke, prod, and cajole until she gets some attention. She's just as curious as Chava, which means the two of them can get into trouble if they aren't careful. As long as

Taima has a job to do, like pulling a pack, she's fine; give her a bit of breathing room though and she will be up to trouble.

"Let's try again," I hear from behind me. Chava has asked several of the others to leave their own horses behind for a few moments while we straighten Taima's heavy pack. This will happen often as we climb up and down the mountains. The twists and steep corners make it nearly impossible to keep the packs in the center of the trail, which only measures three of my feet stepping toe to heel.

As we made the final approach to our summer camp a few months ago, I had worried the trail would be blocked somehow. The men didn't ride ahead of us this time to ensure we had food to eat. Instead, we are all together.

We've heard rumors about the merikac, of course; our scouts have spied their small encampments dotting the hills. Their numbers have continued to grow, but we haven't had any trouble with them this time—at least, not until we pass their small mining town along the creek while making our way up the mountain again. It's the same creek where, as children, Ahwatt and I used to hop from one side of the roaring water to the other; from fresh, thick moss on one bank to small pebbles and mud on the other. The town of Laurette is built along a trail we've used forever. It's the same as all the other little mining towns that are visible as we head up toward our summer camp in the western mountains. Indeed, buildings pop up on either side of the trail in Laurette—meaning we have to walk right through the merikac's little town. I hop off Nublada to walk alongside her and, fearing at least one of the children in our group will be frightened, I look up and down our length.

"Mama," cries a small girl, grabbing for her mother's hand as they pass by the buildings. It's fear-inducing: Men with scraggly beards stop in their tracks to look at us, glaring their hatred through crinkled eyes.

"Get out of our town!" someone cries out. Ahwatt rides up to the man, a heavyset miner in blackened clothing, soot covering him from head to toe. *He must have just come from working,* I think to myself. A group of them draw closer to the man as my brother approaches.

"We don't mean you any harm. It's just that you've placed your buildings along our trail. We have walked this for as long as I can remem—"

The heavyset man walks right up to Ahwatt then stands to his left side, peering up at him with devilish eyes. His peers stay where they were, not courageous enough to come face-to-face with a Native. "Don't care what you done before. We's here. We's stayin'. Find another way around or go somewhere else." He looks back at the other men, perhaps for encouragement. Though the man appears large, he is no match for my brother. Sitting atop Luksi, Ahwatt is enormous.

Ahwatt nods at me to continue moving everyone through the town. Once I start moving everyone behind me will follow.

My brother turns Luksi slightly with what appear to be invisible signs for the horse to follow. He's antagonizing the merikac who stands too close. The pony turns and as he does, the man has to step back or be knocked over by Luksi's shoulder. All the while, Ahwatt keeps his unblinking eyes on the man. Normally, my brother stops conversations by leaving. This time, for all intents and purposes, he's ending the conversation by staying.

It works because the man stands his new ground, but says, "This is the last time you can come through here," waiving a finger for emphasis. His buddies nod their heads in agreement. Ahwatt isn't the least bit bothered by this brief show of force. Then he does something so out of character that I turn almost fully in my saddle.

"We're camping for the night just outside your town. Just one night and then we'll get to our camp up on the mountain. Come," Ahwatt says, "smoke with me tonight. You'll see that we are peaceful and don't want to cause any conflict."

The man looks sheepishly to his buddies who are nodding in the affirmative.

"Awright."

I don't know what Ahwatt has planned, but I can only hope it's truly peaceful.

We pass through the town center now. A walkway of wooden planks connects the buildings on one side of the street. People, mostly men, bustle about, crossing the dirt trail, then climbing up to the walkway to enter one of the many shops. Even burros are walked along the thin line of wooden planks, clip-clopping their hooves in a hollow sound that reminds me of walking on a forest floor beneath tall pines: layers and layers of fallen needles making a soft hollow sound as we tread across it....

A bell rings as one man enters the general store. The squat building stands straight up and down, with a squared-off front. Long lengths of timber have been lain down horizontally then crudely stacked to a height of where my head would be if I were riding Nublada. There's a small opening for the window glass. The door is also made of wood, but those timbers have been set vertically. I can't say how they are held together from my vantage point.

Other buildings are made to look differently. The bank is made of horizontally lain timbers. These aren't rounded like those of the general store. Instead, they are smooth and painted a pale blue. Big square windows hold panes of glass, and a doorway has one little flowerpot next to it. One lonely Columbine grows in the pot. A woman comes out of the door just as I'm passing it, a broom in her hands. She begins to sweep the walkway in front of what must be her store.

"Ah!" she gasps as she looks toward me. Then she makes a noise of anger— "Uh!"—gripping the broom tightly with both hands. A look of fear dashes across her face. Then anger again—she draws her lips up into a smirk.

"Horace!" she bellows.

A deep voice can be heard coming from the depths of the building. "Yes, dear."

"Come out here this instant! A bunch of Injuns are walking through our town."

"Who is coming through the town? Did you say injuns?" asks the husband sounding exasperated by his wife's demands.

"Yes!"

"Well, do they want to trade something?" he asks.

"Horace!"

I just let out a little chuckle to myself. There are fourteen buildings in all, including several that look like miner's homes—small, barely tall enough for a man to walk inside. Wooden logs have been stacked together willy-nilly, barely holding onto one another. The structures, which dot the land here and there, just behind the main buildings in town, look as though they could blow away in the wind.

A hotel or two stand in wait for the passengers to arrive on the stagecoach. Sometimes the coach will pull into town with women dressed fashionably in long-sleeved dresses of calico or all in black. Younger ladies wear hats of beaver fur, while the more refined of the women wear felt hats with feather plumes falling from the sides. Other times, four horses pulling a closed-in coach with doors on either side will be driven by several men who sit high atop the driver's box, driving the horses.

When I pass by the house of ill repute, the Floatin' Horseshoe Saloon, the women outside largely ignore me. They stand on a staircase that wraps around one side of the building. Several smoke cigarettes. They are dressed in a variety of outfits, from brightly colored dresses to shabby gray rags that barely cover them. As Ahwatt rides by them, they start calling to him and giggling.

"Honey!"

"You ever had you a real woman?"

None are brave enough to step off the walkway in front of their saloon. But they keep calling to Ahwatt, nonetheless.

"Take me back to camp with you!"

"Won't you stop a spell?"

Ahwatt ignores them completely. It's as if he hasn't heard the women: His face gives nothing away. If he did make a move, the merikac might see it as a threat and wouldn't be interested in his offer to smoke the peace pipe with them later today. It might put us all in danger.

***

Out of town we finally come to the mine itself, where many of the men in Laurette work. Water-supply ditches guide the creek water into the mine. I don't know what the merikac do underground, but the water coming out of the mine smells sickening and looks even worse. A brown sludge trails out of the mine and into our creek.

Thankfully, our camp is upstream, above their mines, where the water comes straight off the mountainside. Snow melts one drip after another into the rivers and streams that run heavy with icy cold waters. Collectively, the drips create a deluge downstream that flows forcefully over rocks big and small and descends into the valley. Tall lodge pole pines surround us. Vibrantly green, these sentinels, second in command to the ring of mountains, point daggers skyward. The mountains themselves look like one large rock from our camp, but when you climb up to the top, you find it is actually just a mess of large rocks, one on top of the other. As winter turns to spring, the kinnikinic becomes lusher. Here, just below tree line, we feel safe.

***

When I awoke this morning, I felt hopeful. All summer long, the hot western sun has been warming us. Summertime in the Colorado mountains means picking plants, flowers, tree stems, all for *Po'rat,* Medicine Man. He makes teas and tinctures from them all.

"Flowers of elk root, hawthorn, and maple make a tea that soothes sore throats," he explains to Chava, who has joined me today.

"Sticky pine resin is applied to wounds."

"How about this?" Chava asks, holding willow stems. Po'rat peels back the tough outer bark and has my daughter bite into the freshly revealed innards.

"Pain relief," he says. "Yucca roots relieve joint pain."

She and I gathered most of the plants at a nearby pond that is fed by mountain streams: The mountains that surround us there are so high they block the sun.

Other plants are gathered in the long valley we cross each spring and fall. It's the men's hunting grounds, where buffalo are plentiful.

My girls love to hear the story of the valley that I tell often when we are working.

"Buffalo was having trouble walking across all the large rocks that River liked to carry and deposit on her shores. Walking along the river was the only way between the mountains, but her shores were very narrow. So, Buffalo told Creator, 'All these stones hurt me as I walk. Since this is the only way through the mountains, can you help me?' Creator agreed because other animals wanted to walk along River's shores too, but they weren't wide enough. Creator pushed and pushed the eastern mountains and the western mountains apart, forming a large valley."

There are no trees in the valley, just grasslands as far as the eye can see. Antelope, barely visible as they melt into the background of the waving green and golden grasses, run amongst big, brown buffalo.

This summer, food has been plentiful. We've collected tivac, or pine nuts. Some we eat now, and others are crushed into cakes to eat in winter. Small animals like marmot, chipmunk and squirrels are coming out from their long winter inside ground dens. We women fish while the men have hunted the elk and deer as they come back to the mountain: We women dry the meat after carefully separating the sinew and fat from the muscle and skin, stretching the hide over a smoldering fire of green tree limbs. Red chickaree and rabbits have been snared and skinned, and the meat has also been dried. There isn't enough to sustain us through the upcoming winter though. We need one buffalo. And today is the day—*tinay kuc.* The buffalo hunt.

***

A breeze begins to blow up from the valley. A bristlecone pine, almost as old as the Ute tribe, doesn't move: Even as harsh winter winds blow snow up and over its needles, the green cones pinch when picked. The tree has been there, growing just on the ridge top; we pass it year after year. A grove of aspens, all their roots intertwined into one big family, is fluttering yellow and orange leaves. They crackle in the wind as they quake, sounding the way our long elk-skin dresses do when we walk. The gusts tug at the colored leaves, sending one or two down to the earth…I stand watching as they spin silently to the ground. The wind carries the pungent smell of the forest changing seasons. There's something else though, a scent I can't immediately identify. Whatever it is, it makes me shiver from fright.

"First signs of fall," says my oldest daughter, coming up to interlace her fingers with mine. Yes, I nod, looking into her eyes to see if she is aware of the odd sensation the wind carries with it. She looks back to me, smiling contentedly. All this week, colder temperatures and blustery conditions make the pine boughs tremble, bracing for…something.

Shake it off, I think. *This will be a good day.*

After our horrible winter, my anxiety has risen. I sometimes shake with uncontrollable fear. Can't do that today though. I don't want to scare anyone else. I don't want anyone to know of my fears.

As I watch the men prepare to leave in the first light of dawn, the light breeze becomes downright blustery. We are all so proud of our hunters. The food they will provide for us today should calm my nerves.

Squalls of wind rush up from the valley, as if to blow the men back. *Remain where you are!* it howls like the long slow cry of a coyote. I stand shivering with the others, covered in blankets as we watch the hunters leave. I'm partly cold and partly fearful. The gusts of wind pick up dirt and small pieces of bark, sending them our way in a barrage, lodging dust in our eyes and mouths. *Maybe this is a sign,* I think to myself, riled by the wind. *Perhaps they shouldn't go.*

The men are expert hunters. I don't worry about their skills. And the horses don't seem bothered by the wind. In fact, they seem as excited as the men. None are saddled. It's wonderful they can do their part to keep us safe and fed too.

Ahwatt makes his decisions based upon how many animals or people might be killed during the hunt. He's been this way since he was a child, begging to go with the hunters before he was old enough. As a child he mimicked the older warriors, listening to their stories of battles, excited to follow in their footsteps. So, I'm not surprised that before I can reach him, he shouts, "Tinay!" The hunters hop on ponies then race out of camp and down the mountain. The buffaloes make their fall home along the Platte, in the hills and valleys dug by the river long ago.

I again feel a gust of wind. *Maybe I'm just imagining this,* I think to myself. Ever since Mawic and the three other elders died, it's been hard for me to know whether our lives will ever truly be safe again. Truth is, since my parents died, I've lost my ability to ever feel safe anywhere. But this is more than that.

I remain near camp with the other women but try to separate myself from a few of the more vocal ones. More and more, I hear them whispering about Ahwatt, though I often pretend not to hear. They are demanding he fight the white men. I'm the reason he holds back.

Ahwatt is a fierce fighter; negotiation isn't his strong point. More often, he uses his large stature, hovering over people while he speaks. Then, before he makes a decision, he quickly turns on his heels, suggesting the discussion is over. I have always been the negotiator, seeking to maintain relationships, manage emotions, and calm fears. I'm quiet, tiny and thin, but when it comes to the tribe, and especially my children, all I want is to teach the younger members everything I've been taught.

Losing favor with some of the women can be difficult, but I'm willing to take the risk. The merikac simply keep coming. It isn't possible to kill them all. More will replace the dead. Instead, like my father, I believe in negotiating for what we want—which is to live here on the land we've always had, maintaining our culture and traditions. Peace is the answer to our problems.

To avoid some of the women's stares, I gather my children then call to some of the women who also believe in my chosen path. Since our terrible winter, my brother has taught me how to shoot a gun to keep our camp safe when he and the other men are out hunting. We practiced down along the Platte, where it winds through our mountain valley. I always keep the musket nearby now. Sitting with the children and the tribal women I have approached, we separate dark red, ripe chokecherries picked yesterday into piles. These will last through winter, we hope. Although the wind has lessened, there are moments when squalls push up from the valley. Where we sit, on the still-warm earth, soft from the thick layers of pine needles, sunlight comes intermittently through the canopy of boughs swaying above us. We overturn tapered willow baskets one at a time, dumping the fruit onto a clean blanket, separating the cherries from the twigs or leaves that are still attached. The girls try secretly popping cherries into their mouths. Their guilt shows on their faces when their lips pucker and their eyes squeeze together: The fruit's taste is very bitter. They look to me with shamefaced eyes. Because the bitterness means they won't eat many cherries, I simply shake my head at them.

We chat quietly about the day. "Chaska," a friend, Magena, asks me, "how are you feeling about our men's chances this year?" She looks into my eyes, laying a hand gently on my shoulder, and waits to hear the truth.

I want to blurt out that I'm nearly paralyzed by fear. That I can't sleep for the nightmares that torment me. I dream of lying on the ground, starving, blurry eyed from lack of water. I have visions of dead tribesmen, bones showing through flesh eaten by crows, starved. My girls look to me expectantly, dependent upon my strength. I say, confidently, "Wonderful. The men are skillful. They will get us a buffalo."

"Chaska, remember who you are talking to. We grew up together. I can see the fear in your eyes. You're worried and you can talk with me."

Sighing, I give in. "Merikac are everywhere, Magena. I'm worried they are taking over our land. Ahwatt wants to kill them all, but I think that will only start more trouble for us."

"Maybe that's what is best. These people intrude and make their homes here. Why shouldn't we fight back?"

"Magena, there are just too many of them. If we try to kill the ones who are here, more will come. We are a peaceful people and so we should find a peaceful solution."

Magena shakes her head, then looks to me. "You sound just like your father, Chaska. The other women worry that you're putting the wrong ideas into your brother's head and confusing him. They say you should mind your tongue."

I raise my gaze and look in the direction of our camp, where our other tribeswomen are working diligently. They sit apart from our group, probably complaining about my interventions.

"Pia why aren't those women helping us?" asks Chava.

"They have other responsibilities to our tribe," I tell Chava. I purse my lips together so that I don't say more about them. They are tanning hides, working just as hard as we are. It's work we are proud of—scraping the large buffalo or deer hides, softening them, making them waterproof by drying them over a smoldering fire of green branches. How can they not realize Ahwatt cannot win this relentless trespassing by killing the white men in small battles? Why don't they understand: His indecisiveness could cost us our own lives?

I often wish I had been born to become our tribe's leader instead of my brother. At least Ahwatt and I have a relationship in which he listens to my requests. Do I beg? Or nag him? Probably. I know there are fellow tribespeople who think I'm being disrespectful when I confront my brother. *"Why does Ahwatt ask his sister for advice?"* they ask. As a woman, I wasn't allowed to ask for what I wanted from the merikac. I had to convince my brother and the men of our tribe that what I wanted for Kit is the right answer.

Chava comes to sit in my lap. She doesn't seem satisfied by the answer I've given her. She turns to look in my eyes…puts her little hands on both of my cheeks. We are eye to eye, and she says:

"Pia, why do those women stare at us while we work?" She turns my head in the direction of the women. They are huddled together, snickering, watching us.

"Pia wants to create peace with the white men. They don't understand. When I tell them peace is better than fighting, they disagree. I'm trying to convince Ahwatt of that too. A long time ago," I continue, "I tried to convince him I was right, but he didn't believe me. People died because of it. So, for a long time, we used to be so mad at one another we didn't even talk. Auntie made us work together to fix our relationship. Remember the story I told you about us hunting together?"

Mapia turns her head toward us. "I remember that story!" she says. "Tell it again, Mama!"

Despite feeling a bit self-conscious, and after telling the story many times before, I explain it all again....

After our parents died, I was angry at Ahwatt because I thought he could have saved them, though he was only a boy. We fought a lot after that, until there just wasn't anything more to say.

At that time Ahwatt was learning to hunt. I used to taunt him...I was jealous he was allowed to leave camp to hunt while I had to stay close by. "Elk and deer stand still so much of the time; anyone can shoot them for a kill!" I would tell him. He would look at me as if I was crazy. "You have no idea how difficult it is," he'd say, beginning to shake with frustration. I suppressed a giggle while watching him struggle to gain his composure. "If you say so," I replied, shrugging my shoulders and walking away. Inside, though, I was anxious to go out and hunt with him.

Auntie helped build back our relationship. With her encouragement, Ahwatt took me hunting once or twice. I wanted to teach Ahwatt how to pick berries, but I wasn't allowed. Though Ahwatt was willing, the elders said he would be viewed as doing women's work and would have to relinquish his future as the leader in our tribe.

He taught me to use the bow and arrows even though he was the one who made the kill the first day he took me hunting. I was happy to be away from my usual chores—until Ahwatt walked off, making me drag the deer back to camp.

I leaned down and pulled the animal by its back hooves, dragging its carcass along the pine needles strewn over the forest floor. Occasionally, the deer's antlers caught on smaller scrub oaks; I had to stop and untangle them. "Why are you making me drag this deer?" I called to Ahwatt up ahead. I had begun understanding just how difficult the task was—but I wasn't going to admit it.

Ahwatt turned and smiled back at me. "You kill a deer, you carry it, little one."

"Can you at least help me get this animal free instead of just standing there?" I called a short while later.

He shook his head. "No."

He didn't help me at all.

Two years separate us in age, but Ahwatt is stronger physically than I am. I tried giving him a pouty face, which usually made him give in to whatever I'm asking. Not this time.

Ahwatt's stubbornness made me think about his lot in life. Eventually, he would be our leader and assume responsibility for our safety. For our hunger too.

"Sorry," I said.

I knew hunting was hard work, but I hadn't realized our outing would start to fix whatever was broken between us. I picked up the animal to start walking again—but I stopped suddenly, tilting my head in thought, remembering something. Then, I ran ahead, leaving the deer and catching up to Ahwatt while trying to control my anger. I grabbed his arm to make him stop walking; he turned to look at me. "I never see *you* drag the kill!" I cried. "You ride into camp on Luksi, dragging the kill behind your horse!"

Ahwatt doubled over, laughing. "You actually realized I tricked you?" he said. We were almost back to camp by then.

We worked together to drag the deer home. I still don't put up with my brother's tomfooleries. Nor does he let me get away with any either.

***

Chava looks up from her work with excitement.

"What is it?" I ask.

"Luksi is coming! I know his gait anywhere! It's the men!"

She jumps up, spilling the chokecherries near her side of the blanket. Then she rushes down through the meadow where our camp lies and stands at the edge of the ridge to greet the men.

My heart fills with dread. It's much too soon for the men to be back. I stand and walk to where they will come back, up from the valley below. They will have had to ride through Laurette, or skirt around it, I hope....A *woosh* of air blows in triumphantly as Ahwatt and the others in the hunting party reappear. Most of camp has been alerted to their return by my little one, so we prepare to greet the men and see the buffalo they have killed for us. Instead, Ahwatt charges past us, not slowing Luksi, not even making eye contact. His horse, the pinto with intermingling smears of brown and white, takes one look at me then continues right by, sweating generously, ears stiff, pinned down.

The rest of the men ride into camp much more slowly, walking their horses. Normally, they speed into camp to celebrate the kill. Several glare at me as though I did something wrong. They begin hopping off their horses, their heads down. No one makes eye contact with me. The horses seem lethargic too. That's when I realize: There's no buffalo being dragged behind any of the horses.

Just then I hear Mapia ask my husband, "Where is the buffalo?"

When I don't hear Kaib answer, I begin to panic. A burst of anxiety rushes through my body. I want to ask what happened, but no one will meet my eyes. I'm just standing in the middle of hunters walking past me. Finally, Kaib comes to me. Still atop his horse, he comes up next to me so that I can put my hands on his leg. Looking down, his forehead is wrinkled in anger. "Walking down the mountain this morning, we saw buffalo in the valley. Ahwatt instructed us to fan out to surround the herd, but just after his command left his lips, we ourselves were surrounded…by Americans," he says. "Maybe fifty, all told. They came out of the woods," he continues, "just down the mountain. They sat on their horses, guns drawn; Ahwatt tried to reason with them. They said if we wanted to camp on *their* land, we could, but that was all: We're not allowed farther down the mountain. We can't get to the buffalo," Kaib concludes. "The Americans set themselves up to stop us."

All I can do is stare at my husband, bewildered. "*Their* land?" I ask.

Although the Americans have been here for ten years or so, our long history of living here—along these streams, beside the rivers, amid these broad valleys and tall mountains—means nothing to them. We are called Natives to depict our lesser stature in their eyes, but we are not considered native to this land as owners.

"But I thought we had made friends with them.," I say, thinking about how Ahwatt had smoked a peace pipe with the residents of Laurette along Buckskin Creek. Although I wasn't there, I assumed it was a peaceful interaction. Now that I think on it, and knowing my brother, perhaps my belief was wrong.

My husband shakes his head. "No. Any respect we thought we created is gone. They are not our friends. Ahwatt told them how important it is for our tribe to make this hunt. The merikac just laughed, saying the end to the hunt would mean the end to the Indian that much sooner. We thought it best not to fight them. Our camp is so close, they could easily have come and killed all of you. Instead, we turned around and came back."

I'm stunned. I can't imagine the scene our men must have come up on, and how they feel now.

"Perhaps you can go back out again?" I suggest.

Kaib again shakes his head no. "Ahwatt told them we would be leaving in a few weeks. He asked them to allow us safe passage through. The men said they would stay there, keeping their guard against us, until we finally leave."

As my husband and I talk, I begin to feel Ahwatt's gaze on me. I turn to see him stalking up to us. Leaning down he points his finger at me, pressing it hard into my shoulder. "*This*," he bellows, waving his arms now, indicating the lack of a buffalo, "is your fault, Chaska! We had to turn away from our responsibility because the merikac threatened our tribe's safety." He spits at me. Red lines radiate from the browns of his eyes, protruding across his brow. I haven't seen my brother this angry for a long time.

He draws even closer, pointing an accusing finger at me again, this time right in front of my face. "Do you think this could be solved with a piece of paper?" He's so close I can feel his chest trembling in anger. "Would those men have left us alone if we had signed a treaty?"

Ahwatt has been meeting with the territorial governor who would like to sign a peace treaty with us. In my mind, I see all of us getting along and living here together peacefully. In Ahwatt's mind, it will just be a piece of paper—written in English, he won't know what it says, and doesn't believe the merikac would hold to it anyhow.

This too is a trait I dislike about my brother: He does not know right from wrong. Thus, when he is responsible for something, anything, he gets angry. Either way, I'm not deterred.

He turns to walk away so that the conversation cannot continue. Turning back suddenly, he says: "Do you know what's happening out there?"

Well, no I don't, I think. *Other than walking through the town of Laurette, I'm in camp.*

"One day, there are no white men," he says. "The next day, an entire village has been constructed at the edge of the river. They're like us, Chaska. They carry all their belongings on mules. Hundreds of men. But they unload buildings from the mules, they put them up and stay there. Suddenly—a village." He spreads his hands, indicating the breadth of the white men's villages taking up entire swatches of land along the river.

"To do what?" I ask.

"Pull rocks from the river," he tells me.

What nonsense! Is he lying again?

"When they see us coming, they grab their rifles. No one wants to talk to us. They don't care that you think our tribe deserves land of our own. They only want us gone to collect their gold."

He turns on his heels to end the conversation again. But that isn't happening. I know I shouldn't confront him with the entire tribe watching us, but my anger begins spilling out of me.

"Brother!" I cry. "Make them understand! Lead us! Bring the other men and convince them! Find a way! Don't be mediocre!" I say. "Don't make short-term decisions that are good enough. Make long-term strategies that ensure our lives will be great."

Ahwatt stares at me intensely. Forcing him to make a decision is asking for trouble. As the tribe watches, stunned, I realize my usual reserved nature has left me. This is so important to me that the indomitable passion I feel for our tribe overtakes my shyness.

"Chaska," Ahwatt roars, "*I* took on the task of negotiating because *you* asked me to. It can't continue! I cannot let another winter go by where some of our elders have to leave camp for us to survive."

That's it then. He is still upset at the last difficult situation for which he had to take responsibility. Now this. I'm not letting him walk away again. "We sign the paper with

Hunt," I tell him as calmly as possible, "and we move to a safe place. Lead us to land where we can continue as the Ute people." My directness could backfire on me, but I'm done with Ahwatt's cowardly nature.

"Enough of this," my brother replies. "I do *not* want to hear anymore from you about signing a peace agreement."

He isn't getting the last word. Hands on hips I start giving it right back to him: "What are you talking about? I didn't go with you today. I didn't make the Americans block the hunt."

I know the other men in camp have been getting inside Ahwatt's head, trying to convince him not to sign a treaty with the merikac. "No more talking, now we fight," they say. Ahwatt has made several trips to Denver to talk about the situation with the merikac governor, Hunt, trying to either find a way to live together with the Americans or find land just for our tribe to live on. Land where we can continue our culture. Hunt says it may be possible for us to move. But he also says we must become "civilized." *And* he says nomads are not considered American. Farmers are American; landowners are American. Wanderers are not.

Ahwatt usually comes back from his trips to Denver exhausted. "They don't understand us," he tells me. "They say we should grow our food from plants they are willing to provide. I don't see why we can't use the ones that already grow here, as we've always done."

"Why can't we just say we'll do their farming," I ask my brother, "then continue our ways once they're gone?"

"They will live among us, Chaska. They will teach us to farm and watch us as we learn. It isn't that simple."

"But father signed all those treaties with the Americans. Why can't you be like him?"

My question stops Ahwatt dead in his tracks. Starting with Fray Dominguez and Fray Velez, Franciscans who ventured across our lands nine decades ago, our tribe has been making agreements with trespassers. Back then, father was just a boy. He made the trip with the padres, helping them to talk with other Ute Natives along the way. Though the Franciscans were kind, others weren't so friendly. When Mexico became part of America, the merikac signed away our land as if it were their own. My father asked the President to let all Utes become Americans but was turned down.

Ahwatt stares at me. Striding forward he looks furious, balling his fists. It's just me and him.

"Why can't I be like Father? Did you ever think maybe I didn't want to lead the tribe?" he asks.

The men watching the argument take in their breath. All of us stop and look at him. My brother—big, strong, tough, courageous—didn't want to lead us? No wonder he doesn't make decisions. I don't think the admission was something he ever thought he would say out loud, but it makes so much sense to me now. That was probably why he asked my opinion so often.

It's as if my brother comes out of a trance. He looks to me, my mouth hanging open, then he looks to the others, who are just as surprised by his statement. If it were me, I would be apologetic. But not Ahwatt. He quickly regains his footing and continues his rant, directing his vitriol toward me:

"How could you forget all the broken treaties? As soon as Father signed a treaty with the merikac, they broke it."

I had forgotten that. Strange to lose that memory. Father was such a calm soul. To me, as a little girl, he probably put on a strong face, as I do for my girls. But he was probably devastated by the broken treaties. Ahwatt had been invited to the men's council, though I was not. He might have memories of Father's frustration that I've never been able to access. His job was to keep us safe, so these injustices must have crushed his spirit. Surely the merikac have learned that we are all better off finding peace together.

Instead of getting mad, I walk up to Ahwatt and look him in the eyes. "Trust me, brother," I say. "Ever since Mom and Dad died, it has been difficult for both of us, but especially for you. You *will* save us," I tell him empathetically.

We've both carried our pain for over twenty years. Mine, a sadness for our loss. His, a guilt that he could have done more. We've both stuffed down the sorrow, but my brother has also had to assume more responsibility than he wanted.

The wind picks up again, carrying with it a sense of hopelessness. Ahwatt thoughtlessly swats at the wind, trying to make it go away. We have done nothing wrong except live our lives. These people come here thinking the land is wide open, theirs to take. It's uncontrollable…yet we must find a way to survive. We both just want peace but have vastly different ideas of how to manage that. I finally feel confident Ahwatt will listen to me and find accord with the merikac. Until I look in his eyes again. There's anger in them. And hurt. What I thought was an agreement between us was merely his anger at being put in the position I've placed him in. Just when I think we are finally speaking the same language, he says, "Kaguc," using his nickname for me. Little Grandmother. "We have no choice. It is time to fight. Every intruder will be killed."

Chapter 10

The Rendezvous
(Summer, 1865)

The idea of travelling to the Rendezvous this year weighed heavy on Waa-nibe's mind. Although Kit has travelled to the annual event every year since marrying Waa-nibe, this year's gathering of trappers and mountain men from across the West concerns his wife.

"Of course, I'll be safe there," Kit tells her. "Just look at me! I'll be joining all the other trappers in the West. I'm practically their leader!"

He continues packing his saddle bags—matches, a comb and a few dried cakes of piñon nuts Waa-nibe had prepared—not another thought to his safety. When Waa-nibe suggests Natives are looked down upon by most of Kit's associates, Kit scoffs.

"Maybe another man would be afeared a' these folks," he says, "but not me."

But Waa-nibe is right. Most of the trappers at the Rendezvous know Kit lives among the Arapaho; but Natives aren't as well thought of as before. Whereas once Kit and his fellow mountain men traded easily with Natives, perhaps even living among them for a winter, the situation is different now. Sure, they still trade with one another, but on Native terms—meaning one or two men must go into the Indian camps alone, approach the chief and ask permission. Long gone are the days of simply riding in and demanding the Natives trade. Indians now expected more of the Americans, asking for—no, demanding—they be given flour, good weapons, tobacco. The Indians were causing entirely too much trouble, in Kit's mind. Worse, they had gotten in the way of progress. Most Americans agreed, they needed to go—and fast. But Kit isn't about to tell his wife she's right about the dangers of travelling to the Rendezvous. It would worry her too much.

After courting and marrying Waa-nibe in Santa Fe, she insisted they live in her parents' village. At first, her father and the other men were hesitant to allow Kit into the Arapaho camp, but over time, he has been at the very least tolerated.

They moved here three years ago. And looking at his wife now, even as he is packing to leave her, Kit is proud of the position he's assumed within his wife's family—he's developed strong negotiating skills that help both him and them. Villagers are happy when Kit brings them gifts—a few Springfields or Sharps to shoot, or Mackinaws. Once, when he was handed a San Diego belduque, he offered it to the chief, who seemed pleased with the desert ironwood handle knife.

Kit gave his fellow trappers unhindered access to beaver on the villagers' land in exchange for the best cloth, spices, flour, and knives. Which Kit then gave to a variety of favorable or influential people, as necessary. In turn, the overstuffed plews his friends sold at the Rendezvous or in St. Louis made anyone who hadn't been invited quite envious. Kit hadn't thought to ask permission from Waa-nibe's tribe, but he was sure they were fine with it.

Losing his independence for the winter hadn't been pleasant, but at least he still gets to leave the village for trapping and scouting. And, of course, he leaves every summer for the Rendezvous. After marrying Waa-nibe she insisted they stay with her family. Kit knew she had originally been intended for another villager, but once Waa-nibe had a look at Kit he felt confident that her betrothed was forgotten. Avipani, his name was. The village scout. He had fully expected to wed Waa-nibe, it would have increased his standing within the tribe significantly. Kit thinks he still pines for her. It was difficult for Kit to understand why the man was the scout, in charge of the tribe's safety: As far as Kit was concerned, he was trouble. Besides being a braggart, Avipani extended the truth to make himself appear more powerful than he was. Kit had seen right through him, but not the others in the tribe. When Kit had just been allowed into the camp and before he knew of Avipani's ways, the man had sold Kit out. Kit found himself begging for grace after Avipani told Waa-nibe's father that Kit was an Indian killer.

"What? No sir. I ain't nothin' like that. I've learned to live with the natives, not kill 'em." The trust Kit needed to live with Waa-nibe's tribe and take her hand was shaky at best. Even now, Kit isn't sure who is a friend and who is a foe.

They had continued to look upon him favorably; he was one of the tribe's most eligible men. But the man eyed Kit with eyes that burned with desire to kill him. So much so that Kit often wondered whether the day might come when he didn't wake up. Something about that man just didn't sit well with Kit. Avipani might even try to get what he wanted most—Kit's wife. Sometimes it burned Kit to the core to think of his wife left alone in the village with that man while he wasn't around. But Kit had to make a living. Trapping and tracking is all he knows, thanks to Kaib. Honestly, once the Native had shown him the basics, Kit picked up everything else quickly. He hoped to use the skills and knowledge he had learned to his own advantage…maybe even be named an Indian Agent for the Ute territory. He would have more control over who lives, who dies, who is forced to move or do his bidding. It went without saying that they'd all be better off with him, he believed. He had earned their respect.

***

After he finishes packing the saddle bags for the Rendezvous, he brings them out of the small house he built for himself, and his family then carries them over to where Taos is hitched. He grabs the saddle by the horn on the front end and the cantle at the back, then heaves it up onto Taos' back. He sinches the billet then puts his foot into the thick wooden stirrup and swings himself up and over. He's got a bag not unlike a gunny sack that he will carry over his back by the drawstrings. Inside are a few scraps of dried meat, some berries his daughter gathered for him, and the sourdough starter he was given by Cookie. A burro tied to Taos carries the flour, Dutch oven and cast-iron skillet he'll use to cook along the way. He waves to his daughter, his wife and her family as he walks Taos out of the village. *They practically worship me,* he thinks, bidding the villagers goodbye. They track his every step leaving town toward the endless lands he loves.

The attention Kit commands is no less impressive when he arrives at the Rendezvous. His swagger alone makes heads turn as he strolls into camp. He and Taos make a handsome pair—Kit sitting high up on the horse's back, the fringe of his long hunting jacket prancing with each step…Taos' buckskin coloration shining brightly in the sunshine, the animal's dark mane and tail flowing carelessly as he moves, shaking gently as a morning breeze….Kit believes his horse understands the other men's esteem: Taos high steps as he approaches the encampment.

Kit selects a prime camping spot, just along the river, where water and thick green grasses are abundant. The spot is close enough to the action that everyone will be able to access him easily. Why make them walk to his tent? They need him far more than he needs them.

Indeed, Kit knows all the younger trappers at the Rendezvous are eager to hear him crow about his adventures and display his uncanny skills with the rifle, hitting targets no one else can make. He may have been shy and quiet in his younger days—but only because he was inexperienced. Now, Kit believes his gifts are meant to be shared with his fellow mountain men, who aren't as fortunate as him. His sphere of influence has expanded.

***

The first to greet Kit is a man named Beckwourth, his constant friend from his earliest days roaming the West.

"Come here, you ol' bangtail," Beckwourth says to Kit. He tries to wrap his six-foot frame around Kit in a bear hug. But Kit, too wily for the tall man, dodges with quicker reflexes.

"You still claim to be the chief of the Crows?" Kit asks sarcastically.

Beckwourth ignores the insult. Instead, he looks for Kit's wife.

"She stayed back this year," Kit tells him.

Beckwourth nudges Kit. "Heard they ain't letting no injuns in this year," he says, bending low to be heard. "I ain't surprised you left her home."

Rumors had been flying across the Rendezvous that the Indians had been caught stealing.

"They ain't welcome," Beckwourth tells him now.

Kit nods. But he doesn't like what he's heard. *Gossip like that can give all Indians a bad name,* he thinks, remembering his family.

***

"There I was. Gots ta take a leak like a cloudy sky's gotta rain," says Beckwourth, smiling and looking from one man to the next as he tells the story of his undoing. "I sees an outhouse back behind the saloon, but I can't tell if it's fer the house next door." These men, sitting on stumps set around the campfire, scruffy, not one clean shirt between them, quietly nod in agreement, picturing the scene in their inebriated minds. "I's almost done ma business when I hear a lass callin' ta me. I peek out to see she's coming at me with a musket. Must'a been her old man's cause she couldn't point that thing straight if her life depended on it, barely able to hang to it at all. She come straight up, and props open that shitter door."

Beckwourth takes a swig of something and pauses for emphasis. Probably drinking Taos Lightning like the rest of the mountain men gathered around. "So, I stands up…Now, mind ya, ma pants are still open cuz I ain't quite done what I come in for." Another swig. "She had me ten days to Sunday. Little thing, all she could do was shoot at ma feet. Well, you know ol' Beckwourth. I just button up and start talking." He stretches his long body and stands for further emphasis. Kit stands removed from the circle, facing the backs of the men.

"I says to her, 'Sweetie pie, I ain't doin' nothin' wrong here. Just relievin' myself. Run along now wit' your daddy's gun, honey,' I says to her.

"Little biddy holds her ground. I make to leave the privy but she ain't gonna budge. She stands only to ma belt buckle, musket still in her hands, looking at me like I'm half-cocked." Beckwourth takes a breath. He knows how to make a story extend all night long. Stringing along his listeners. Likes the attention.

"All of a sudden, her daddy come outta their home, fit to be tied. He's yellin', 'What you doin' with my woman?' Another long slow swig.

"I tell him, 'She's teachin' me how ta piss.'

The men, half drunk, fall over laughing, knee slapping and shaking their heads. Kit forgot how good Beckwourth's stories could be. He tells some humdingers. Like saving his boss from a bear that was just about to take a bite out of him. Or saving his captain from a raging river, grabbing his hand just as he was about to go over the falls. Beckwourth sure kept the tall tales coming.

The drink had been sizzling through the men for most of the day. Not much to do at the Rendezvous except chatter to one another. In the evenings, gathered around the fire telling whoppers, if someone passes out, they are just pushed off the stump where they rested their butt so another reveler can take the place. Kit isn't one to partake but does enjoy the stories. Just a bunch of loners taking a long overdue break. Competing too.

So, it surprises Kit when a well-dressed, comparatively clean gentleman stands to address the collection of well-oiled, wild explorers. "In all seriousness, men, can we have a chat about the Indian problem?"

As the man stands there, a second foreign-looking man stands up. Long in the face, clean shaven, his blond hair combed to fall neatly over his left eye. He sports a black overcoat and matching buttoned vest. A single black ribbon sits tied in a bow at the neck of his white button-down shirt. It all looks out of place in the wilderness campsite. But then Kit looks closer. *That ain't no trapper.*

Hunt. What was the governor doing here at the Rendezvous? Most of the men here came to the far corners of America to get away from the government. Hunt wasn't welcome to simply walk in on their party.

"Gentlemen let's face facts," Hunt says. "The Indians have our land, and we want it back. What do you say we demand those Indians give it to us? We tell them we'll make it worth their while. Heard they might even leave if they have a certain piece of paper. We've got a right to improve ourselves. Let's make America the gold standard of countries around the world. Far as I can tell, these Indians don't know any better. We'll take what we want and if they die so be it. Hell, they can't even read!"

Hunt chuckles at himself, but Kit doesn't think his words were all that funny considering he can't read or write. Hunt and his sidekick have caught most of the men at what Kit likes to call the "drowning in their sorrows" stage, a perfect time to lay it on thick, when most of the hearty souls gathered at the campfire have lost their gumption—and most of their hope. The governor did have a point about the land though. If the Indians remained in the trappers' country, its value would remain at only half its worth.

"We take the land, get what we want off it and let the homesteaders on," Hunt says.

Kit stands back a bit, listening. Around the campfire, a few men who are still upright shake their heads in agreement at Hunt's comments. Long ago, Kit thought the white man could share with the Natives, live together peacefully. Chaska had been the first to bring up the subject. She had said all sides should sign a treaty of understanding, something that would give each a fair share of the land. Hearing her talk about it broke his heart. At that time, he would have done anything to help her. She had foresight…she had known it would come to this. "Fighting isn't the answer," she would say. Kit had no idea what she was talking about at the time. Heck, he was just a kid trying to make his way west. Now, though, it was obvious. One or the other had to go.

More and more he's coming to believe as most Americans believe: The Indians need to go, and fast. He'd be the first to sign up to move them into settlements far away from America. If Kit could ever become an Indian Agent, he'd have the power to do just that. He's been hearing it from everyone he meets too. Homesteaders ask him if they can just kill the red men where they intend to set up a farm. Miners don't want the Indians to disrupt the streams for fear the motherload will become dislodged. Although he's not quite to the point to out-and-out kill the Natives and continues to encourage all to find peace, he's thinking on it all the time. Providing for his family means venturing into Indian country; he's got to be able to sell product or his family starves. If the Indians stopped his way of life so he couldn't provide for his wife and daughter, there'd be hell to pay.

"Them injuns might be without the might of our military, but they's dreadful smart," notes Beckwourth. "They'll know you is taken' them for a ride and bark you right there." He stands, rising a head above the territorial governor.

A few men nod their agreement. Others sit staring, eyes glazed over from too much booze.

"Eh, just put 'em under the sod."

"What you think, Kit?" somebody asks.

Kit frowns. He's frustrated by Hunt's intrusion but can't find a way to get the governor and his sidekick out of here. He stares at Hunt with piercing blue eyes.

"Move 'em out," he says.

Heads nod in approval. Before a breath can be taken, Kit hears, "Pass the Lightnin'…."

Hunt and Kit continue to stare at one another. Eventually, the governor and his mysterious partner sit down. Soon enough, the men are back at their antics. Beckwourth starts up another tale, and all that talk about Indians—and the governor's speech—is soon forgotten.

Over the next few days though, it seems more men were sober than Kit had thought. Or at least they remembered what was discussed around the fire. Everywhere he walks, Kit hears chattering about removing the Indians.

"I've got a plan to get those Utes off our land. Them vigilantes won't stand a chance."

"The Gov told me this morning, if we take their food away, if we take their water, they ain't got a reason to stick around. Mining gunks up the water so bad, ain't nobody can drink it. Not deer. Not buffalo. Nobody."

Kit pinches the bridge of his nose. He can't believe his ears. "That's a fool's errand, man," he says. "If there ain't no deer drinkin' the water, there ain't no beaver. What's we gonna drink?"

Chaska might be right, he thinks. Getting the Indians to a place of their own may be the safest way for everyone.

***

"You got a plan, Mr. Governor?" Kit asks as the man gets ready to mount his horse near the entrance to the Rendezvous.

"I do, Mr. Carson," says Hunt, turning to face Kit and stepping back from his horse.

Kit notes the man's face is covered by a well-groomed beard. Hunt explains a swath of land that nobody wants lies on the western side of the Colorado Territory. "Desolate, not good farming country," he says. "We'll give them that and be done with them."

Just then, Hunt is joined by the mystery man from the previous night. Kit extends a hand, hoping to find out who the man is and what he wants. Delicately, the man takes just Kit's fingers in his. "Nathan Meeker at your service," he says. He then extends his leg backward and bends from the waist.

Kit stares at Meeker. Is the man bowing to him? Or just reacting to the difference in their heights? Before Kit can respond Meeker abruptly stands to his full height, looming over Kit. He begins telling him more than he ever wanted to know about his town. "It's called Greeley, after my mentor," says Meeker. "A Utopian society that will make even Plato's Republic look like a plebeian little village." Kit has no idea what the man is on about and would prefer to talk with Hunt. Thankfully, the governor interrupts his associate. "How do you propose to keep the Utes in line, Kit?"

Finally, Kit has the chance to explain his connection to Chaska—and thereby to Ahwatt, the Ute chief.

***

Shortly after he left Chaska's camp, Kit had set out south for Santa Fe. He made his way along the Fountain River while the Ute tribe headed west to Bayou Salade, their summer camp. He'd been mostly a loner, tending to keep to himself. And although his journey had started off with him as a naïve, inexperienced teenager, he'd made it through his first three years without getting arrested while the bounty had been on his head, and he'd learned to trap with the best of them. In fact, over the past four years, he'd become one of the best—if not *the* best—trapper and trailblazer in the West. Probably in all of America for that matter. *Didn't come easy,* he knows. *If it wasn't for Chaska, I'd probably be lying dead somewhere.* But once Chaska's tribe had shown him the basics, he taught himself all he knew now.

At this point in his life, Kit thinks of Chaska as a one-off. She embodied peace and kindness—but she was probably the only Indian left who thought that way. Ahwatt certainly hadn't helped matters. Sure, he let Kaib teach Kit to hunt and scout, but Kit believes he couldn't wait to get the white man out from under the security of his tribe.

***

"So, by going through his sister, you believe you can make them move out of the area?" Hunt asks. He is still standing by Meeker and the horses.

"Been in contact with Chaska on and off for years," Kit tells Hunt. "Heck, she's the best one to talk with about this kind'a stuff. Ahwatt and I have met numerous times. He's so…what's the word…indecisive. His negotiating skills aren't worth a damn. The noncommittal fool."

A moment later, when Kit offers to be the go-between, Hunt is pleased to take him up on the offer.

"What do you want for your time?" Hunt asks. This is the moment Kit has been waiting for. He hadn't seen it coming, but now that it has arrived, he's not about to let the opportunity pass by. He says, slow and confidently, "The power I need to make it happen."

***

"Father, oh father! You're home!"

Kit's daughter, Adeline, runs to meet Kit as he rides into camp on Taos, returning from the Rendezvous. As Kit's in-laws trail behind Adeline, she raises her arms and sets her hands on Kit's boot, still in the stirrups. His daughter is always the first to meet him when he comes back to camp. Instead of the happy reunion he expected, though, his daughter looks as though she's been crying. Her tear-stained face is distraught—big eyes looking up at him from below.

Kit hops off Taos then bends down to be eye to eye with his young daughter. She jumps into his arms, hugging him close, and he gathers her in, delighted to be home. "Oh, Adeline!" Gently, he takes her shoulders in his hands and pulls her away to look into her eyes.

"What is it, my little Addy?" Kit asks. *Can't be nothin' too bad,* he thinks. *Probably lost a favorite dolly is all.*

"It's mother…she's nearly gone!" Adeline says, sobbing into her hands.

Kit's stomach drops.

"Gone?"

Fear builds inside him. He makes a groaning sound then drops to his knees. Clasping his daughter's hands in his, he searches her eyes for answers.

Adeline breaks into more tears. "Avipani almost killed her," she says quietly.

Kit's hands tighten. Jumping up from his knees, he rushes over to his in-laws, examining their faces for answers. But the two of them are searching the ground with their eyes, not meeting Kit's stare of anger. He doesn't have time for their humility, or their pity.

"What happened?" he screams at them. "What's wrong with my wife?"

Waa-nibe's father steps forward, still not meeting Kit's eyes. In a whisper, he tells Kit Avipani came into their teepee during the night. He had come to kill Kit, but in the darkness mistook Waa-nibe for her husband and stabbed her. She tried to escape, but Avipani shoved her down to the ground. She hit her head on a rock; now she lies in a coma.

Kit feels his knees buckle; the news is more than he can stand. Before his body can hit the ground, his father-in-law catches him. Quickly, Kit sees a look flash across the man's face—anger? pain? frustration? Kit can't be sure. The guilt of not being here for his family when they needed him most sears deeply into his chest.

Kit's not one to feel emotions for others. His sadness is for his own loss—the deep love he and his wife shared for one another. His sadness quickly turns to anger. "And you did nothing?" Kit says, jumping up and putting his face close to his father-in-law's. He realizes the look in the man's face had been revenge. Toward Kit. For marrying his daughter. He knows his actions aren't respectful, but he had left his wife and daughter to travel to the Rendezvous because he trusted they would be safe.

Adeline takes the opportunity to run to her grandmother, who stands amid a group of Arapaho who are watching the scene unfold. Waa-nibe's father ignores Kit's rant. "Adeline escaped and came to us. When we arrived

Waa-nibe was nearly dead. We called for Medicine Man, but he refuses to enter your tent. Waa-nibe is alive," Kit's father-in-law reminds Kit, "although we don't know for how long."

"No, no…!" Kit whispers. *Did I do this?* he questions himself. Perhaps he has been gone too long. Perhaps he should have stayed home to protect them.

Looking up, Kit sees his enemy. Avipani. The proud Arapaho is standing apart from the group of his tribesmen, his challenging gaze staring into Kit. Kit shakes with anger at the one man who can't be trusted in the village.

"You make me sick," Kit spits out at his father-in-law. Adeline, huddling with her grandmother, runs to Kit. He takes her hand. Together, they head for the teepee where his wife now lies near death.

***

For weeks, Kit and Adeline sit by Waa-nibe, holding her hand, talking to her softly. And for weeks, she lies still, barely breathing. Her husband and daughter take turns soaking clean rags in the dipper then gently swabbing her lips. Only Waa-nibe's mother comes to check on them, leaving Kit and Adeline to fend for themselves as they care for Waa-nibe. Then Kit hears Adeline ask her grandmother, "Why aren't others coming to see Pia?" Kit finds himself surprised by the response. "Your father has brought a lot of pain to your mother's family. He's not one of us; we need him to leave, so we don't want to help him."

Other whispering surprises Kit. "Why won't he leave?" the Arapaho ask one another, speaking of Kit. *Are they crazy?* Kit asks himself. *Why would I leave my wife?*

Adeline comes into the tent crying often because the other children tell her she's a half blood. She's not one of them…she doesn't belong. They don't want to even touch her.

At this point Kit begins to realize he's just being used.

***

One morning, as the sun shines in the sky, Waa-nibe's breathing becomes erratic—for every breath in and out, her throat rattles, gurgling. Slowly, she draws her last breath then breathes it out in a soft, slow moan. Kit rages out of the tent, his heart feeling as though it is breaking in half. He screams his discontent, frightening his daughter. Kit needs all his concentration to stop himself from slitting Avipani's throat: He crosses paths with his enemy nearly every day when the tribe assembles for a meal. Thankfully, Avipani is soon ostracized from the tribe; the leader forces him to leave them for killing Waa-nibe, one of their own. If they ever meet again, Kit vows, he will kill the man.

***

Two days of mourning is enough for Kit. He had spent the last two weeks preparing for his wife's death. As the only white man in the village, he wasn't allowed to attend her family's funeral for her, a private ceremony meant only for Arapahos.

Kit had already begun to realize neither he nor his daughter were safe in his wife's village. He has already packed up his wagon. Waa-nibe's family has provided him one kindness: a horse to pull the tiny conveyance. The wagon's planks are old and worn, struggling to hold on to one another. Taos is tied to the back. *See if they survive without me,* Kit thinks as he steps into the wagon.

Adeline weeps when she has to say goodbye to her grandparents, but Kit doesn't take a second look. *She'll be better off with my sister in Missouri.* He clucks at the horses, snapping the reins. Soon enough he and his daughter are long past being able to see the village behind them. Kit can find his way even though there is hardly a trail to follow. Thanks to Chaska and her tribe. They showed him how to look for signs. Smell the air. Listen. He and his daughter will be on the Santa Fe, heading east to St. Louis, in no time.

***

Prairie grasses sway as Kit makes his way to the main trail. Clumps of prickly pear cacti grow in colonies, their reddish fruit sticking straight up from the cactus pad, making them easy to spot. Kit carefully steers his wagon around them.

***

Father and daughter don't say much during the trip…Unfocused eyes stare ahead at the ocean of grasses, grief swirling through their minds. No sounds except the jingling of the spurs encircling Kit's dusty old boots and the clip-clop of the horses in front.

Kit's sun-parched skin displays wrinkles that seem to have dug deeper into his face after the recent turn of events. Adeline too seems lost in thought. *She just lost her mother*, Kit thinks. He knows his sister will be better at helping her heal than he could ever be. With his daughter safe in the East, he can continue his treks through the wild. It's the only job he's ever known.

***

Before too long a cloud of dust rises on the horizon. Kit and Adeline watch as a wagon heading their way flips on its side. Several passengers appear to jump from inside the wagon's poke bonnet. The two horses are still yoked and stamping their feet, eyes wide, trying to view the disaster spilling across the prairie behind them: In their fear the animals are still dragging the wagon cattywampus through the field. A man quickly runs up next to them, desperately trying to calm them. The bodies of those who jumped lie unmoving in the prairie grasses.

"Now, what do we have here?" Kit mutters under his breath. Adeline, by his side, stands up to see the commotion.

"Father…the family?" sweet Adeline queries.

Kit's heart skips a beat, panicking. He's seen the family strewn about but isn't sure whether they have been run over by the wagon, which even now makes its way through the weeds.

Adeline points toward movement. "There!"

She directs Kit to three people stirring: a woman reaching for a tiny baby nearby, and a girl who looks to be Adeline's age. She sports a flowered bonnet, pink and cheerful.

"How do?" Kit says, tipping his John B at the woman. Then he continues toward the man, who has successfully stopped the stampeding horses. "You've gone topsy-turvy," he shouts.

He halts his own charge then takes his time before hopping down from the seat. It isn't often he gets the chance to sit in a wagon rather than warming a saddle.

The man looks a bit worse for wear. Maybe this is the first time he's found himself in such a predicament. "Don't you worry none," says Adeline. "This happens all the time."

Kit looks over. Her daughter's eyebrows are raised. *Darn,* he thinks. *She does know what to say to make people feel at ease.* Before helping the man, Kit means to lift Adeline down from the wagon: She currently stands atop the wagon's toe board. "Hope this don't take too long, darlin'. I'd hate to make you late to school." He stands and stretches then carefully scoops her up and plants her safely on the ground. Instantly, she runs to the girl who has spilled onto the prairie, her own bonnet bobbling along as she goes.

Always empathetic, his daughter is as nurturing as her mama. Adeline rushes over to the little girl, helping to straighten her pink bonnet. This is the adventure of a lifetime for this family, Kit understands. To build a home and live on the open prairie, so different from back home. He breathes in their infectious hope and joy. Even in their current predicament. A welcome change he can enjoy for a short bit.

Kit helps to right the wagon. Then he heaves wooden trunks up over the sideboards, stuffing the contents of the family's life back inside. Fortunately, the wagon's bonnet is still intact.

While they work, Kit asks why the family is all alone on the trail.

"Had to stop," the man says. "Little Jackie was sick from the sun."

He points to a tiny boy, maybe only a year old, sunburned, lethargic in his mother's arms.

"It's not safe out here alone," Kit says. He calls Adeline over so that she and her new friend can collect a few cacti. "Careful 'a them prickers," he says to her quietly.

"The rest of the train went on," the man explains. "We were supposed to catch up to them. Just can't seem to get there. It's been one issue after another," he says.

Adeline carries the prickly cactus pads to her father. "Let's get your boy fixed up," Kit says carefully.

He carries the nopals toward the little one. The girls kneel near Kit and the man watches too as Kit shows the family how to remove the spines with a rock, gently scraping them away. Kit carefully squeezes the pad until it leaks an oozy liquid. Applying it to the tips of his fingers, he gently slathers the goo on the young boy's face. His mama, seeing the cure, breathes an audible sigh of relief. Kit leaves her with the rest of the remedy and heads back to the man. Taking him aside Kit asks if it wouldn't be better for them to ride along to St. Louis with he and Adeline. They could catch the next wagon train. Apparently too proud to take the help, the man insists he can handle the situation.

"No harm will come to the ladies. I've got my rifle," is all he says.

"Okay then, good luck to ya," Kit wishes him.

***

As the sole wagon heads east, Kit looks back one more time at the family. He easily swings himself up onto the jockey box. Then he extends his arms and helps Adeline back into their own wagon.

"By hook or by crook, I wish them luck," he says.

***

"Daddy," Adeline cries, "I'll miss you!" He and Adeline have taken to sitting out on the front porch of Eliza's home in Franklin. The two-story log home, built by her husband Robert sits not far from where Kit grew up. "Come here, my little prairie flower," Kit says, reaching his arms to her. Adeline gets up and kneels next to her father, arms strewn about his neck, not letting go.

Kit feels a tear in his eye himself. He knows he won't see Adeline often, but she'll be much safer here at school than in his wife's village. His sisters are nearby—they will look after his beautiful daughter.

"Darlin', I'll miss you too, and I'll think about you every day," Kit tells her.

Striding across the yard, Eliza comes up to the two, her long dress clip-clapping from her quick gate, a basket of just collected eggs under one arm. "She'll be just fine, won't you, Adeline?"

"Liz promises to come and visit you at your school, and bring you home for the holidays," Kit says to his daughter, though she is trembling in his arms.

"That's right," says Eliza. Stepping around the two, she places her hand on Kit's shoulder, saying reassuringly, "Don't you worry a bit, little brother. She's got loads of cousins here to play with, and Aunt Matilda said she will help out too."

"Why do I have to go to boarding school, Daddy? I could stay here and go to school with my cousins," Adeline whines. Eliza and Kit exchange glances. "Kit, she could—"

"Stop. She's already enrolled. She'll get a great education and can be anything she wants afterward," he says, hugging his daughter close.

"But it's so soon after her moth,—"

"Eliza," Kit says in his deep baritone. "She will be fine."

"Could Aunt Eliza come with us when you drop me off? Pleeease?"

Eliza lets out a laugh. "Of course, honey. That way, I'll know where to come and get you when we bring you back home."

***

Riding up to the school, Adeline had demanded she sit inside the box surrounded by the bonnet so that she couldn't see her new school. Kit and Eliza sat up front, chatting here and there, but mostly just keeping to themselves. Kit desperately wanted to get back out west, but he was also concerned about Adeline. He found himself to be much more emotional than he'd expected, even holding back tears a few times at the thought of his little girl, motherless at such a young age and now being placed in a home much different than her experiences so far. Living in her mother's Arapaho village was much different than living at the school with only other girls for friends.

Eliza had told Kit, "Girls these days need a proper education."

"I don't have much educating," Kit notes. "You don't either and we turned out all right." Eliza had just glared at her brother, then reminded him that he had made a life for himself that was all his own. "Do you really think Adeline would like to become a trapper like her daddy?" Kit admitted that his daughter needed a good foundation, which he just couldn't provide to her.

"Relax, Kit. She'll make so many friends and be exposed to more social activities than she could here in Franklin." Though Eliza's children attended school part-time in town, Kit was sure she would have wanted more of an education for them. It was the cost of the school that kept her from enrolling them. Besides becoming an excellent trapper and scout, Kit made good money.

"Darlin', we're rollin' up on your school," Kit called to his daughter. Though he and Eliza kept their gazes forward, a small head pushed through the bonnet just enough for the face to show. Neither Kit nor Eliza moved, not wanting to encourage Adeline to miss the first sites of her school.

The whitewashed, three-story building was massive. Three separate entry doors opened into the building that would be Adeline's dormitory. Girls of all ages were playing in the field just outside the dorm. Several female schoolteachers stood nearby, looking neat and tidy in long dresses of calico, their hair pulled into buns pinned at the back of their heads. All looked serene and pleasant, not stern and foreboding, as Kit had thought they might look.

Several other wagons were hitched along the fence that separated the dormitory from the field. Fathers of children were helping their wives from wagon driver's seats as girls hopped from the wagon beds. Teachers greeted the timid new students with smiles and hugs.

"Look, Daddy." Adeline pointed to the new students. "They're just like me."

Kit put on a brave face, pulling the wagon near to the fence. He hopped down, helped Eliza from the seat and then held out his arms. Adeline smiled then hopped into his arms, where she got a strong hug.

"Hold my hand," she demanded. Aunt Eliza and Kit each took a hand, then headed toward the others.

A woman strode toward them, her skirts hanging just above her lace-up boots with very tiny heels that clicked on the ground as she walked. Bending to one knee, she looked Adeline in the eyes.

"Welcome, welcome! I'm Miss Elizabeth. I'll be your teacher this year. And what's your name?" Adeline had inherited her father's shyness: She crept backward until being completely hidden behind her aunt's skirts.

"This is Adeline, her father Kit, and I'm her aunt Eliza."

"People call me Eliza too."

This elicited just the right reaction: Adeline peeked from her aunt's skirts. "Really?" she asked quietly.

"Yes. I can't wait for you to meet all the other girls. There are thirteen new girls starting this year, and three of them will be in your grade, Adeline. Would you all care to follow me? I'll show you around and get Adeline settled into her room. By the way, Adeline, I live on campus too." At this, Adeline smiled and looked from her aunt to her father.

As the four of them stepped inside the building Kit could see the kitchen and dining hall on one side and a small office on the other. The second floor was an enormous room lined with metal beds sitting next to little wooden dressers. There was one bed and one dresser for every student. The mattresses were thin but spread with sheets and a thick wool blanket all tucked in and neat. Miss Elizabeth led Kit, Eliza and Adeline to a bed near a window. White curtains hung down, leaving a small space of windowpane out of which Adeline could see the children in the field playing.

"This will be your bed, Adeline. You may place your things inside the dresser. At night, your shoes should be placed under your bed," said Miss Elizabeth. Adeline sheepishly sat at the edge of the bed, looking to her father glumly until she saw a young girl sitting in the bed next to hers, blond braids hanging down her gingham dress. Miss

Elizabeth noticed and took the opportunity to introduce the girls.

"Adeline, meet Patrice. She is in the same grade as you. This is her first day here also." The two girls locked eyes and awkwardly smiled at one another. Kit looked at Eliza, who gave him a happy grin while Patrice and Adeline said hello.

"Do you want to go play?" Patrice asked. Adeline nodded yes, and the two took off down the steps, giggling nervously.

Kit had thought he would share a teary-eyed goodbye with Adeline. Instead, he shouted a goodbye to her while she and Patrice ran through the grassy field. His heart aches bleakly from the pain of missing his wife and now his little daughter, but it's obvious Adeline will be safe and happy here.

***

Kit knows his sisters will take good care of his daughter, so with mixed feelings he rides the steamboat back to St. Louis, back to the only job he's ever known. He'll come see Adeline next season when the plews are hauled in. For now, he'll collect Taos and head back out west. He's got more than trapping on his mind. He wants to be a part of creating the Colorado treaty, to get land back for America.

Chapter 11

Mining in Colorado
(Summer, 1866)

It's been five seasons since I found the white man named Kit. Kaib was allowed to show him how to track animals, to hunt and find trails. My instinct tells me he is a good young man who wants to help us. I'm sure of it. Moving up into our mountaintop summer camp, we pass by more white men than any previous year. Their towns are sprawling—gobbling up entire hillsides, taverns and saloons spilling into rivers, mines belching black clouds that blot out the sun. Why anyone would build homes that stay in one place is outside my comprehension. Before the tribe passes each town, Ahwatt sends scouts forward to talk with the merikac to secure our safe passage. Last year, they weren't very happy we were on *their* land. Ever since we left, I wondered if they would allow us back. My nervous energy makes me shake all over. I have the same nightmare night after night. The Americans watch us as we pass. Their faces are covered in soot so that I can just see their eyes, which are bloodshot. Their eyes seem to glow as they watch, focusing solely on me. The miners stand perfectly still. Just their eyes follow us as we pass.

Suddenly, as if coming to life, they shout, "They're here!" The miners come at us wielding sharp pickaxes. "Go, go! Ride!" I yell. Kaib is ahead of me: He rides fast toward the hills. My children cluck to their horses and kick at their girth to make them move away, but the girls scatter in all directions. Even little Chipara sits atop a mustang, but the horse steers her toward the men instead of away from them. "Chipara! No!" I yell to her, but she can't hear me over the men's screams to get us! Kill us! Nublada, normally good in stressful situations, won't move. She lopes along no matter how much I kick her belly with my heels. Suddenly, I'm the only one left. Everyone else has found a hiding spot or ridden away. The white men are all around me, raising the picks to my face....

I sit up suddenly, sweat is running down my face, and my breathing is erratic. I'm shaking. Then, looking around the quiet tent, Kaib is at my side, sleeping. It's just a dream.

For weeks, it's the same nightmare, over and over.

***

My girls enter the teepee. "Did you find the cottonwood buds?" I ask. Kaib looks up as they come inside.

"No, Pia," Mapia says.

I'm prepared to shout at them for not taking my request seriously. Collecting cottonwood buds at summer camp is one of our most important tasks: Without the buds, puss will ooze from any cut or wound our tribe members suffer. But when I look over, Mapia and Chava are holding dead cottonwood branches. Their shriveled brown leaves are covered in a thick layer of dust. Kaib grabs at one and inspects it.

"What is it?" I ask, trying to swallow down my concern.

"Oh, Mama!" Chava cries. She runs to hug my legs. "The trees," she tells me, "They all look like that!"

"There were deer too, Pia," Mapia whispers. "Three dead, but one just lying on the ground staring at the sky."

Kaib looks to our children. "Did you touch anything besides this branch?"

"No, Pia," they say together.

"Did you drink the water along the creek?"

Mapia nods then bursts into tears. "I didn't know, Mama! It was so bitter!"

I draw in a few deep breaths, letting them out slowly. Chava explains that her sister drank the water before they realized anything was wrong.

Kaib and I exchange glances. Maybe the water is fine, but the plants are dead from the coat of soot.

"Tell me more about the deer." It's all I can think to say. Letting the girls talk gives me time to think. Up here at camp, the leaves and trees are green and lush. But Ahwatt will need to know what my girls have found.

***

"The air burned in my eyes and nose," Mapia declares.

Ahwatt has let us come into his teepee after we told him our message is urgent. Kneeling before the girls so he is eye level with my daughters, Ahwatt listens to their venture. My daughters call him The Tree, to which he will reply that his branches are coming to get them. Not today though. Ahwatt sighs loudly; Kaib ran to tell him we had news. I think they both know more than they are telling me because neither man allows me to catch their eye.

Finally, Ahwatt stands. He puts out his hand for each of the girls to hold onto. "Show me where," he says.

***

The small stream the girls have lead us to feeds into the Platte. Along the riverbanks great swaths of trees, normally green with leaves or sharp pine needles, are barren. Other trees merely have leaves clinging to dead branches.

I glance down at the river and raise my hand to my mouth. "Ahh!" I gasp.

Normally, a multitude of fish would glint pinks and yellows in the sunlight. Now, hundreds of fish float belly-up in the slow-moving water, their sickly-looking fins drifting in the current. The smell is overwhelming. Like burnt meat.

"I've seen this before..." Ahwatt says.

"Is it the Americans?" I ask.

Ahwatt nods. "The men and I came across a similar area last year. I had hoped it was just one impure place, but everywhere I've been in South Park over the last year is the same. This may be our last summer here."

Heading around the mountain is already difficult for my tribe: We've got to skirt one white man's settlement after another. Early on, the white men walked the creeks, pulling shiny rocks from the water to make their fortunes. Now, the rumbling, crushing rocks the men shovel into the mouths of their machines is causing the dirty water left behind here.

My brother stands quietly along the banks of the river. "I don't know if we should drink this or not," he says. "I've watched the men coming out of their holes in the ground, coughing, heaving for breath, spitting blood."

The white man, his greed. It kills the fish, the trees...I can only assume it will eventually kill us. I can't help myself, but I start crying. It's so much. Why would Ahwatt be unsure of us drinking the water? Is his uncertainty a product of his usual irresolute nature? Between his dithering and our situation, I'm not able to think straight.

I look over to see Mapia: She has walked her horse down to the stream and is standing along the bitter water. Reins in my daughter's hand, the horse backs away from the stream, apparently aware of the poison. Mapia observes a half-dead fish that has become stranded along the water's edge. It's struggling to breathe, its bloated body heaving, mouth open, eyes wide. My daughter's tears fall from her face onto the doomed land.

***

"Here, catch," I say to my oldest daughter, tossing her a basket. I'm standing only a few feet from her; her head is turned away from me, but I know she can see me here, on her left side. But she doesn't catch the basket. Or even turn her head when I pitch it to her. Only when it hits her in the shoulder does she jump.

"Pia," she says, agitated. "Why did you throw that at me?" Her face in a pout she shakes her head at my perceived carelessness.

My almost teenaged daughter is changing in so many ways. Her face is a cluster of red bumps, especially her forehead and cheeks. The almost flush redness started right around her twelfth birthday. We all go through that phase at this age. Some more than others. I remember having red splotches on my face for a few years. Up until I got married, really.

Her moods are ever changing too. I never know which Mapia will appear each day. She has only a few more years before it's time for her to marry, make a family of her own. Last year, she won just about every race she and her pony entered. She will be able to find a wonderful husband now that she's won races, a coming-of-age tradition. Unfortunately, Mapia's current obsession is a tall good-looking boy whose most obvious trait is his love for himself.

The Ute people have been known for centuries for our pony racing. It's something we're very proud of: We take time out of our days to race one another.

This past spring was rainy and muddy, but one afternoon, when the sun finally dries out the race field, every member of our tribe leads their pony out to the field.

"Hear that?" Chava asks me. I'd been busy with sorting piñon nuts, but now I can hear the drumming. Our men are chanting too, asking the ancestors to come and join us for an afternoon of fun.

"Cov-våh-nåns-ûb!" Chava yells. *Horse race!* My daughter is already running across the field to fetch her horse. I'm feeling a bit giddy myself at the idea of racing today. We work so hard to stay fed and safe, that a race day will give us all the chance to have some fun and relax.

Even Nublada knows what is happening. When I reach her and throw the bridle over her neck, she gives a happy nicker.

"Yes, girl, we're going for a race!" I exclaim. I'm so happy that I lead her to a boulder, hop onto it and then swing my legs over her girth. I give Nublada a little kick—and she's off, galloping toward the race field. With my legs wrapped around her barrel, I lean my head back, breathing in a deep, delighted sigh. I won't take the time to paint her body this time, but others will paint circles around their pony's eyes and lightning bolts across their bodies. When Ahwatt was younger, he painted his horse with white polka dots across the animal's hind quarters.

"Oh, look out!" I shout gleefully. Ponies are galloping onto the field left and right. One of them gives their rider a joyful buck, kicking his back hooves up in the air. When we ride, we feel the horse's strength and they feel our excitement. We feed off one another's energy. They nicker to one another, as though saying, *It's time for some fun.*

The way the races work is this: Teams of one rider and two holders compete against each other. The rider hops onto a pony held by the first holder at the starting line, then rides bareback to the other end of the field. There, the rider jumps off their pony, then leaps onto the second pony being held by the reins by the other holder; then the rider races back to the start. The first competitor to cross the line wins.

I'm in the first group of riders, five of us in all. These are women my age who have been racing like this since we were able to sit atop a pony. I'll ride Kaib's pony named Wäh-păn-a-kär down the field, then switch to Nublada on the way back. Mapia will be my second holder.

Two elder men will be the judges. They stand on either side of the makeshift starting line, which looks more like a jagged line because our holders are trying desperately to keep the ponies steady. The five of us stand back from the starting line, preparing to run and take a flying leap onto our ponies. On either side of the field, families watch with nervous excitement. The women go first, then teenagers, children and, finally, the men.

"Ready?" I hear a judge shout. My body shakes with excitement. Kaib and I make eye contact, and I nod to him, signaling that I'm all set.

"Go!"

My feet start hitting the ground as my arms pump vigorously back and forth. I squat down and use all my momentum to leap up onto the left flank of Kaib's pony. Wrapping my arms around the pony's neck, I push my left elbow into Wäh-păn-a-kär's shoulder, then use that leverage to swing my right leg up and over the gold-colored pony. "Yah!" I shout, kicking Wäh-păn-a-kär with the heels of my moccasins, snapping the reins about her neck. I don't sit on her back but grip tightly with my knees around her girth. My body leans forward. My head is almost touching Wäh-păn-a-kär's neck, who is eyeing her competitors.

It's tight with riders and horses bumping sideways into one another. The valley could fit ten horses racing side by side, but in this race, the five of us have huddled up next to one another. The ponies around me are all giving everything they've got, legs driving into the ground, heads bobbing up and down, reaching for the end of the field. The ground goes past so fast, I can't make out one single blade of grass; instead it's just a blur of green.

Halfway down the length of the field, Wäh-păn-a-kär has taken at least twelve large charges forward. I can hear the shouts of the spectators, cheering for their favorite. The entire tribe is here.

As I approach Mapia holding Nublada, I sit even higher off Wäh-păn-a-kär's back. Mapia will need to catch Kaib's pony while still holding Nublada. It's tricky and demands a lot of my daughter.

With two or three pony lengths before I come to Mapia, I slow Wäh-păn-a-kär only slightly. Using my hands at her withers, I push myself up and off her, swinging my right leg backward while she's still moving. I keep one hand on the reins, and as my feet hit the ground, I start running toward Mapia to hand her Wäh-păn-a-kär's reins. As she's grabbing for the exhausted pony, I release my grip, then take another big leap onto Nublada. She needs no encouragement to sprint back to the starting line. As soon as she feels my knees on either side of her barrel, she's galloping.

I'm neck and neck with my good friend Magena, whose dark-brown pony Tish-um is charging forward. Smiling, I urge Nublada on, snapping the reins for show. Magena does the same. "Yah!" I hear her shout. I turn to my right. She's grinning too.

We're headed for the judges, who are standing at the finish line, craning their necks to see who crosses the line first. Shouts of encouragement are drowned out by the sound of pounding hooves. With each stride, one pony's nose is ahead. Then the other. Nublada. Tish-um. Nublada. Tish-um. We fly over the finish line, laughing at our good fortune to race against one another. Neither of us gains anything, other than to know we won the spring race.

The judges confer briefly, putting their heads together.

"Magena wins!" the judges shout.

"Good girl," I tell Nublada, patting her lathered neck. Kaib comes over to hold her while I hop off, giving me a quick hug and a smile.

Next up are the teenagers, but as they ready themselves, a blurring rain sweeps through. The storm had been forming over the mountains that surround us. Slowly, thick gray clouds skimmed over the top of the peaks, then slid heavy with water down the mountainside. Substantial raindrops pelt us quickly, soaking the field, leaving puddles where pony hooves dug in from my race. It races by us as quickly as it came in, but now the air is thick.

Mapia seems unfazed by the storm though her pony has steam rising off his back while rivulets of water drain from his shoulders. The pony hasn't yet shed his thick winter coat, so the rainwater doesn't release very fast. Po, the boy who came to our rescue a few years back, is also racing. He's won every spring race since that horrible winter, so we are all watching to see if he can win another.

"Ready?

"Go!"

Mapia easily hops onto her pony with a splat, then takes off down the field toward her father, who holds his pony Wäh-păn-a-kär for her to ride. As the teens race from their holders, strings of mud fly from their hooves, hurtling straight at us. Magena, who held a pony for her daughter, looks at me and belly laughs.

"You're covered too, you know!" I shout at her, laughing despite tasting a mound of mud that must have clung to my lips.

Mapia got started easily, but Po seems more affected by the rain. Though he effortlessly hops onto his own mount, he slides off the slippery animal, landing with a thud on the ground. Nonetheless, his pony takes off for the end of the field with Po still holding the reins. As Po and pony whip past us, the teen is dragged through the muck. His arms are taut while his legs are flailing behind him. Finally, Po lets go. I giggle despite myself. He is absolutely covered head to toes in dark brown slimy muck.

During the children's race, one young boy, tall for his age, takes a flying leap behind his horse, planting both hands on the pony's hind quarters. The boy straddles the horse, sending his legs around the girth, but the pony won't have it. Instead of running, the pony plants his feet firmly into the ground, refusing to race. Looking back once, as if to shake his head, the pony lowers his muzzle and begins nipping at a patch of tender green grass, to the horror of the rider. Those of us watching howl with laughter.

A young girl just isn't tall enough to get herself up and over her pony. Instead, as she leaps toward her mount, her body slams into the pony's side and she crumples to the ground in embarrassment.

The ponies like the fun just as much as we do, nickering their pleasure at competing against one another. They may be smaller, and lower to the ground than the horses the merikac ride, but their explosive speed is a wonder. These ponies love to run, so when it comes to racing, they all want one thing: to win. Once they finish a race with sides heaving, nostrils flared wide, sweat frothed white at the neck, they're ready and eager to go again. After the day's races are over the ponies get loads of attention and petting from the riders.

I watch as Mapia nuzzles her pony as the two walk back toward where we stable the animals for the evening.

***

It's been a few weeks since the girls found the dead trees. Ahwatt has come across more dead deer and dead fish. He says perhaps my plan to have land expressly designated as our own is a good idea after all. Several women have confided to me they would feel safer if land were set aside for us. Most of their husbands, though, are willing to fight. Most times, when another tribe trespasses, we can work it out with a peaceful solution; the white men's intrusions, however, feel different.

The Americans' battles are different, for one thing. Before, tribes tried to encroach on one another's hunting grounds. A war party was sent out to fight them back. My husband tells me the merikac believe this land is theirs and *we* are trespassing. If there's a place the Americans haven't yet settled, this could be our chance.

There's a split among the tribe. Some women and a few men are willing to sign a treaty. Those who are against it have gone so far as to pull their teepees close to one another. The rift isn't good. Ahwatt is in the middle, but he also has the final say. Those in favor of fighting are angry at my constant nagging to my brother; they think I should stay out of tribal affairs.

For as long as my brother fails to make decisions, I'll be nagging.

Some, including myself, think the white man's power is so overwhelming they could come to our camp and leave the entire tribe dead. But there are those who disagree and are willing to fight to the death. Irrespective of losses. And the merikac seem to work together, maybe they all know one another, because they work to make our lives miserable with one shared purpose—expand their country. My ideas for peace haven't made the summer peaceful for me, that's for sure. I get threatening glances. There's whispering behind my back. Sometimes I wish I didn't have such a strong urge to keep us safe. I want a good life for my daughters. The brutal facts are that we are being overtaken. My father had this same strong will to keep us safe. Ahwatt didn't get that trait. Maybe my father guides me. I can't explain it, but I'm willing to bear the brunt of the criticism to see it through. So, I focus my energy on what we always do in the summer—gather what we can to dry, snare small animals, and keep everyone fed.

***

I see my mother and father standing next to their horses. Pia's long hair is braided and lies along her back, just as I fix my hair every day. My father is in his regalia, as if going to the Bear Dance. Tilting my head, I ask him, "Father, why are you dressed like that?" "I am going on a long trek, and you are coming with me," he says. "Me? Why me? I don't leave camp; I cannot go with you." He shakes his head in sadness, pulling his lips together as he used to do when Ahwatt or I disappointed him. "Send Ahwatt then," he says, with Pia nodding her agreement. "Where?" I ask. "To get it," is all they say together, before turning to walk away, their horses in tow. "What? I don't understand!" I shout, but they don't turn around, just keep walking.

"What do you think, Kaib?" I ask my husband after explaining my dream.

"So, your parents said to send your brother to get 'it'?"

As a hunter, a warrior, and a trader, Kaib ventures outside the camp much more than I do. He tells me the merikac are building villages that nearly surround us now.

"Should Ahwatt go into their village?" he wonders, considering the dream. "Is 'it' the treaty, Chaska?"

I look at him, considering. A good suggestion, but I don't feel that's the answer.

As we sit thinking, our oldest daughter screams. "Mama!" her frightened voice calls through the night.

"I'm here," I say.

"I'm afraid," my daughter says.

Again. It's been like this for weeks. Her fear lies purely within.

"There's nothing to fear," I tell her, exchanging glances with Kaib. I reach for her hand in the dark teepee; when I find it, it feels bony and thin. Her teenage body, once rounding out, has turned into skin stretched over bones. It seemed to happen overnight.

"My belly," she says. "The pain keeps getting worse!"

The rest of the family begins to stir in the confined space of our teepee. Every night is like this. Mapia wakes, frightened of an imaginary dread. Then the pain starts again. Yet she hasn't eaten enough to keep even the smallest child alive. And none of us has slept for weeks.

Through another fit of coughing, she croaks, "I need Po'rat." Medicine Man.

Mapia gasps for air; I draw her close then rub her back, trying to calm her body. "Sit up straight…take in a breath," I say.

Every day seems to bring on a new issue for my oldest girl. Yesterday she looked at me with watery eyes, saying she sees more than one of everything.

"It's nearly light anyway," Kaib says. "I'll fetch him."

Before he goes, I grab his arm. "Medicine! That's it, Kaib!"

He looks at me, waiting for an explanation.

When my parents were sick, I begged Ahwatt to get merikac medicines. We had heard of other tribal leaders who had taken the medicines and survived. Medicine Man said my parents had done bad things and couldn't survive, but I think they had caught an American sickness.

"That's it," I tell Kaib again. "We need to ask Ahwatt to get the medicine to cure Mapia."

I can tell Kaib isn't convinced of my interpretation. "I'll get Medicine Man," he says, ducking through the flap of the teepee. He grew up with my brother and me. Never have I heard him agree with my suggestion that our parents died of a sickness other than what Medicine Man could conjure. I know it sounds far-fetched too, but all I've got is hope.

While he's out, I stir the fire to revive it. Po'rat will need the flames. He's sought so many therapies already for Mapia—pine resin for her breathing issues, maple and willow barks cooked into a tea for pain. Nothing helps. He can't find a cure for her. He says perhaps Mapia has a spirit inside her, or she's committed an evil act and is paying for it through the sickness. He said the same of my parents. But my beautiful, sweet daughter wouldn't hurt anyone.

He's not on my side when it comes to finding accord with the merikac either. The anger he displays when I insist on negotiating a treaty with the Americans surprises me; he is generally a peaceful quiet soul. He's seen other treaties broken in the past. We all have. But he has told me on more than one occasion that I'm sick in the head for thinking there can be peace.

Tonight, when he arrives, he decides to chant to heal my daughter, hoping the evil spirit inside her will leave.

Sitting at the fire, Medicine Man slips into deep reflection. We all sit silently to let his work heal our daughter. My husband catches my eyes. He believes Mapia could have taken in an evil ancestor. "With her sweet nature, she couldn't say no," he says.

Suddenly, Medicine Man stops chanting. His eyes pop open and he jumps to standing. Shaking his head, he seems distraught. Slowly he turns to look at each of us until his eyes lock with mine. "She hasn't been bad," he says. "You have."

Chapter 12

Coats to the Utes/Dead Homesteaders, Summer 1867

Standing at the bow of the steamboat heading south toward St. Louis, Kit notices a well-groomed man coming his way. The gentleman sports a deep blue coat with gold detail embossed along the collar. His shirt has a long lace collar and matching lace at his wrists. What looks to be a newly minted beaver skin hat rests on his head of full hair. *An aristocrat,* Kit thinks, hoping the man passes him by without a word.

Kit himself is wearing a borrowed, oversized shirt—and borrowed, oversized trousers—from his brother-in-law, a six-foot-four giant. The only clothes Kit owns are his skins, but because he has to look presentable at his daughter's boarding school, he has been loaned the clothing. The borrowed, oversized thick wool black jacket he sports extends past Kit's fingertips. And although the borrowed white cotton shirt is buttoned to the top, the collar hangs loosely from Kit's neck. The waist of the oversized pants is rolled over a few times so that the length fits. Overall, Kit looks like a child wearing his father's clothing.

The aristocrat's skin shows white as snow. *He's illy looking*. Tall and thin, lathy as a twig.

Sure, enough the man tips his hat toward Kit: "Good day." Kit nods in reply then turns to the boat's stern to make his getaway. *Best to keep my distance from this one*, he thinks. The man instills Kit with a general feeling of fear that shakes his entire body. He seems a bad egg. Or, perhaps, a bamboozler. But the man turns in Kit's direction and follows him with the confidence of a self-absorbed Easterner. "John C. Fremont," the man says, extending a hand toward Kit. "I need a man such as yourself," he continues. "I've been hired by the Corps to find a way west. The railroad wishes to send their trains across our good country. Could you lead me?"

Kit's first thought is of his newly found independence.

"I'm to write a summation of my travels and present it to Congress," the man continues. "It won't just be Congress reading this. Thousands of homesteaders heading west will use my report as their guide," the man boasts. "Don't worry, man, I won't ask you to accompany me there. Not in that getup anyway," the man says, looking Kit up and down. He places a finger over his upper lip and breathes out a small laugh.

The blusterations of the man! Such a braggart!

"I had hired a man to keep us on the trail, but you, my man, will do much better. So, it's settled then?"

Fremont stares at Kit, who is dumbfounded. Without uttering one word Kit has been called a poor dresser and been hired on to lead the unknown man across the West. But how does Fremont know Kit is capable of leading them? And what if he doesn't want to?

"Pay is one hundred dollars a month," says Fremont, all but sealing the deal.

Kit considers. *Money or independence?*

He decides his independence can wait.

***

One of the best things about scouting for Fremont is the chance it gives Kit to keep an eye on the Utes. After learning he had been named as an Indian Agent, Kit finds himself obliged to check in on them much more often. One of the worst things about scouting for Fremont is the man himself. His demands verge on the ridiculous. On the first night of the expedition Fremont expects his camp to be set up differently than the camps of the other men on the expedition. Delicate map-making instruments must be unpacked and carefully set down on polished mahogany tables Fremont has brought in his wagon. A meticulously crafted oak desk imported from Europe is carefully placed in his tent each night then returned to a safe spot in the wagon each morning. Although his spy glass and compass are always kept on his person, he is fussy about where his other tools are to be set out.

The man is as delicate as his precious instruments, Kit thinks.

Fremont is the captain of the expedition, but Kit is the principal guide. At least according to the men. They would follow him anywhere. Fremont, on the other hand? The men joke he's just a mail-order cowboy.

Those assigned to the march are all seasoned frontiersmen, capable of standing on their own if need be. Fremont is an entirely different story. "That Fremont, he'd be better as a porch-percher than an expeditioner," Maxwell, the principal hunter says. The men follow Kit, but he can tell they have their issues with him too. When nobody thinks he is listening, Kit can overhear their conversations.

"Looks like he's been rode hard and put away wet," Preuss, Fremont's assistant claims.

Most days Kit pushes the men to march between ten to sixteen miles. He tries to bring them over to his side of thinking by shooting targets with them. Mostly they just shoot at birds that fly along the river where they camp each evening. Each night before the horses are barricaded with wagons, they are shod then turned loose to graze. Cookie sets up his crumb castle to prepare the evening meal. He was a last-minute addition to the crew when he and Kit crossed paths.

"No mystery meat in there, right, Cookie?"

The men hate the sausages Cookie makes toward the end of a patch because all that is left of the meat—some of it gone bad—is stuffed into casings for dinner.

"You'll put your nose in the bag of whatever I make," Cookie replies.

At nightfall, the expedition's caviada pickets the animals, connecting their halters to a steel-shod picket driven into the ground. Because Kit had acted as cavvy boy all those years ago, he feels obliged to teach the naïve boy as much as possible, explaining how best to coax the animals toward him. Kit advised, "Grab you a handful a' coffee beans and stick 'em in an old can. Shake it to make some noise. Them horses, they'll think you gots a handful a' grain and come runnin."

Kit takes his turn as guard with the others, working two-hour shifts. Often, a less experienced guard sets off alarms, declaring he's seen Indians. One morning, well into Colorado territory, Kit and the men are fixing to leave their encampment along a quit stream when the lead guard comes up quickly, spurring his horse along. "Indians!" he yells, pointing up a nearby hill. "Twenty-seven at least!"

Kit asks Fremont to bring his glass for a look—but there's nothing. He decides to ride up and check for himself, so the cavvy boy releases an unsaddled horse for Kit. Riding bareback, rifle in one hand, reins in the other, and his legs wrapped tightly around the horse's barrel, Kit races up the hill to advance upon the Indians. Upon his return thirty minutes later, Kit shakes his head calmly, his blue eyes tranquil. "It was only six elk."

***

Back on the trail, as the principal guide, Kit usually rides Taos far out in front of the rest of the wagon train. Today is no different. Fremont may be called the Pathfinder back home but here it's Kit's job to either follow existing Indian trails or blaze new ones.

The morning has that shimmery feeling…Kit can just tell it's going to be sweltering by afternoon. Though he's shed his heavy leather coat, he can already feel sweat dripping through his cotton button up shirt. Waving his Stetson back and forth in front of his face just seems to move the hot air around, not provide relief.

Off in the distance, oh about twenty feet ahead, a billow of sailcloth sits idle among the branches of a pine. As Kit approaches, he sees bits and pieces of a wagon, scattered along the trail and lying in the high grasses alongside. He waits in the hot sunshine of the trail then halts the wagon train when it finally catches up. Maxwell, the team's hunter, comes forward, his rifle already to fight. The man calls his gun The Equalizer.

Kit and Maxwell eye the area. Pieces of a broken schooner—a sideboard here, a toe board there, pieces of wheel spokes broken off—lie haphazard along the trail and in the nearby grasses. The wagon harnesses and the yoke, smashed to bits, also lie among the wreckage.

The family's trunks lie open, scavenged through completely. No sign of the horses.

"Could be an ambush," Maxwell says. He swings his head back and forth, scanning for trouble. "Natives?" he wonders.

Fremont, who is usually the last man to help wherever danger is a possibility, is riding with the chuckwagon, which draws slowly up to the others.

"This calls for all hands—including the cook," Kit says quietly. A few of the other wagons have stopped short.

"It appears they took the wagon off the trail," Maxwell offers.

"Why bushwhack through the brush?" Kit asks. "Nothing's movin…It's not an ambush." Kit says.

His trained eyes scan the area again, not landing on anything of importance…until he sees a pink flowered bonnet trampled into the trail. His mind harkens back. *No, no.* That sweet girl was Adeline's age…jubilant even though she'd just been thrown from her family's wagon. He smiles at the thought. So little, so naïve, so willing to be a part of her family's new adventure. Now this.

"Look."

Maxwell points to an arrow that appears to be standing straight up in the grass. Kit leads Taos to it as the other men search the tall grasses for survivors. The husband lies flat on his back: the arrow had bored through his chest. Probably killed him instantly. The little girl's mother isn't too far away, still holding her little boy, still red-faced from too much sun. But the girl is nowhere to be found. Probably kidnapped. Or killed.

I had a hunch, Kit thinks, remembering his conversation with the father. The next moment Kit feels the rage build inside him: his arms and hands shake at the horse's reins, his entire body trembles with fury and guilt....Killing an innocent man just trying to make a better life for his family, his beautiful wife murdered, and a young girl starting a wonderful adventure probably kidnapped

Kit senses the others surrounding him, looking on the family lying dead. "Buzzard food," one of the men says.

Kit lets out a scream. It's loud and uncharacteristic—a shriek that has built within him, fueled by rage. Even Taos is surprised by the noise: his ears stand up and his nostrils flare.

"That could wake snakes," says Maxwell. He's known Kit for a long time and hasn't ever seen him act like this.

"Let's make them a nice bone orchard here in the grasses," says one of the wagon train.

"I have a schedule to keep," Fremont whines.

The others stop to help anyway.

Once the family is buried, the wagon train heads out. But now Kit's scouting has ulterior motives—more than just getting Fremont safely through Colorado territory. He can't shake the feeling that he could have saved the murdered family…the sight of them reminded him of his own wife, killed. And then he'd had to leave his daughter in the east, just to stay safe….

Fremont might be oblivious to the unusual extent of Kit's scouting, but Maxwell isn't. "Kit," he says, "what're you doing taking the wagons this way?"

"I can't stand it, Maxwell. The feelin' is so strong…I got to get to the bottom of that family's killer."

"I know you lost your wife, but you got a job to do. Fremont'll be madder than a hornet if he finds out."

Kit gives Maxwell a steely look. "He's not gonna find out."

Maxwell shakes his head. "Well, then let me help you."

***

Day after day, the two men take turns scouting farther and farther from the wagon train. Kit took chances riding far out from the caravan, through tall prairie grasses far off the wagon trail, searching for the family's killer. After five days of searching, Kit finds a makeshift camp along a stream. Tying Taos to a nearby tree, the horse is obviously uncomfortable with being left tied here alone. "Don't you give me grief," Kit tells the horse as he backs up. "I have the do this." Kit crawls on his stomach, approaching the camp hand over hand, slowly, quietly. When the man at the camp turns Kit's way, he knows he's found the killer. It's Avipani.

I'm gonna kill him. Kit had been around when infantrymen killed Indians, but he's never been one who take part. He's guided them, finding trails that lead to the complete obliteration of an Indian camp. But this is different. And personal.

"You'll do no such thing," Fremont informs him when Kit describes his plans for revenge. "As your commanding officer, I tell you: there will be no more killing. That family deserved what they got, leaving themselves vulnerable."

Kit can't say he disagrees that the family left themselves vulnerable, but that shouldn't mean they had to pay for their mistake with their lives.

"We'll ask for a parley tomorrow," Fremont says. It's a command not a suggestion.

"We'll leave at midnight," Kit tells the men he's convinced to help him. It's not his way to disobey orders, but this is revenge. And Kit has convinced himself he must kill his enemy. It's payback. Besides, when he spotted Avipani's camp, the Indian was with only a few other Ute men. A renegade troop banished along with his wife's killer. Arapaho tradition. Kit knows no additional tribal support will hunt for these killers.

That night, under the cover of darkness, Kit and the others secret themselves out of their tents. Each has been instructed to meet at the Creekside. When they've all arrived, they walk through darkness, with only the moon's light, toward Avipani's camp. Kit leads the men, then halts them when he senses the tents are nearby. Down onto the cold, hard flat earth, the men crawl hand over fist tamping down dried grasses before leaning their bodies through them. Kit wonders if the dank smell of deadening grasses will give away their location. The sudden hoot of an owl causes Maxwell to flinch, scraping the ground as he lifts himself to standing. He quickly lays back down to his stomach. Only three tents are standing. Kit has dreamed of this moment for so long. He's imagined coming face to face with his enemy, wishing he could drive a knife into his body. Now that this chance is finally here, he's suddenly so excited that his body shakes with anticipation.

"They must have heard us coming," Maxwell whispers. "Which means they are in the brush here with us? Kit, your wife is Arapaho. Call to them. Maybe it will draw them out."

Kit breaks the silence of the night with a slow, deep moan, that echoes over the prairie, signifying it's safe. The first man to come out of hiding from the woods is Avipani.

Kit tells those around him to stay quiet. *I'll affect his demise.* With cold determination, he stands. It takes Avipani only a few moments to spot him in the moonlight and realize who stands before him in the darkness. When Avipani begins charging, Kit raises his pistol. Instead of firing, though, he pulls his knife just as Avipani reaches him. The two fall backward, Avipani's arms wrapped around Kit's body. The next moment, Kit's knife plunges into Avipani—the Ute's eyes convey surprise when he pushes himself up on one arm. As he rises, Kit drags his knife upward, catching it on Avipani's rib cage. Then, he shoves him to the ground, faceup.

With the combatants' gazes locked on each other, Avipani whispers, "Your wife was my favorite kill …."

Kit lifts his boot just over Avipani's head. He pounds his heel down on his enemy's face, bones breaking under his foot.

A short while later, as Kit leads the men back to their camp, he hears them whispering among themselves. Apparently, there is general surprise that Kit maintained his composure during his confrontation with Avipani. "I ain't never seen him kill," said Maxwell, who had hunted with Kit this whole time. Preuss said, "Maybe the rumor is true. Maybe he took his wife's life?"

***

"Amass the Utahs, Kit. I want them here as soon as they can get down off the mountain." Kit turns to look at his new boss, Superintendent David Merriweather. The man has little knowledge of Ute territory, so Kit was immediately put in charge of Ute land. He found the job consisted mostly of hearing complaints from Americans while convincing the Indians they were trespassing. After killing Avipani, his patience with the Utes has dwindled to nearly nothing.

Merriweather explains: "The goal is twofold. First, we need to convince the Utahs not to join forces with the Apache. Then, we continue to push for our treaty. We need them off our land!"

Although Kit has tried to explain his long-standing relationship with the Utes, Merriweather isn't interested. Nor will the man consider the possibility of approaching the Ute tribe to determine if they are willing to negotiate peacefully. Instead, he expects Kit to travel to the Ute territory and retrieve the men then bring them here to the office in Santa Fe.

***

Days after Merriweather makes his opinions known, Kit is headed northwest toward Chaska's camp. During the long, hot days of walking Kit can only wonder at the changes he's seeing in Ute country. Towns of shacks that have been hastily constructed from recently felled pine trees barely tall enough for the likes of Kit to fit inside. The smell of sulfur overwhelms him at times by the burning in his eyes and throat.

Tipping his John B as he passes one such town, Kit is surprised to see a mountain man walking toward him. Dressed top to bottom in elk skins, Kit can't help but wonder why this guy would stay here rather than be out in the mountains.

"Good day."

"Good day yourself. What's a man such as yourself doing comin' through Laurette?"

"I got business with the Utes," Kit says stopping Taos as the man saunters toward him, his white beard and hair bobbing slightly as he walks along the dirt road splitting the town in two.

"Higginbottom's the name," he says stretching his hand toward Kit.

"Agent Carson," Kit says in his deep gravelly voice, grabbing the man's hand and shaking it vigorously.

"An agent? Say, what business you got with them Indians?"

"Meetin' up with their leader. Hopefully convince him to move outta here."

"Good! Good! 'Bout time somebody moved them along. Hell, I've just put in for claims all along this valley and up onto the side 'a this here mountain. I ain't puttin' up with much more from those people—walked right through our little town last time they got here. Showin' off like they owns the place. I's cussin' them out so bad—one of 'em had the nerve to ask me to smoke with him. I know I dresses in their gear, but I ain't no injun," Higginbottom proclaims.

Kit can't disagree with the man's claim to the land. And after killing Avipani, Kit has convinced himself that his enemy and the Ute are inextricably connected. He wishes it was as easy as telling Ahwatt to move along. It would be much better all-around if Kit cold negotiate with his sister. At the very least he can talk with her, build their friendship, her trust. Maybe, just maybe, she can convince her obstinate brother to do the right thing.

Once his bidden good day to Higginbottom and promised to do his best to get the Ute out of here, Kit starts to daunting trek up the mountain trail toward the tribe's camp. The miners don't usually come up with way, mostly because the Ute scouts would stop them in their tracks. It's slow going, up and foot path that winds through clumps of scrub brush and tall, thin pine trees.

Kit has left Buckskin Creek far behind when he arrives at the Chaska's camp. He's been followed by Ute scouts most of the way up. Thankfully, they allowed him to continue rather than killing him and taking Taos. When he finally climbs up and over the lip of the outcropping where the Ute make their summer camp, Kit is in awe. Treeless mountains so high they nearly block the sun surround the camp that lies along a flat meadow of grasses. Bluebells, Sago Lilies and yellow Buttercups bloom along the edges of a high-altitude pond. Lush and green, Wheatgrass has sprouted everywhere, covering the ground with a green blanket that gently undulates in the breeze. And there, in the middle of it, is Chaska, smiling and walking briskly to greet him. Kit raises a hand as a hello.

"Chaska!" Kit feels an immediate connection with this woman, who helped him to become the man he is today. Despite his wavering feelings about the Ute, he will always feel a bond with this friend.

"Kit, what a lovely surprise." His friend walks right up to Taos, touching his nose. After wrapping an arm around the horse's neck for a squeeze to say hello, she looks up at Kit, covering her eyes to the sun's glare with a hand above her eyes.

"What brings you up here?"

"Thought I could have a talk with Ahwatt. First though, can you and I parlay a bit?"

Chaska quickly looks to see who has noticed Kit's arrival. He suspects she's looking for her brother, though he doesn't seem to be around. She nods and walks in the direction of the forest that surrounds the camp.

"I am surprised to see so many miners along the Platte," Kit offers.

"The *merikac* have trapped us here, not even allowing our men to hunt buffalo." Kit frowns. He and Chaska walk through the tall pines, the coolness there feels refreshing after riding so far through the hot sun.

"The water is bitter," Chaska says, "My daughter has been sick. Her belly aches. She wakes up every night screaming."

Kit swallows hard. "Chaska." He stops deliberately to face her. "Don't drink the water. You and your people must leave here as soon as possible."

"Kit, it's our home. Where else would we go?"

He ignores her question. "Look, Chaska, the miners, their poisoning the water. They pull the gold out of rocks, then that contaminated water flows into the Platte."

As he and Chaska emerge from the woods and head back to camp, Kit turns to see Ahwatt standing in tall grasses, staring at them.

"He won't like the fact that you and I are talking," Kit says.

"No," Chaska agrees. "He's always been apprehensive about it." She turns to him. "I'll let you two along to discuss what you came here for." She quickly makes her way back to camp, leaving Kit staring at the big Ute leader.

All told the Ute tribe consists of five thousand to six thousand souls though living all over Colorado territory. Here on the mountaintop, Kit needs to convince Ahwatt, the leader chosen by the Americans to speak for all the Ute people, to send men for the meeting.

Kit stalks toward Ahwatt, lifting his boots to step over the grasses. The sun has snuck behind a passing cloud, creating an ominous darkness. He fully removes his hat, placing it over his heart. Looking Ahwatt in the eyes, Kit claims, "I'm here as a friend."

"No, you're here as an agent who wants this land."

Kit acknowledges the truth with a nod. "Either way, you've got to come to Santa Fe. Once we discuss the plans—"

"Plans? For you to move us away from here? Kill everything in your path? Then make neat rows of wooden homes here instead of letting us alone?"

Kit reaches for his ear tugging hard. "You need your own land Ahwatt. This is your chance to get it. For the peace Chaska wants. Come to Santa Fe and talk with Merriweather. I'll make it worth your while."

Ahwatt turns and walks away, effectively ending the discussion. Kit's seen this from him before. Instead of pushing the big man, he'll head to camp for the night and try again tomorrow.

Though the tribe has come to know Kit, few except Chaska seem to trust him. He and Taos spends the nights just far enough away from the tribe's camp to make Ahwatt and the other men feel secure. The horse appears to feel perfectly comfortable in their camp in the woods.

As he lights a campfire to cook a small slab of bacon, Kit knows they have a scout or two watching his every move; he'd do the same if the tables were turned.

***

The next day, Kit climbs back up the mountain atop Taos for a huddle with the men, explaining their trip will give them to peace they need to carry on all their traditions.

"Why doesn't this Merriweather come to us?" Ahwatt demands. I wonder that myself, Kit thinks, but makes up a lie instead. "We have gifts for you at the fort, that he can't carry alone." Ute men stare at him but say nothing. The silence eats at Kit's nerves.

"Fine," Ahwatt concedes.

"But there's a wrinkle in the contract negotiations."

No one moves. Kit has spoken before the Ute leader turns to leave as is normally the case. Again, an unnerving silence. No one moves to leave the teepee where the negotiations have been taking place.

Kit continues, trying to hide a shakiness to his voice that he just can't stop. "The Americans will sign on only if your tribe promises not to hunt."

Ahwatt stands and draws closer, hovering just above Kit, but Kit has long since realized Ahwatt's aggressive stance is just a scare tactic.

"That won't work for us."

Kit holds his ground. He looks up into Ahwatt's eyes. "Let me make myself perfectly clear. If you don't sign the treaty as it's written, your entire tribe will be killed, including Chaska."

A collective gasp from the Utes fills the strained atmosphere. The men's anxiety is thick with unanswered questions. One small head nod from Ahwatt—and the men trickle out from the teepee, leaving just he and Kit, standing toe to toe. Though Kit feels unsafe in the confines of the space, he's secretly glad to finally have the Utes where he wants them. Perhaps the prohibition on hunting will make the decision that much easier for Ahwatt.

"What will we eat then?" Ahwatt asks somberly.

"The Americans will provide you with food."

Ahwatt paces back and forth in front of Kit, then stops to regard the merikac in front of him, his eyes pulled together in thought. "I'm not putting the lives of my tribe in more danger," he says. "If we must give up hunting on our land, then we won't hunt."

Ahwatt turns to leave, but then stops. He turns his big body fully facing Kit.

"I'll be the one to tell my tribe," he says, "not you."

***

"Men," Kit says amiably, "thank you for coming. The long trip you've made will be well worth your effort. We continue to hold the leadership of your tribe in the highest esteem."

Ute men sit on the dirt floor of the single-story fort, the window and door left ajar for air to circulate and let in light. Just outside the window, the Sangre de Christo mountains loom, already frosted with snow. Ute ponies are tied to the post just outside under the shade of one of three cottonwoods that grow inside the fort walls.

The talk regarding how to ensure the Utes stay away from their sworn enemies, the Apache, should be easy.

Merriweather continues in his usual brusque, unempathetic manner. "You don't like the Apache and they don't like you. I expect you will stay away from them from here on out." The Apache have become a real problem for Kit: they consistently kill homesteaders traveling through their territory. Men heading west to make their fortune are left for dead as they cross Apache land. Everyone at Indian Affairs is worried the Apache will convince the Utahs to do the same, especially since Ute country holds the richest source of gold this side of California.

Merriweather walks to each Ute man in turn, handing him a blanket made of thick wools. "A blanket for all," he says, handing each person a three-point Hudson Bay covering. Each looks the same: the entire covering is an off-white with two black stripes on either end.

"Riding the distance from South Park to Santa Fe, more than two hundred miles, has meant keeping you from your families. These blankets are tokens of my appreciation."

Kit knows there is a stash of muskets, knives and other products he and Merriweather could also bestow upon the men if they need more convincing to stay away from the Apache. This is only the short-term solution to Kit's problem. The treaty, he hopes, will solve his long-term issues.

Kit hopes those who haven't favored signing the treaty may be convinced after this meeting. Ahwatt has remained at South Park to keep the camp safe, which is all the better for Kit— he doesn't trust the man anyway.

"The treaty will give you most of the Colorado Territory," Merriweather lies. He knows full well the Utes will be confined to Western Colorado. "Everything will be provided for you to be successful civilized members of society. You will farm the land and become one with us," he says. Kaib asks, "We will hunt on the land also?" Merriweather simply nods in agreement.

"No farming," Kaib confirms. "We have plants already." As Merriweather nods again, the men sitting around him nod in agreement also. Kit turns to look out the window at the Sangre's off in the distance. He knows he will be free to roam the mountains he loves once more, but the men in this room will be cut off from them.

Kit pinches the bridge of his nose to tamp down his frustration. He realizes the men don't understand the implications of not following the treaty to the letter. The treaty isn't a request. Merriweather's demands aren't a request. This is an ultimatum. The Utes *will* grow crops and *will* become civilized. Otherwise, the Americans see the Natives as wild, and untamed. They haven't even heard the worst of it—no more wandering around the territory; the entire tribe has to live in one, small, designated place. A reservation.

"Indians will be provided a stipend of American dollars," Kit says, hoping the men will like it. "And animals—cows and sheep."

Merriweather squirms a bit in his chair. He and Kit know the reservation won't meet the Ute's expectations. Looking around, the room feels smaller than when they started this meeting. Twelve sets of Ute eyes look upon him leery of his intentions. As they should. Kit feels the anxiety growing in the room too. A prickle of concern rises along the back of Kit's neck. He shakes it off, squaring his broad shoulders and focusing his icy blue eyes on the Ute men. Telling the Utes any more than they already know might cause a revolt.

***

After the meeting, the Ute thankfully return to their own land. The patience it took for Kit to meet with them was overwhelming and he found himself exhausted by it. To calm his nerves, Kit takes time out of his workday to ride another expedition with Fremont. It felt good, a relief too. But out on the open prairies, Kit's mind turns killing Avipani. He remembers the satisfaction of turning the knife in Avipani's body. He wonders if all killing was this easy, or if his feelings are only because Avipani took his wife from him.

Kit's remembrance is interrupted when shouts go up, "Indians ahead!" Kit's heart races in anticipation. The march halts, and the men bring out their arms. In the lead, Kit imagines the feeling he had only the night before—euphoria, excitement, control. His anger has only grown stronger since killing Avipani.

As the Indians draw closer to the wagon train, however, Kit recognizes Ahwatt. Somber as usual, the leader has locked his gaze on Kit; he seems intent on riding straight toward him. Apparently, Maxwell recognizes Ahwatt too, because he starts grinning. When the Ute leader reaches him, Maxwell says, "Ahwatt, I haven't seen you in years."

The leader seems surprised by the interruption in his thoughts. He gives a quick greeting to Maxwell but continues to focus on Kit. Fremont, as usual, remains ignorant of the anger the chief is demonstrating. "I welcome the Spanish Yutahs to our camp," he says. Then, he smiles.

Ahwatt ignores Fremont's chatter. Pointing at Kit he says, "We need the white man's medicines. Now."

Kit imagines the leader has allowed his tribe to drink the poisoned water of the stream he had warned Chaska about. Or, put his people in some other kind of trouble because of his inability to make well-reasoned decisions.

"Chaska remembers," Ahwatt starts. "Our parents, they could have survived with the American's cure. Now you are withholding your medicines from us again," he accuses, "and we are dying."

"No, Ahwatt!" Kit yells, furious that he would accuse him of killing anyone. "I told you not to drink the water. The water is bad, bitter, from the mining. It's your fault they are all sick," he continues, "you've poisoned them by staying in that place. Our medicines can't fix your problems; I told you to move."

Kit's body shakes with anger at the fact that Ahwatt didn't listen to him. Although the "Indian problem" has become Kit's problem, he would rather see Chaska's family alive. She might be the only one he cares about at this point.

"Chaska's daughter is sick too."

Kit stares at the tall chief. *No. Not Chaska.* Whatever he felt about other Indians, Chaska will always hold a dear place in his heart. But that place is growing smaller.

Kit moves Taos close beside Ahwatt, who is still sitting atop his horse. Shifting his body to draw his face close to the Native's, Kit says, "You are killing your niece, not me. You haven't listened to anything I've told you!"

Ahwatt grabs for Kit's jacket. He pulls, trying to force Kit down from Taos. Finally, Maxwell rides up next to the two men. "That's enough!" he tells Ahwatt, grabbing him to release Kit.

"We need your help *now*," Ahwatt repeats.

"God dammit!" Kit cries.

He knows nothing can be done at this point. He wouldn't do anything anyway. Not for Ahwatt. If he could have helped Chaska and her daughter, he might have, but it's too late.

Chapter 13
Merikac Come Too Close
(Winter, 1867)

After Medicine Man declared it was I who had caused my daughter's illness, he wouldn't help Mapia any longer. He claimed my fear of fighting the merikac was causing my daughter's illness, and that I should change my ways. Although others in the tribe agree peaceful means are the answer to our problems, he singled me out. As the leader of the movement to sign a treaty, he claims there may even be others who become sick because of my meddling. I'm the problem, he said. "There will be no peace with the white man," he told us, packing up his herbs, his tools. "Give up that absurd idea and your daughter will heal."

Then he left.

Medicine Man is well respected for curing our illnesses. He was born a healer, just as his father was born to heal us. His powers are not questioned. I'm guilt ridden, knowing I've caused my daughter's illness. As Mapia's mother, I'd never do anything to hurt her. I want to comfort her, protect her and help her to become a strong woman. It's distressing to think that I have caused her problems.

Apparently, Medicine Man isn't the only one in the tribe who thinks I'm the problem. Those who had agreed with me that peace through a treaty is our answer, are now hesitant to let their opinions be known. They fear their family members could become ill too.

For now, I care for my daughter and try to forget my ideas for peace. All I do is watch over her, by myself. Kaib can't watch his daughter slowly weaken. All I can do is think about it. The best solution for now is to stop talking about it and focus on Mapia, to ease her suffering. Rubbing her hair gently as she leans against me, I think of all my oldest daughter has brought to me. She's been mesmerized by life ever since she could first experience it. She's found joy in every little crevice of the world, from tiny bugs and new buds on trees to horses and deer. Her wonderment has brought so much joy to me too—she's allowed me to see all we have and to be thankful for it, to be in awe of it.

What I had thought were the usual skin changes every teenager goes through have been something so much worse. They've turned her face and neck pink and red with blotches. She breathes in fits and starts, sometimes gasping for air. It sounds as if she is breathing water. Today, Mapia lies near me in our teepee, her head in my lap. I look down at her, only to realize clumps of my daughter's hair are sticking to my fingers. Whole tufts of her long, dark hair fall to the floor. I gasp. When Mapia looks to me concerned, I quickly regain my composure. I smile at her, as if everything is all right. But she has a fit of coughing. When I release her so she can take a breath, blood trickles from her mouth. I reach for a blanket to wipe the blood before she can see it, but I'm too late. She wipes at it, then sees the blood and immediately lets out a scream. Pulling her close, I say, "Everything will be all right," though I know that's a lie. My body shakes violently, and I can feel tears running down my face. We stay here until nightfall, when she finally falls asleep.

The next morning, Kaib carries her outside for fresh air, but her eyesight has worsened. Immediately, she lifts her hands to her eyes, squeezing them shut. "No! I can't! The sunshine is like a knife slicing through my eyes!" she yells. My husband looks to me with such sadness, but he gently picks up Mapia to bring her back to the relative darkness of the tent.

The guilt I feel for causing Mapia's illness is physical. My stomach feels as though someone has punched me—if I try to eat, I feel nauseous.

All that night I feel Mapia's warmth as I draw her close. *How can I be a mother to my other daughters when I feel such agony for Mapia?* I wonder. I'm rocking her gently back and forth when I suddenly realize her breathing has become shallow. I'm so frightened that I begin to shake her. "Mapia! Wake up!" My screams awake Kaib and the girls. Tears are streaming from my eyes—my oldest daughter is dying in my arms! Kaib sets one hand on Mapia's back and the other on mine. It's not long before Mapia's body is limp. At first, I'm numb. "No…" I whisper. My husband rubs my back. Suddenly, I hear big heaving sobs, followed by a long, drawn-out scream of grief. My own.

***

"He's retching again," says Medicine Man as I enter Tawoot's teepee.

The man used to be as fast as a jack rabbit, but now lies dying.

No need to tell me. I can smell the sour, rotten stench of vomit. Taking in a breath through my mouth so as not to further smell the stink, I say, "I've brought the herbs you asked for." Waving away the smell, I sit to his side, uncovering the variety of herbs I've collected for Medicine Man to inspect. I hope he won't need me to stay long; I might throw up too if I'm required to remain here too long.

We don't get along, me and Medicine Man. I haven't cared for him since he allowed my parents to die when I was merely a child. Him telling me I caused my daughter's death is one more reason for me to dislike him. He's never helped me heal from illness, although I've had only a broken heart repeatedly.

He goes from tent to tent tending the men who have fallen sick and asks me to accompany him because I'm always finding herbs and plants. Also, after Mapia's death, I feel nothing. I'm numb. Chava and Chipara bring me flowers to cheer me; I pretend they make me happy. Inside though, it's as if nothing is happening. I may or may not be breathing. I may or may not be living. I don't care. I'll never be the same after my daughter's death. The hole I feel where Mapia once dwelled within me has broken me. If the men are sick, it doesn't matter. Nothing matters. So, Medicine Man probably brings me along because I'm not one of the wives, crying at the sight of her man in pain.

The men's illnesses are different than my daughter's. It starts with strange spots on their tongues and inside their mouths; it appears on their skin as a red rash. Scratching leaves bloody scabs that pit on the skin. Severe fever leaves the men sweating horribly.

Po'rat sends me to the next teepee to check on its occupant. I step carefully along the icy path that extends from one teepee to the next. Snow has drifted up to the teepee, covering the bottom in a blanket of white. Opening the flap, I see a man who lies still as death, but his face is flush. He is just at the beginning of the disease. Sweat glistens along his neck and head even though the day is cold, so I quickly pick up a cloth, take it outside and wrap a ball of snow inside of it. I head back into the teepee and dab the cold cloth onto his forehead.

"How are you feeling?" I ask.

The man shakes his head from side to side and rubs his stomach.

This sickness reminds me of the one that killed my parents. Father traded with Spaniards and white men in Taos, as did many in our tribe. He would carry tanned hides to them, and then he'd come back with knives, sometimes a musket, or even a horse. I remember him leaving every year when I was just a small child up until he passed. He and a few other men would travel during the fall before winter's cold set in. Within two weeks of returning from his last expedition, Father had strange red spots on his tongue and in his mouth. Ahwatt was the one who noticed them first. Father was teaching my brother to use a gun he had brought back. Innocently, Ahwatt asked Father about the spots. I remember it like it was yesterday because I had been sitting near them, watching, trying to find a way to join them, although it wasn't my place. "Why do you have those spots, Mowac?" Ahwatt had asked, pointing to Father's mouth. A sudden flash of fear had passed across our father's face, and he'd let out a little gasp before composing himself.

That night, he and Pia talked about the spots quietly in our teepee. There was alarm in their voices. They'd seen this before and it didn't end well. "What can we do?" Pia had asked, but Father only shook his head.

Over the next few weeks, he became quite hot with fever.

"Pia…will Towac die?" I remember asking. Rather than answer me directly, she sent me out to collect the cottonwood buds that start forming toward the end of winter. Father complained of head and body aches. "Here, my love," Mother had said, giving Father cottonwood leaf buds to chew to reduce his fever and lessen the pain. When he held himself from pain, Mother would gently rub his back, trying to lessen his discomfort.

One cold winter morning, we all awoke and looked to Father. He was cleaning tools in our teepee, as the winter winds were blowing outside. Again, poor Ahwatt was the one who noticed a red rash on Father's face and hands. "Towac! Your face!" Mother had gasped and pulled her hand up to her mouth. Their eyes met, and they had stared at one another a long time. No one said a word for hours after that. We each just kept our thoughts to ourselves, although we were all thinking the same thing.

When the rash blistered, then scabbed over, father was left with deep pits in his face and hands. We all thought that was the end of it.

It was a few days of uneasy hope, but those joyful thoughts were swept away when the vomiting started. It never stopped. Every day, Mother propped up my father's back against the teepee poles and forced him to take a few sips of water from the gourd she kept near her sleeping mat. My father weakly sipped the water, but he could never keep it down. My mother would quietly wipe up his bile from the floor of the teepee with a cotton cloth.

Medicine Man said he couldn't save my parents because they had encountered a negative spirit—either as a result of evil acts my parents had taken or because the spirit disliked them—that refused to leave their bodies. At first, my brother fully believed our parents had made terrible mistakes in their lives, but I convinced him otherwise. "No, brother, no. Think about it. When have you known either of our parents to go against tradition? Has anyone ever said a bad word about either of our parents? No!" Ahwatt agreed after much prodding and developed a new theory: The merikac intentionally put the harmful spirit into Father. Upon much contemplation, my brother claimed that when Father returned from that last trip, he seemed different: impatient and quick to anger. I didn't notice a difference, but then again, Ahwatt spent more time with Father. Ahwatt took to this theory so strongly that it informs his decisions to this day. He has never forgiven the merikac for it. They passed on a spirit that was so strong it could overtake a living person.

By the time my mother came down with similar symptoms, we all knew her fate.

Medicine Man tried everything he could think of, but nothing worked: washing Father's skin with agave soap, brewing teas of echinacea, hawthorn and maple, picking willow leaves for father to chew. The spirits wouldn't leave my parents: Their fever and rash only became worse. Medicine Man said only the merikac themselves could rid my parents of the sickness.

I begged Ahwatt to ask the Americans to help. He was just riding in from a hunt with the men. He was on the verge of becoming a teenager, when boys learned their future tasks in earnest. As he hopped off Luksi, I ran to him, desperately begging him to do something. "Only the merikac know which spirits they've sent to Father," I told my brother. "Only they can force them to leave."

"No, Chaska," Ahwatt replied. "They have to live with the consequences of their actions." This was before he realized the merikac were responsible for the sickness. By then, it was too late.

We were both very young. Ahwatt was just becoming a man—he wanted desperately to hunt with the older men. I don't think he considered the consequences of his actions. Usually, the men were gone for days, taking time to prepare themselves mentally and physically to take the life of an animal that would feed us. This time had been no different. As Ahwatt told it, the men left camp and built a fire around which they prayed to Creator, asking them to provide for us as they have always done.

Ahwatt never regained his confidence after his decision not to save our parents. It's probably the reason he's been hesitant to make choices ever since their death. I could say I forgave him, but that would be a lie.

That's probably where some of my anxiety comes from today. After our parents died, I have never felt fully safe. Ahwatt doesn't help. As more merikac arrive, his desire to kill has risen too. That's most likely why I fight for our tribe's safety. My trust in Ahwatt to make difficult decisions has decreased far too much at this point.

***

Tawoot, the sick man, looks into my eyes as I wipe the sweat from his face and neck. "Am I going to live?" he asks. I nod though I know it's a lie. I can't see another person die right in front of me. If he knows of the other men we've buried just this week—seven to date, and the man in the next tent doesn't have long—he isn't making it known to me.

No one can figure how the men became ill. It started a few weeks after they met for the council. Ahwatt has had much more exposure to the merikac while talking about making a treaty, and he isn't sick. Kaib isn't ill either, thankfully.

Ahwatt has gone to ask Kit for help. He left last night under the cover of darkness, choosing to go alone. After he helped to bury the seven. Kaib was the one who convinced him to go. "It's time," Kaib told him. But so far, nothing.

***

"Good, Chipara, now flick her forward," I say, watching my youngest become a better rider than most children her age. She has a strong emotional connection to Nublada, who reminds me so much of Auntie's horse, Kyra. Like Kyra, Nublada is genuinely concerned when it comes to children. Like Kyra, Nublada gently rocks her rider back to a sitting position when a child loses her balance, seeming to make her smooth gate more graceful, smoother.

As much as I've always loved racing ponies, I feel my body resisting close contact with any member of my tribe. I'm barely able to stand my ground here on the racing field, so I can watch my daughter compete.

Chipara whispers to Nublada. The horse's ears prick backwards. Whatever my daughter is telling the horse, her words are between her and Nublada. My now seven-year-old has been riding horses even before she could sit up without any help. She used to ride with me and Mapia, sitting in front of us. Mapia was the one who really sparked Chipara's interest in racing. It had been one of my oldest daughter's favorite pastimes. Mapia was silly, she would have fun teasing the other riders by saying her skills at racing were far superior to theirs. Oh, my sweet, sweet girl. The thought of her brings tears to my eyes. In comparison, Chipara just races hard and wins. No funny stuff. But Mapia will always be connected to my soul, reaching for me from her grave.

I will myself to stop thinking of the past, of Mapia sitting high on a horse, laughing and enjoying her time racing.

Focus, Chaska. Just like Mapia, Chipara has a gift for befriending any horse she rides. Today is no different. The bond between her and Nublada is so strong that even I, an accomplished racer myself, can barely see Chipara's cues to her mount.

When Chipara races, she hugs Nublada as I do. But she also screams a high-pitched, loud scream of joy. The faster the horse, the happier she is.

"Pia! Pia!"

My daughter Chava hollers then runs onto the racing field. After what happened to Mapia last year, I have a heightened fear for my children's safety. At the same time though, I can feel my stomach drop—what if Chava brings news of something else bad that's happened, can I handle it? I'm barely able to mother as it is. *Please, please, Chava! Don't let your news threaten what little peace I still have!* I remove my focus from Chipara to tend to Chava's needs.

"I know, Mama," is all Chava says as she reaches me.

"You know what?" I ask her.

She looks at me quizzically, then all she says is, "Kit gave us the blankets."

I have to wonder if my daughter was hit in the head. She's telling me something I already know. I want to scold her for scaring me so badly, but instead I try to stay calm. Kneeling to meet her at eye level, I say, "Yes, Chava. Kit gave each man who met with him a blanket." I turn, closing my eyes and tensing my jaw at her nonsense, but she grabs my skirt. "No, Mama, you don't understand. The blankets are making the men sick. They carry the bad spirits. The spirits were put into the blankets to make our men die."

All I can do is stare at her. *No, that's not possible. He wouldn't do that. Kit wouldn't poison our tribe.* Shaking my head, I'm certain Chava is mistaken.

***

"Chaska, I told you the man was bad!" Ahwatt says when I relay what Chava told me. "He was at the council. He translated for the tribe when he spoke to Sherman!" my brother snarls.

"I just don't think he would deliberately give us blankets he knew might be contaminated," I tell him. Kit wouldn't do that…would he? The last time he came by camp I barely recognized him. His eyes had changed. In his younger days, his eyes were warm, caring, compassionate. Now, something had changed. Perhaps it was just me, but he looked sharper, hardened and maybe even distrustful of us.

"Leave me!" is all Ahwatt says.

Shortly thereafter Ahwatt summons my husband and the other men who aren't sick to meet with him. Their meet lasts long into the night. When Kaib finally returns, he doesn't say a word. But I can tell something significant is about to take place: My husband's energy is intense. He moves swiftly around the teepee we share, gathering his bow, arrows and knives.

"What's going on, Kaib?" I ask.

I beg him to give me information, but he refuses to even look at me. It's obvious. He and the other men are going to war. I can only imagine it's to fight the merikac. Again. The guilt I've felt since causing Mapia's death has left me questioning myself. I know in my heart that a treaty will help us address our contentious relationship with the merikac, but I can't bring myself to act on my feelings. I don't want to lose anyone else in my family due to my actions. So, I've kept silent. Even when I hear men and women encouraging Ahwatt to fight as many battles as it takes for the Americans to leave us alone.

"No. Please, don't do this, Kaib"—though I don't quite know what "this" is yet. "Don't go. *Don't* do this!" I repeat.

He won't look at me, and simply pushes me away when I plead with him.

"Kaib! I can't lose you too. Please! Please, spare me! If you die, I can't go on any longer. It's just too much death. Please, stay!"

He merely walks out of the teepee.

The girls are huddled together, frightened by our interaction. We don't usually fight with one another. Telling

Kaib I'm lost without him probably didn't help my daughters to stop worrying about me either.

I could run and try to stop Ahwatt, but that would make him look weak to the other men—and make me look a fool. My husband tells me Ahwatt has spent much time with Hunt recently—without the need for me to intervene. I had thought a treaty was imminent. It's been a long time coming, but I thought he was finally listening to me. Now, with the men leaving, I'm not sure what's happening.

***

I hear them long before I see them. The ground begins shaking under me. It sounds like a herd of buffalo stampeding wildly up the mountain. The fresh snow hasn't stopped the men from riding their horses hard. "Whoop! Whoop!" they cry.

It's our men. They ride into camp, bloodied from battle. Most trail a horse behind them. The men hold the reins of their own ponies with one hand, and a long yucca rope that has been fashioned into a bridle for the stolen horses. Eastern horses. Their tall, lean bodies completely overshadow our ponies.

Then I look to Magena's husband and lose my breath. In his fist he carries a scalp. Long hair has been wrapped around and around his hand. A swath of bloody skin swings from the end. He brings it up and over his head, just as I've seen the merikac do to our own. Why follow such a horrid merikac tradition? His celebration rings in my ears, and I know then we are doomed.

I lock eyes with Ahwatt as he rides into camp—mine questioning, his wild. He rides his paint horse so close that Luksi's shoulder rams me. As I stumble to regain my footing, my brother sneers at me: "Just got rid of our problems!"

Which problems? I wonder.

My husband also rides full speed into camp. We lock eyes for a moment before he plows past me. Behind him he too leads a horse whose nostrils are flaring from the effort of running. He swings his own pony around, powerfully twisting the reins hard. "We stopped the merikac today. The

Apache helped." He says this almost maniacally. His mouth laughs out the words, his eyes large and fierce. "We killed the merikac, Chaska!"

I've counted ten new horses. Scared and angry, I can't speak.

Where had the men collected the scalps they carry? And where did they commit such a slaughter? They had left our camp before sunup. It's not hunting season, but winter, cold. Snow lies on the ground, and a storm is coming in. Normally, they do not leave for long in these conditions. They've come back quickly though, and they carry at least fifteen scalps.

"El Pueblo is gone!" the men yell.

Fort Pueblo. A trading post that sits between the Arkansas River and Fountain Creek. We have camped there in the past, when white men and Spaniards came up from Santa Fe to trade with us; that was before they intruded on our lands and constructed a fort there. The adobe walls that surround the fort should have been enough of a barricade to halt Ahwatt's surprise attack.

Women come out into the cold to see what is happening. They run to their husbands, finding reassurance when they learn they've come back safely. But one woman runs from horse to horse, frantic, screaming her husband's name. "Tierra? Where is my husband!"

Ahwatt jumps down from his pony and leads Luksi over to the woman while holding the reins with a blood-stained hand. He speaks quietly to the woman, telling her Tierra is gone. Her shrieks become ever louder, openly raging at his absence. "No! No!" she begs. "Please…no!" But the men ignore her. They are frenzied—still whooping and circling their horses—it's as if they've all gone mad—still whooping and circling their horses. But as frenetic as the scene is, I can't care.

All I can do is stare. My heart beats faster…my understanding of what has transpired gradually grows. As I stand there, something starts heating my gut. It rises slowly, up to my mouth. I expel a shout: *"No!"* Running full sprint at Ahwatt, I reach my hands up when I get to him and shove him hard in the chest. Stunned, still wild-looking, he stares at me. "They are peaceful! We have *always* been peaceful with them. Trade with them has *benefited* us! *Why* did you do this?"

I'm screaming. So loud my throat hurts.

Ahwatt hovers over me. "They won't leave, Chaska! They stay here, taking our water, our animals, even taking our land! We've been promised their help, but it never comes!"

I shake my head, not believing the spark he may have ignited by his provocation.

Ahwatt continues: "They brought the illness that killed our parents. I know it! Now the merikac have paid for the guilt I've carried ever since their deaths."

"You pretended to be friendly, didn't you?" I spit the words from my mouth. "That's how you got into the fort. You used my name!" I'm shaking from anger, and my skin is hot despite the full-blown snowstorm that has begun blowing around us. It dawns on me: This act of violence makes our tribe no better than the merikac. I've been quietly hoping Ahwatt would make prudent decisions that would finally resolve our endless conflicts. Instead, I realize I have to save the tribe from themselves.

Chapter 14

Resolving the Indian Problem
(Winter, 1868)

Several men ride toward Kit as he advances upon the newly built Camp Alexis, a splotch of tents and hastily constructed wooden buildings just north of Red Willow Creek in Nebraska country. Rough-hewn logs seem to have been notched and stacked carelessly by an overabundance of underlings. So much so that when Kit reaches the stables, they are leaning to one side, ready to topple. All this for a man he will never see again.

Normally, Taos is a peaceful example of a horse that is comfortable with his surroundings, but not today. He is skittish for some reason. “Easy, boy,” Kit says, calming Taos. “Don’t go catawampus on me now. I don’t want to be here either.” He grips the horse’s barrel tightly with his legs, just in case. Sure enough, Taos pushes off his front legs to rear up. A surge of panic rushes through Kit’s body as if he’d just shot whiskey. As experienced as he is, sending him askew like this can be surprisingly uncomfortable.

"Let's just have ourselves a little visit with the archduke and get out of here," Kit says more to himself than to his distraught pony. The military has been tasked with showing the Russian Czar's only son the western country while he visits America. Kit has been told he is the embodiment of the American dream, so his presence is expected. It upsets him to be so far away from Ute territory and his work; the Czar's son is just a side show.

***

At first glance, General Philip Sheridan and his horse, a seventeen-hand giant, don't seem to get on well. While the general twists and turns, kicking the horse's flanks hard, trying to get his mount near enough to Kit for a handshake, the animal pins his ears flat at the abuse and comes to a stop just shy of Kit and Taos. Amused, Kit watches as the animal swings his head around and opens his mouth, trying to bite his abuser. *Good thing he can't reach.*

"How do you do, Agent Carson?" General Sheridan says.

Gently nudging Taos toward the commanding officer and his horse, Kit puts himself at arm's length so he can offer a firm handshake. "Pleased to meet you, General," Kit says. He's not pleased though. This trip will cost him days of travelling that could be spent identifying the best ways to beat the Utes out of Colorado. The complaints from Americans heading west could keep Kit busy for ten years. *Damn Indians!* The Natives' constant attacks on the new homeowners are driving Kit mad.

"You'll make a good show for the Czar's son, the Archduke Alexis, during his visit," says the general. Kit grits his teeth at the thought of being part of the show. "I trust you're willing to give our young guest a shooting lesson," Sheridan commands.

"Uh, no—" Kit begins, but is ignored by Sheridan.

Once the homesteaders crossed the Mississippi River, they expected free land. More than one of them has observed to Kit: "I's told to head west and pick a spot in the dirt. Once I put up a house, it's mine." *As if I don't know that,* Kit has always grumbled to himself. What they didn't count on were Indians living on their patch of land. "We've built our home, we are working the land in an effort to own it, just as the government has asked, but we have to deal with these Indians constantly trampling through our crops, irrespective of the obvious rows of corn and wheat we've planted." Kit tries to explain the Indians have been using the land long before they moved to the spot, but the homesteaders simply expect Kit to move them. "Tell them we live here now. They don't own this land. It ain't theirs no more."

Townies dislike the Indians hanging around their settlements. With few laws in these upshot towns, who's to say a few Indians might not get killed when miners get drunk and shoot randomly or hit a few Indians at the outskirts of town. No one cares. Heck, maybe Kit would be better off if that happened more often. Take the law into their own hands.

Kit is shaken back to reality when a second man and horse approach quickly. The rider appears to be considerably out of control of his horse. "Spravka!" the man shrieks.

Neither Kit nor Sheridan move. "What was that he said?" Kit asks.

A young man who could only be the Archduke Alexis, Czar Romanov's son, surges past the two men on a horse hellbent on freedom. "Said he was inexperienced," is all the general says, but doesn't make a move. Alexis' mount must stand a good sixteen hands. The horse pulls his two front legs off the ground, and Kit prepares himself for what happens next. Alexis grabs the reins and seems to tighten his legs even more around the horse's girth. At the request, the animal kicks up his back legs to complete the jump. Surprisingly, Alexis stays seated, although his arms are now wrapped solidly around the animal's neck, the young duke howling for help.

Finally, Sheridan kicks his stallion in a weak attempt to chase down the runaway. The animal isn't having it though. Through nonstop kicking, Sheridan digs heeled boots into his horse's flanks, but the horse just backs up as calmly as possible, seemingly intent on making his master furious. "Miserable animal! We should take you out and shoot you too!" The horse gives Kit a quick glance before stopping altogether.

Kit says, "Oh, for heaven's sake," swinging his reins and clucking to Taos, who seems to read Kit's mind. He swings around to give chase. Whipping the reins about the horse's neck, more for show than anything, Kit gallops away from the general, quickly overtaking Alexis' horse. He grabs the reins easily then gently pulls on them while Taos slows himself down. Alexis' giant, uncooperative horse listens to Kit's command and halts. "Thank you, sir," Alexis says, using perfect English. "Your efforts are commendable. You've saved me from sure death."

Kit simply tips his John B and says, "Ain't the first time me and Taos had to chase down a runaway."

With the runaway horse's reins in hand, Taos and Kit turn the lot around to head back to camp. Now that he isn't running headlong toward death, the Russian takes the opportunity to look Kit up and down. "Those clothes you wear…dear me! You must be what the general calls a mountain man, I presume?"

Feeling slightly offended Kit nods his head in agreement. Alexis' voice is that of a teen boy just before his voice changes. It's in opposition to Kit's deep baritone. "My good man. Are you the famous Kit Carson about whom I've heard so much?"

Briefly, Kit finds his chivalrous side. "At your service!" he booms.

The well-groomed teenager sitting across from Kit is dressed in a deep blue coat embossed in gold detail along the collar and sleeves. A long lace-collared shirt with matching lace at the cuffs finishes his attire. What looks to be a newly minted beaver skin hat rests on his head of full hair. *Another aristocrat,* Kit thinks. Just like Fremont.

"You are to be my shooting instructor," Alexis discloses with a sly smile.

"So, I've been informed," Kit says, although he doesn't know any more about what's going on than the archduke. *I'm just here to put on a show,* thinks Kit dejectedly as he leads Alexis and the horses around the makeshift stable. Sheridan has excused himself for the moment to attend to "urgent" matters.

***

Two hundred men standing atop a distant hill riding tall, lanky horses, all dolled up: Shiny English bridles and well-oiled saddles. Archduke Alexis is here, carrying a rifle, as he wonders aimlessly. Buffalo gather in the field just below them, standing in groups of twos and threes, meandering and nipping off grass. Sheridan hops off his horse with surprising ease and hands the reins over to what looks like a boy in a soldier's costume. The youthful soldier hesitates, then asks, "Did you have any trouble with the ice, sir?" A crushing stare from the general has the young man turning on his heel before he can be reprimanded.

"Come on, I'll take you to the front," Sheridan says, walking toward the crowd of men.

The front? Kit thinks. *Is this a war?*

Approaching the men, Kit is surprised to see an Indian leader standing just off to the side. Wrapped in a thick buffalo hide, the man seems out of place surrounded by American soldiers, who wear dark-blue jackets lined with gold buttons down the front. A variety of insignias denote the privates from the officers, then on up the line to the generals. Kit eyes the Indian leader warily. The chief returns the favor. Kit nods and tips his hat to the man, although he's unsure why. Custom, he supposes. Without an ounce of empathy, the general says: "Let's show the red men the power of America's military. Only then will they give up and stop their barbarism." Kit wonders what type of "power" the general is talking about, but he doesn't have to wait long to find out. Sheridan grabs at the closest rifle, raises the gun high above his head and shouts, "Kill the buffalo! For every one we slaughter, we kill an injun too."

Huh?

Kit's surprise is genuine. When he realizes his mouth is hanging open, he quickly closes it, standing back from "the front." Without a buffalo to kill and eat each year most tribes will starve. There simply isn't enough sustenance in other animals to keep the entire tribe alive.

Years ago, Kit would have seen the sadness in the moment, but not anymore. The land was their land. If they couldn't share it with the Indians, then the Indians would have to leave. In fact, Kit finds himself quickly coming to terms with the idea of removing all the Indians from the land. Years ago, when he first started as a trapper, people made fun of him because he was green. His was a lonely existence, for a while. He'd prefer to be in the majority now.

A man runs through the crowd, giddily yelling, "Save the tongues! I've got a request for twelve dozen buffalo tongues!"

Sheridan walks proudly over to Kit, who stands only a few feet from the Indian chief. Clapping Kit on the shoulder, the general says, "A medal for every man who kills a beast. We'll position an Indian atop every dead animal as a reminder."

Kit turns to look at the Indian leader, but the man is looking off into the distance. He appears to not have heard the general. "Is this just for show?" Kit asks, wondering if the buffalo hunt is simply a carnival act for the Czar's son.

"No," Sheridan replies. "Government orders. All across the West, we've been told to kill as many buffalo as possible. Used this technique in the Shenandoah Valley, it worked like a charm."

Kit hasn't heard this before and is taken aback. Apparently, he isn't the only one with an Indian problem.

"Later today, if there are any left, we'll fire cannons into the herd," Sheridan says to no one in particular.

Cannons? As surprised as Kit had been to hear the buffalo would be killed collectively, today, he considers the end result. This could be the beginning of the end to his problems.

"The Indians must settle down, become civilized," Sheridan continues. "The best way for us to do that is to shoot buffalo. When they are scarce, the red men will be dependent upon us."

Or dead.

Kit spies Alexis. He pushes through the crowd to where the Czar's son is already shooting into the herd. The young man takes a quick glance sideways. Realizing Kit is standing next to him now, he makes eye contact and stops shooting. Alexis has changed clothing for the kill. He's dressed in silks that flow gently. His outfit stands in contradiction to the tight lines of military jackets all around him. It appears the young visitor isn't very good either with horses *or* a gun.

Kit notices a nearby female cow, her calf standing just off to the side of her. Alexis raises his gun, attempting to aim for the nearby animal, then pulls the trigger too soon. The cow falls to the ground, writhing in pain after being shot in the midsection. The teen boy quickly switches guns and discharges another round without the slightest attention, shooting off the ear of the calf. Then he moves on to the next target. Kit finds himself wondering if the boy is just another hard-hearted nobleman allowing the wild and majestic animals he shoots for pleasure to suffer then die a terrible death. The cow and her calf haven't died but lie nearby, grunting through their suffering. Looking around, Kit finds animals in similar predicaments all over the field: ears missing…a nose blown off the face of another….Although Kit wants the Indians gone just as much as the next person, he is disgusted by the lack of empathy on display. *This has got to stop,* he thinks. *Now.*

"Lovely to see you out here, Agent Carson. Let's begin my lesson."

Alexis is apparently unaware of—or uncaring toward—the animals suffering from his wounding.

Kit says nothing. First, he's got to kill the wounded animals properly. He aims his own gun and pulls the trigger, killing the animals in agony nearby. The thrill of killing Avipani isn't comparable to this; it's a letdown really. Once he realized what he needed to do, Kit had hoped the feeling of exuberance he had experienced while taking the Indian's life might be re-created here. Sadly, the only thing he feels is repulsion. Kit makes his living trapping and killing animals, but he does so with respect to the life he's taking. Chaska and Kaib taught him that. But he's also an Indian agent in charge of moving the Indians out of American territory. If the buffalo represents an Indian killed, Kit is happy to oblige.

Alexis has stopped shooting. He watches Kit. Standing by his side, Kit sees the boy is about his height. *Time for that lesson.* "Aim for the shoulder," Kit says, keeping his focus forward.

Thankfully, the boy is a quick learner. The two spend the better part of the afternoon shooting side by side in relative silence. Herds of buffalo mosey toward Kit and Alexis, completely unsuspecting, sadly oblivious to what awaits them. Probably fifty dead animals lie below them when a handsome yet stern-looking man with a heavy mustache introduces himself as Captain Thornburg. Kit's heard about him—he might very well be the person who's killed the most

Indians of anyone. And apparently, he's more than willing to talk about it.

"Nice work, gentlemen," Thornburg says. "Although I haven't killed many buffalo, I've killed more Indians than the entirety of this gathering," he asserts, confirming Kit's suspicion. "In fact, I keep newspaper clippings of my accomplishments just to remind myself of the task at hand. Some nights, just before I lay my head down to sleep, I look through it, proud of the way I conduct myself." He pauses a moment. Probably expects to be hit with an overflow of compliments.

"Kill them all!" he yells, breaking the silence.

Kit ignores the egotistic jerk. Alexis follows his new friend's lead. When Thornburg doesn't manage to elicit a reaction from the prince, he thankfully walks away to bother another group of men with his self-aggrandizement.

By late afternoon, lumps of brown fur lie dead all about the high brown grasses: winter white mixed with crimson pools of congealed blood.

Chapter 15

Plans to Denver
(Spring, 1868)

Merikac women walk along the streets of Denver in bonnets that surround their heads and then are secured at their necks with colorful ribbons. Their dresses flow to the ground and pick up mud along the way. Men in dark hats and long, black boots trudge by, as do handymen in filthy, baggy clothes, dirty from their toils.

No trees stand along the muddy track. No vegetation of any kind. Buildings seem to have grown into their spots lining the roadway. Most have whitewashed outer walls and red rooftops. As we ride our horses through the town, Ahwatt directs us toward a building of bricks the color of fallen oak leaves, just off the road, where the treaty will be signed. I've waited so long for this day I can't believe it's finally here.

To be honest, I shouldn't be going to the treaty signing. Women aren't supposed to travel with the men like this, but they all agreed I needed to come. I've been pushing for the treaty all along; if anything happens to the tribe, it should happen to me first. Then they will know the whole thing is wrong and prepare for a war that will most likely kill everyone....I felt like a prisoner, riding with them for three days from our camp, the tiny spark of hope I'd been carrying inside growing all the time. The weather was warm and the skies sunny. I tried to capture the blue sky in my heart as hope. Early March in the mountains can still be a ferocious beast, sending blowing snow, high winds and frigid temperatures our way.

Not while we traveled to Denver though.

I was confronted with the landmarks of my life as we made our way north—the camp where we endured winter's harshness lies just to the east of where we ride now. I remembered the awful winds howling through the trees...the spot where I first found Kit...where I thought this would all be okay.

It was probably the last time I would ever see that camp.

Over to the west the bones of the earth stood up straight, reaching for the sky…That was where we made our winter camp amongst the tall, red rocks. Oh, how I'll miss those red rocks! My brother and the other warriors hunted buffalo along that trail for so many years. Although I'd never been a part of the hunt, I'd known that was a place that had much to offer us.

As much as I hated the thought, the good of the tribe took precedence over my family. I still couldn't say whether I was right, but it made sense to me: to live with the merikac, not to kill them. We had always found ways to live with all that had been handed to us, and this shouldn't have been any different. I was more nervous than ever that my actions might cause me to watch another of my children suffer or die. My only hope was that if any of us had to suffer, *I* would become the one who grew sick and died. And I think Ahwatt realized the guilt he had lived with after doing nothing to save our parents. I only hoped he had finally realized he must live with the consequences of his actions. And that those actions made the tribe less safe rather than more secure. I was proud of him: He had travelled to Denver many times already to confer with Hunt, although when he went, he never brought any of the other men with him. Perhaps he was finally using the time to grow into his position as our leader. That seemed to be the case. In any case, one night after Ahwatt returned from Denver, Kaib snuggled up next to me. "The treaty is done," he told me simply. "No Americans will be allowed on our land."

"No intrusions?" I asked, incredulous at my brother's newly found negotiating skills.

"None at all," Kaib confirmed. "And we will still be allowed to hunt and fish, live just as we used to on our land." Then he did something I'd seen Ahwatt do throughout his life—he swiped at his mouth.

Curious, I asked, "We still move with the seasons, right?"

"Yes," my husband replied. But he again brushed his hand against his lips.

***

I say very little as we ride through town, preferring to keep to myself. Ahwatt has been designated our leader by the merikac, so of course he's headed north. Riding with us are leaders of the other seven bands of Ute that make up our tribe—Tabeguache, Mouache, Caputa, Weenuchiu, Yamparika, Grand River and Uintah. They have come to Denver to hear and sign the treaty too. Anxieties swirl in my mind, not allowing me to think clearly about the future. I'm to walk into the room where the signing is to take place, stand with the men and keep the peace simply by my presence. "If there's a woman in the room, there's less likely to be a fight," Ahwatt claims.

"Thank you, Ahwatt," I tell him as I dismount Nublada. "I know this will be difficult, but it's best."

I tie Nublada to the post in front of the building, but Ahwatt ignores me. My horse warily eyes passing wagons that come close to where she stands. "It will be all right," I tell her, patting nervously at her neck, wondering if what I've said is true. She and I lock eyes, and I wish for a moment I could race her out of town and forget all of this is happening. Let her take me to the open country or into a forest of trees where nothing matters….

To calm my fears Nublada draws her muzzle up to my face, rubbing the soft bristles of her chin along my cheek. I'm struggling to find a tiny bit of hope that will somehow reassure me the treaty is the answer to all our problems.

Kit rides up. He removes his hat then signs hello. He's the cheeriest I think I've ever seen him.

"I think you'll be pleased as punch with your new land," he says, dismounting Taos. "You'll have half the Colorado Territory!"

I know Kit means well but leaving our home will be difficult. I've come to realize he doesn't understand this. Probably because he doesn't seem to have any ties to his own home. He's a drifter, just like us, making his way wherever possible. Too bad he doesn't see it that way.

***

The doorway to the building is level with the dirt roadway. Ahwatt pushes at the entrance to our fate, quickly opening the heavy wooden door, as if he could change our future with his strength alone. Dressed in leather breeches and an elk skin tunic, Ahwatt couldn't be mistaken for any of the other men who are already in the room when we arrive. After a life spent in the elements, he looks tough, hard-edged and resilient: a Native American. Today, his long black hair is in braids, flowing past his shoulders.

I push in, as do the others. The closed-in room holds stifling hot air even though the air outdoors is cold. The thick air hits me like a wall. The room's low ceiling makes the chamber feel even more oppressive. With the thick-paned windows closed tight, the stale air hangs in the room. It hits me like a wall.

All around me stand men in black overcoats and knee-length cotton breeches the color of the gold prairie grasses. Their thick wool stockings and cotton, button-down shirts can't fend off the repressive heat. Many take only a brief sideways glance at us then turn away without a greeting. Kit makes his way to visit with them, and an odd-looking man presses his hand into Kit's. Never smiling, the man begins talking while still shaking Kit's hand. His long face and big nose draw quite close to Kit's face. He wears a bow tied at his neck and a thick wool suit that looks brutally hot in this room. I watch as Kit reaches out with his other hand to grab hold of the man's shoulder, pushing him away. The man had been practically shaking Kit up and down.

Some other mountain men are here too. They wear buffalo hide pants and antelope skin shirts. Their shabby raccoon pelt hats are stuffed atop unkempt hair. Although a few of them often trade with us, as does Kit, it's too late for any of them to encourage the Americans to allow us to stay on the land. And we won't trade anymore once we move. The Americans have seen to that. I can only hope our new land offers decent hunting and fishing, although the merikac emphasize that we are to become farmers. But I continue to wonder: Why do we need to grow plants when we are already surrounded by them?

Nathan Taylor, Commissioner of Indian Affairs, is here too, wearing a necktie and a dark jacket over a white cotton shirt. Sweat shines on his face: The outfit he is wearing is perfect for the cold winter weather outside, but uncomfortably hot in the crowded room. He is part of the group said to have been created to build better communications with us, but he seems to want to kill us more than he wants to move us. Perhaps I'll learn his thinking firsthand: Soon enough, Kit brings Taylor and Governor Hunt over to us. He tries to show the two men sign language, gesturing for them to follow. They simply stand there, staring at the trapper, unsure whether it's a trick. Finally, Hunt looks toward our group.

"Thank you for coming," he says. "I hope you understand our position. If we don't move you to a safer location, your culture and land will be trampled." He speaks kindly, although I don't feel his sentiment is honest. He moves to the middle of the room and begins to read the treaty....

"Commencing at that point on the southern boundary line of the Territory of Colorado where the meridian of longitude 107 degrees west from Greenwich crosses the same, running then north…"

I lose track of what the governor is saying. I don't understand anything coming out of his mouth.

"…thence east with said southern boundary line to the place of beginning shall be set apart for the absolute and undisturbed use and occupation of the Indians." Hunt speaks these words only after an endless time of reading.

"Several other small points before signing," he continues. "I know you can't read the document nor can your interpreter, so let me tell you the other portions agreed to by Ahwatt…."

Will he make me proud? I wonder. *What has he done?*

"First, no more wandering over hill and dale trying to find food under every rock and crevice. All the meat, fish and bread will be provided for you. You won't need to hunt or fish anymore. All your needs will be provided for you."

I look to my brother, but he won't meet my eyes. He simply wipes his mouth calmly with the back of his hand. *No,* I think. *This can't be happening.* No wonder he wouldn't allow any of the other men to come to the negotiations....I wanted us to be safe, yes, but to continue our ways—the ways our ancestors found to be helpful, successful, sustainable. That's always been my goal. That's always been what I want. Not...*this*! But before I can say anything, Hunt continues, laying down the final blow.

"You will receive clothing and blankets. Any roads, or railroads, America builds will have full right of way through the reservation...."

I'm desperate to figure out why Ahwatt has agreed to this. I should have known he couldn't be trusted with our safety. Kaib, as confused as me, says, "But you just said we would have full access to the land without any intrusions?"

The energy in our group grows frenzied. How can Hunt tell us we have the land to ourselves, to be ourselves—and yet this? When we move as one toward the governor,

Hunt looks to Kit for help, but the man either isn't paying attention or doesn't want to get involved. Instead, he's already making his way to the table where the Po-kent, the papers, lie on the safer side of Hunt. Though at first the table appeared to be situated in the middle of the room, in reality it sits farther from us, as if separating the two sides of the chamber: the merikac side, and our side. Kit is ready to sign our lives away….He's supposed to be our interpreter. Our agent. On *our* side. Yet he doesn't even seem to notice our anger. Either he knew all along the terms of the treaty, or he doesn't care one way or the other. Did he realize the Pån-å-kår-ro could run right through our land? Did he realize the Po, the roads, would be traveled by merikac?

When Hunt sees Kit reaching for the pen, he moves toward the desk. The other merikac line up behind Kit and Hunt. Why is Kit so willing to sign away our land? I must remember to send up a prayer for the man. I barely recognize the sweet-natured boy he once was.

Hunt waves his hand at us, saying, "This is what's best for you. Trust us." Then he quickly grabs the pen from Kit and unceremoniously signs away our rights. Even Ahwatt is stepping forward to sign, but the leader of the Yamparika band, who is dressed in full ceremonial regalia, pulls my brother back. None would speak against Ahwatt in public unless the matter was one of the utmost importance. He stands as tall as possible to whisper into Ahwatt's ear: "I was against signing their treaty before we arrived and still think it is a bad idea!" We've all huddled around them. Most are able to hear the chief's sentiment and nod their agreement. Ahwatt calmly shakes his head at us. Then comes his telltale sign of lying. "I agreed to these terms prior to the meeting," Ahwatt says, swiping at his mouth, refusing to make eye contact with any of us. The others don't realize what is happening, but I do. "They will kill all of us if we don't move now. No more fighting," he says to our group, focusing his eyes above all our heads toward a closed window. "We will find a way to continue our culture," he adds, rubbing his face.

Aha! He knew about this all along. He's been lying to us!

We're beyond distressed by the changes to the treaty. I had truly believed Ahwatt would be courageous and speak in our favor. Once again, the merikac have promised one thing but then approved another. And my own brother is complicit. Father would be furious.

Each merikac man signs the paper in their turn, then each quickly turns and leaves the room. Nathan Taylor seems to sneer at us before he signs. He also retreats so fast, none of us has the chance to ask him why he's done this to us. None of the men, including Taylor, feels the need to come to us to apologize for signing away land our ancestors lived on for millennia. Kit and Taylor stand by the paper as each of our men take their turn to sign. One after the other unconfidently handing the pen to the next, each making a cross-mark on the page where Taylor points.

Once we're outside again, I can't hold my anger any longer. It's wrong of me to disrespect my brother like this, but all is lost anyway. "Ahwatt!" I yell. "You knew, didn't you? You knew they had demanded to use our land as they see fit and you did nothing!"

At first, the men around us are surprised by my outburst. They stare at me, but they don't make any moves to silence me. Ahwatt stands looking from one to the other of us, his hand completely covering his mouth. "I didn't want to tell any of you. No one would have signed. They've threatened our entire family. If we don't sign," he says again, "they will kill us. They've promised me our camp will be gone before the Falling Leaf Moon," he finally tells us.

This fall. They would have come to our camp and killed us. I'm realizing—as are the men surrounding me—that Ahwatt couldn't win. No matter how many times he explained to the Americans that we were here first, they simply wouldn't listen. Their sense of entitlement to our land is overwhelming.

The weight of the moment causes me to feel dizzy. It's as though I've been blown over by an unseen wind: I can feel myself falling toward the ground, crumpling under the burden of our situation. I feel the future of every one of us has just changed.

***

My mind is a cloud of sorrow as we make our way back home. My stomach feels as if I've swallowed a rock that won't ever be digested. It was as if I had watched a loved one draw their last breath, sucking the air with the last bit of energy their body could muster to move lungs that would never fill again.

The same prairie that we had passed on our way east—the prairie that earlier shimmered golden—is bleak, empty of color. I don't recognize even one landmark that would usually make me happy—a meadow where we once raced ponies, the mountains far off to the west—as we ride southward. Once proud men ride horses while staring out at nothing, slumped with indignity.

As if hearing my thoughts, Ahwatt says, "At the end of the season, we will pack, as always, and not look back." He sounds so matter of fact, so confident. All I can do is stare at my brother, our leader. "We will follow the paths our ancestors forged long ago until they stop. Then, we will create new paths for the future."

The skills we've mastered to navigate the wide-open prairie and up and over the mountains will lead us to our new home. We'll use those skills to hunt and fish, to gather berries, to snare small animals. And figure out what to do with one cow and five sheep. Whatever those are.

Book 3

Chapter 16

Kit's Dilemma, No. 1
(1878)

"Plant the seeds you were given!" Kit says defiantly.

He's sick and tired of Chaska's tribe asking requests of him. Over the last ten years, their complaining has only increased. Eight or so Indian agents have come and gone. Kit himself assigned each of them to the Ute territory. He's all but lost count of how many were too exhausted with constant demands from the Ute to continue. In winter, the Ute expect food and blankets, which makes Kit wonder how Chaska's people took care of themselves before they signed the treaty and moved to the reservation. Ahwatt informs him weekly that if he were simply allowed to move his tribe, they would be all right.

"We were told a farmer would teach us how to work the land," he whines.

Kit glares at him. *How hard can it be? You dig a hole, put in a few seeds, add water – and there you are.*

It has made Kit angry to watch his agents become dejected by the Utes' constant nagging and whining. Most of his men refused to live in the tiny wooden house built specifically for them in the Natives' camp. Instead, they live as far away as possible from the turmoil.

"Just be more…*American*!" Kit tells Ahwatt whenever the Utes complain. *If you can't, you die.*

Kit remembers when he first spoke those words to Ahwatt. Chaska had been standing a few steps off to one side. She and Ahwatt had stared blankly at Kit. "Be more American?" Chaska asked.

"Look," he told them, "your ways and ours don't match. You will either be made more American, or you will die. Period."

Far back, when the treaty was signed, neither Kit nor any member of the Ute tribe could read English. For all Kit knew, the treaty might not have even included winter allotments. Or a farmer, for that matter. But part of being an agent was ensuring the Ute stayed on the reservation so the

Americans who wanted to move west might be able to do so in peace. The reservation itself is a big parcel of land—half of Colorado—and Kit is just one man. During the last ten years, while he was still working with Fremont, he was able to traverse the reservation—albeit illegally—to keep tabs on the Ute. Now, in order to understand what is happening with the Utes on the reservation, Kit needs a legitimate excuse to travel back and forth through the land given to them.

Kit is equally tired of dealing with homesteaders. They make demands of him that he just can't deliver. "I's told if I build a house here, I own the land. If that ain't so, it's on you." Kit has been told the same thing by many a disgruntled homesteading family man. Most of the time, he can solve mishaps by investigating complaints—a horse stolen here, a field set on fire there. Typically, the culprits are long gone before Kit arrives.

"You're the agent in this here parts," homesteaders tell him. "Kill 'em if you has to. If you don't, I will."

Kit wants to tell the homesteaders to go ahead, kill the Natives…but that goes against his job description. He knows the homesteaders have every right to complain. The Indians have been in this part of the country for years, yet they don't have the culture of Americans. *It's a shame,* Kit frets. *Wasting all that time wandering these parts and winding up with nothing to show for it.*

This is our land, Kit believes. Are the Indians considered trespassers? *Yup.* To keep his sanity, he needs to get rid of one side—the Indians or the Americans. He certainly can't begin to kill Americans. And the move to kill Indians has already started. He can hitch his ride on that train.

***

Kit has known trapper Ewing Young for years. The man had wanted to be a cabinet maker but ended up working in the West running sheep between California and Santa Fe and trespassing through Indian country. He buys six thousand head for sixty dollars in Taos, then he and a team herd the sheep up through Colorado Territory and into Utah, where they sell them in California at five dollars apiece.

Kit joins up with the caravan as often as possible. *Ain't no laws against me runnin' sheep and keeping track 'a them Indians at the same time.*

"Havin' you around is like our own private lawman," Young says of Kit's ability to walk through reservations legally. It's a constant battle between the Indians and the Americans—Young just wants to make a profit; the Indians want the Americans off their land. Yes, the treaty stipulates no Americans can be on a reservation, but who's to know? The Utes are supposed to stay in camp; they just got the worst of the land to appease them—nothing's down south of the White River agency except rocks and cactus. "We been attacked so many times, I can't count 'em anymore," Young says of his trips through Indian country. Kit has traded his dealings with homesteaders for dealings with disgruntled sheepherders. Each night, the group sets up camp; then most of the fifteen men head out to hunt for dinner. One or two stay behind to watch over the sheep and the camp. Just the other day, Kit had been left at camp when twenty Indian men rode up.

"Who are you and why are you here?" asked one of the Ute men dressed in buckskin pants. "I am the man who will kill you if you don't leave here by morning," he also told Kit.

"The men from camp will be back soon," Kit replied. He pointed in the direction where the others had gone to hunt.

Kit ignored the Ute when he asked how many men were out hunting. No sense telling the man that Kit was outnumbered by his tribesmen. He should probably have asked the group why they weren't in their camp to the north, but he didn't want to start more trouble.

The Utes left peacefully after their brief talk, but Kit had the feeling it wouldn't be the last time he saw them.

***

The morning after Young praised Kit's ability to walk around the reservation legally, sixty sheep of the herd have been stolen. Kit rides out looking for the animals but doesn't have to go far, finding them happily grazing in a meadow, under the watchful eyes of three Ute men on horseback. Just down from the meadow, a creek runs slow and quiet. There, amongst the cottonwoods, are a whole slew of Ute—children, wives. A few elders too.

He rides back to where the caravan is camping, just a stone's throw from the Indian camp and tells the others. Tents have been pitched atop browning grasses that crackle when moved. "Let's have a parley with the three Ute guards to start," Kit suggests. "We'll be on their land for a long portion of the trek. If we head off the Ute now, we'll have fewer worries later."

"Sure, we can have a parley," Young says with a gleam in his eyes. "We invite 'em over then shoot 'em up when they arrive!"

Cheers rise up from the other men, but Kit can only frown and look away.

"Look, Kit," Young continues, "I know you aren't for killing, but this is business. A few sheep stolen wouldn't be too much of a nuisance. Sixty is another story."

Young looks his friend in the eyes. Kit isn't *not* for killing. The last time was a rush. He just doesn't want to lose his status as an agent if anyone finds out.

"Let's teach 'em a lesson," Young suggests. "How about this, we kill most of 'em now, but let one or two survive. As they run back to tell the others, we just set our guns on 'em. Kill the whole camp."

Kit isn't sure how he feels about Young's plan. There are women there. Children too. At the thought of the chance to kill, his heart starts racing. Perhaps he'd be all right with killing just men?

Young must see Kit's reluctance because he puts it another way. "This is our way of life. If my men don't get paid, they have nothing to bring home to their families." He looks to the men in the caravan—all equally scraggly haired and long bearded…all just trying to make a living. Whereas Kit is an Indian Agent; he doesn't have to run sheep to keep his family fed. *Maybe I can lead them to the camp, but not do the killin',* he thinks. As if reading his mind, Young offers: "You lead us to the sheep and then to the camp, Kit. I'll bring my men to the camp for the kill." Kit must have had a strange look on his face because just then Young claps Kit on the shoulder. "You gots a problem killing all them Indians, Kit?" he asks.

"Nah," is all Kit can say, giddy at the suggestion. *Heck, they deserve to be killed, camping off the reservation.* He can't tell Young that though.

***

Just as the sun is setting, a few men begin to make themselves comfortable in camp; the others, led by Kit, head out on foot to retrieve their stolen animals and set the camp ablaze. Two men go to either side of the meadow, a wide swath of grass surrounded by pine trees. Kit directs all the others to crawl hand over fist to the edge of the meadow then lie in wait on the ground until dark. By that time, the Ute men guarding the sheep have slipped off their ponies and tied them to a nearby branch. They're now lying in the cool pine needles under a tall tree. Kit knows this is the time for him to remain motionless, but the excitement at the prospect of killing another Indian is making his body physically shake with delight. And he won't get caught. When the evening finally sets, he and his party easily sneak up behind the sleeping Utes, slitting their throats. In Kit's case, once the knife plunges into his victim's neck, he takes his time dragging the blade through the skin so he can see the man's eyes—first surprise, then fear, then nothing. His eyes go blank. Kit thought the Utes would likely hear him approaching as their ponies were signaling danger, giving guttural whinnies. But as he looks around now, he realizes he was wrong. *Ain't no survivors here to escape.* Kit and his two men corral the sheep between them; then they use the Ute ponies to herd the animals safely back to their own camp.

When all Young's men have gotten back to camp safely, they sit around boasting. A heavy-set man with a long red beard says, "We'd been right under their noses all afternoon and nary a one caught on," Young crows. "We charged that camp. Sent a load a' bullets straight for anyone who might be outside." A tall, lanky guy who looks to be about eighteen had been in the party too. He explains how he charged the teepees, entering and killing on sight with his hunting knife. "That was right satisfying," says an older man who seems to have only one tooth; then he brags lustily about leaving "a heap a' bloody bodies" behind.

One of the Ute children has been taken prisoner; she cowers in the trees as the men enjoy their success. "Make a fine bride one day," the man who claims her says. She's a bit younger than Kit's daughter now. He thinks about all that happened today, not sure how he feels. No young girl should be taken as a bride, or kidnapped at all, leaving her mama like that. *Bad enough the adults act like children.* He thinks of how Ahwatt and his tribe behave. They don't listen to him. "Don't drink the water." What did they do? They drank the water, and many of them are still sick and dying. "Come for a council to talk about peace." Rode two hundred miles out of his way just to bring them in for a talk. Then they have the nerve to say he poisoned their tribes' men? Unbelievable. To hell with them. *It's time to be on the right side.* The American side, he means. No more investigating crimes against homesteaders. Next time, they'll be dead if he finds them. If it happens that women and children are killed in the process, so be it. After killing Avipani, Kit recalls, he felt good. It was an honest kill, he thinks. And there are about to be a lot more of those.

***

Ten days into the trek, the caravan is squarely in Ute territory. They walk along the Uncompahgre, the river running clear with plumes of reddish water here and there, where the river picks up the red dust of the rocks. The valley floor lies hundreds of feet below banded rocks, red then white, layer upon layer. Kit watches as small boulders skitter downward then smash to bits as they hit the valley floor. As the dust settles, he ponders his newfound interest in killing Indians. It is puzzling. Will his thirst for vengeance one day include those in Chaska's tribe? He's not sure yet.

Kit has ridden far enough ahead of the caravan that he can't see the dust the sheep kick up. Just a few hundred feet from him, just as the valley turns a bend, are two or three Utes on horseback, herding about two hundred ponies. Indian ponies, low to the ground, with short stubby legs. Ornery little critters. Kit chuckles to himself then pats Taos on the neck.

"I wouldn't have any other animal as my partner out here in these parts," he says.

Taos ignores the compliment.

Turning, Kit sees Young bounding along ahead of the caravan. He's seen the Utes—and their ponies too. When he reaches Kit, he stops fast, then smirks slyly. "We could make us fine money with them animals," he says. Tilting his head toward the herd, he just grins.

Pinching the bridge of his nose, Kits says, "I'm so dang frustrated..." What are the Utes doing here? And where'd they get so many animals this far from camp? Although the Indians are on the reservation, they are supposed to be up north along the White River, about a hundred and fifty miles north and east.

"Let's charge 'em," Kit says uncharacteristically.

"Yeh?" Young asks, smiling.

"Yep."

Young grins again then heads back toward the caravan to collect his men. So far, the Utes haven't seen Kit or Young's men, which is surprising. They must assume no one is on their land, as the treaty stipulates.

When the men charge, they charge hard and fast, Kit and Young leading, plowing through the herd of horses, scattering them all along the canyon floor. Though the Indians appear surprised at first, they quickly get up to speed, riding their ponies in hot pursuit. Kit's having a ball, although a little voice in his head asks him what happens if he gets caught: *Indian agent attacks those he serves to protect*. He can already see the headlines. Right now, Young rides up next to Kit, galloping and whooping "Yeeha!" — luring the Indians from the herd while a few of his men tend to the herd, bringing it back as a group, leading them away from the Utes.

In the end, Young's men have captured twenty-five horses. "We can't keep 'em all," he declares. "It'd be too much to herd sheep *and* horses along the trail."

The next part of the trail is usually not as fertile as the canyon. It consists of mostly thick slabs of red rocks that have cleaved from one another. The rocks get so hot in the desert sun the men will need to be careful of burning through worn boots. And they'll need to look for rattlesnakes. Also, though some grass will root in the cracks, there won't be enough for all the ponies to eat. So, the group decides to kill ten: They'll eat off a few now and dry the meat of the others. The rest of the herd is going to California to be sold.

While the horses are led off to be shot, men take turns walking a few at a time to the edge of the river, where they can eat their fill of waterlogged grasses. The amount of money they will eventually take home to their families has suddenly risen significantly. "We can pass time freely without nary a worry about food," one man says, grateful for Kit's help in securing the horses. Kit, however, is concerned about the young girl who was stolen from camp. Knowing the Utes, they'll come and get her at some point. She has already been used for any needs of the men—the cook makes her dish out supper each evening, and she's constantly fetching water for the men. Young takes the girl to bed every night too: Kit has to walk out of camp to keep from hearing the screams. The girl must be just a teenager. Kit is honestly distraught…the thought of the girl and her life over the last few days! He could kill, but he won't go so far as to lie with a child.

***

Upon scouting another Ute camp, Kit relays the information he's learned to Young: The camp is no different than the one before. But it's full of families—Kit saw at least three women tending to nine or ten children.

Hearing Kit's information, Young has a new suggestion. "Our only recourse is to set fire to the camp."

Kit considers. Then he does something he hasn't in a long time. He tugs on his ear. Now he's killing entire families—and he's not sure he's all right with it.

That night, under a sky with no moon, Kit sneaks up to the Ute camp, as Kaib had taught him all those years ago. The men have wrapped old cloths around sticks to set aflame and use as torches. Young's men are getting good at surrounding the Indians without being heard. Kit nods silently to himself. *Thank you, Chaska!*

By the time the Utes realize what is happening, their camp is surrounded by fire. Standing back from the heat, Kit watches, thinking the fire is beautiful—and effective. He can make out women and children running just on the other side of the flames. The tiny pain he feels in his stomach, wrenching it into distress, is easily ignored.

***

Kit can tell the caravan is approaching California coastline by the change in scenery. He sees fewer and fewer yucca and agave plants exchanged for blue beardtongue, snaking chola, and thick hairy milkweeds. High in the mountains, there is still snow aplenty, but not enough to stop the wagon train entirely. By the time the caravan reaches

California territory, the horses and sheep have been run hard over cold, dry, desert country.

After some consultation with one another, Kit and Young decide the caravan will halt to turn out the animals to graze. The group has only a few more days of travel before off-loading the sheep and horses.

That night, Indians sneak into camp and steal most of the horses—both those meant for sale and those ridden by the men. Apologizing profusely, the guard on duty tells Kit, “I'm dreadful sorry. I turned around for a minute to take a leak. Them sons a bitches must'a snuck in and took 'em!”

The rest of the camp had been sleeping, depending on the guard to watch over the herd.

“Well, I'm done!” says Samuel, an overly hungry man who looks like he could miss a few meals. The Indians taking the caravan's stock is the last straw. Most of the men have been dreaming of how they would spend their money after selling the animals.

So, when Kit heads back from California and has the chance to pass through Bayou Salade, Chaska's family's former summer camp, he knows he has to tread lightly. Chaska's family is long gone by now, to the Ute camp in the western territory—the part of the reservation the Indians are supposed to confine themselves to. But Kit knows the Ute camp used to be high above the American towns the men had hunted all through the area.

"Indians ahead," says the lead man in the caravan.

"No, they ain't," Kit says, perplexed. None of them should be here. And if they are here, whoever they are, Kit's had enough.

A hawk circles above the caravan as the men stop along a length of dry creek bed. The bird lets out a prolonged, high shriek then disappears above a butte that juts out to Kit's right. Three Indians gallop ponies along the creek bed, heading toward the caravan. Kit, Young and the other trappers sit atop their horses, waiting for the newcomers to ride up. Out of the corner of his eye, Kit sees movement. At first, he just imagines it to be the hawk circling back, but he quickly realizes it's a trap.

Indians on horseback flood down into the valley from the butte, charging toward the caravan. There are probably thirty to forty men shouting, raising guns high above their heads as their ponies fly straight toward Kit and Young.

The only thing to do is turn about-face and ride as fast as possible back down toward the little shanty-town of Alma. It hugs the river, spreading out along a meadow. Kit and Taos lead the charge down the mountain, a previously well-traveled but slim Ute trail. All Kit hears is the pounding of hooves against dirt and rocks, the occasional low-hanging pine bough blasting him in the gut or swiping at his face, nearly knocking his John B to the ground. Then he smells a campfire—dry wood and browning leaves—probably from the Indians.

Fortunately, it's obvious there isn't any intent to kill, just to scare the caravan from what looks to be an illegal camp. Once in the clear, Kit suggests the men stay the night outside

Alma then go back to continue their trapping. The Indians should have left by the time they get back up there. "If not," Kit says, "we'll arrest them." But, during the night, two of the four horses Kit and his caravan have ridden are stolen. The next day, Kit rides out alone in search of the Indians and the stolen animals. Instead of heading back up the mountain, he walks Taos out toward the Arkansas River. Funny how the river has been with him all these years…A constant reminder of where he came from—a naïve teenager headed west to make his fortune.

Kit steers Taos up a small incline for a good look around. The river has carved a valley surrounded by high mountains. Off in the distance, Kit guesses about ten miles from camp, he sees movement. Taos wades into the fast-moving water of the Arkansas. Kit leads him along a shallow sandbar. As the two climb up from the river's edge, Kit spots the stolen horses.

The land is flat as a pan. There's not likely to be an ambush.

Kit gallops his pony to the stolen horses. Two Indians lie in wait nearby, but Kit's ready. He shoots them dead before they realize he's got his rifle out.

It's two fewer Indians to move on later.

Chapter 17

Ten Years On
(Summer, 1878)

"What are you wearing?" I say to my husband as he pulls the elk tunic over his head. "You can't go outside in that!"

Every month, the Indian Agents leave clothes for us. Merikac clothes. Men are expected to wear a buttoned cotton shirt with full-length sleeves and wool pants. They are expected to wear a wool overcoat when travelling to meet the Indian Agents who care for us. We women wear cotton dresses that touch the ground. The dresses are long sleeved and high necked, even in summer. In winter, they give us wool blankets. If they show up at the White River Agency, that is.

"I don't care anymore, Chaska," my husband replies. He's taken off the merikac clothes and donned elk skin leggings. "Those clothes are uncomfortable and hot. I don't feel like myself in them."

None of us do.

Looking Kaib in the eyes I whisper: "I understand, but if Father Meeker finds you in those skins he'll punish you."

The other agents we've had in the past lived off the reservation and made surprise visits to our camp. They had no interest in getting to know us. Most of the previous agents simply left sacks of grain or whatever rations we were allowed along the trail. Few if any would come out to greet us, choosing to stay in the safety of their little wooden house in White River Agency. Even today, if we aren't wearing the assigned merikac clothing, the entire tribe loses its allotment for the week. This means no one eats. When Agent Meeker arrived, he told us to call him Father Meeker. He's the first agent to live on the reservation, in the wooden house right next to our camp. He watches us so closely it's put us all on edge.

My husband asks, "What's the difference? We can't hunt or fish. I stay in camp day in and day out with nothing to do. It's hopeless."

He's not wrong. At the treaty signing ten years ago, right before we moved here, we were surprised to learn there would be no more hunting. Now, the men who kept us safe and provided our food have no purpose. They won't meet anyone's eyes, too proud and embarrassed to be in camp all day long. I watch them slowly fall into a depression.

It's my fault. I had foolishly thought the merikac would allow us to live our lives, to practice our culture; but this has been a nightmare. In the night, I'm hounded by horrible dreams…in the daytime, I live them. We've changed and aren't the Ute people we had once been gone. The merikac have us between their world and ours.

Instead of hunting, we were told to farm; but we don't know how to work the land or plant the seeds we were provided. "Someone will come live among you," the Americans told us. No one came. The seeds still sit with the farming tools they gave us. Before Father Meeker, we would gather, hunt and fish without the Americans knowing.

We were told they would care for us; so, every week, we travel to the agency to pick up whatever food they've decided to drop off. In winter, there's often nothing, because the merikac don't want to make the trek from Denver—two hundred and twenty-five miles through the Rocky Mountains. Now, my hip bones stick out on either side of me, covered with tight skin. The other women's faces are tight too, cheek bones protruding on either side of their faces. The entire Ute nation is here, all three thousand of us. Instead of allowing each family unit to travel and live separately from the others, the merikac have forced us all to live on the reservation. We are tired, and hungry, and angry. It makes little difference to us who our agent is.

***

Meeker, his family and his staff arrived on a cold spring morning. I stood beside Ahwatt as he greeted them. "Agent Meeker…Welcome to your new home. We're here to introduce you to our council." Ahwatt had been selected by the merikac to represent us; even today he remains our leader, but there isn't anything he and the other men can do to change our situation.

That day, Ahwatt extended his hand to shake with Meeker, as the merikac do. But Meeker merely looked at my brother's outstretched hand then gazed into Ahwatt's eyes with disgust. Instead of engaging with us, he simply pushed aside, leading his family up a short hill to his home—the same wooden structure that all the other agents had left empty. Then he slammed the door behind him.

"They've left their belongings in the wagon," Chava said.

"Leave them," Ahwatt replied. "We won't carry their items; they can come for them when they're ready."

***

Later that day, once he and his family were settled, Meeker gathered the tribe together out in front of his wooden home. We stood in the grassy field while he stood on the stoop, his family and the workers who came along with him at his side. "We begin farming tomorrow," he said. "Line up for inspection at daybreak. Anyone not wearing the American clothing provided for you will lose their provisions for the week. After we farm, we will gather your animal-skin clothing and burn it."

Burn our clothing? I should have known then. Our skins aren't just coverups. We wear them to be nearer to the animals that gave of themselves so that we could eat, so that we could keep warm. The animals are a part of us. Father Meeker didn't understand that.

Father Meeker next told us we would become civilized only if he watches us day and night. "I'm here to change you," he said. But having a merikac, his workers and his family watching us all the time turns out to be unnerving. Most of Meeker's men—there are five of them—stand and stare at us when we walk by them. The man named Fred Shepard, however, seems to be less judgmental toward us. He will say hello and has learned a bit of our language—enough to say, "good day" and ask how we are doing. But he's the only one.

"You will be well cared for," Meeker promised that day. But that was a year ago now. And anyway, we had heard it all before from the previous seven agents who "cared" for us. With Meeker, however, our lives have gotten worse. I didn't think it possible.

***

Before Kaib can leave the teepee in his skins, I hear a woman yelling, "No! Leave me be!"

Chava.

Kaib and I rush out and find her cradling my granddaughter, Kam, in her arms. Meeker is there: He has a firm grip on Chava's right arm. Chava is holding some berries in her hand, and she's crying. That's the problem.

Chava's generation of women have lost many of the children they conceived: Their bodies can't feed and nourish a baby when they themselves are starving. We, the Ute people, our culture, our ways of living, will vanish from the face of the earth. If the merikac don't kill us outright, our culture will vanish simply because of malnutrition. After losing several children right after they were born, the granddaughter in Chava's arms has fought her way to six months of age. I call her *me pooch tivac*, my little pine nut. She's going to be a racer, just like Mapia, and just like her mom too. My other daughter isn't so lucky. Though both Chava and Chipara are married to highly respected men, Chipara constantly loses the babies she carries.

I should have grandchildren racing their ponies. I wish I could *give* them ponies….

Chava is still crying, and Meeker still has a firm grip on her arm. "I went out into the woods to gather berries for my daughter," Chava says. "She's starving…look at her!"

I'm surprised my granddaughter has made it this far. As thin as a corn husk doll, her head looks oversized compared to her little body. My own daughter is so frail and thin that Meeker easily wraps his fingers around her upper arm. Once a stunning nineteen-year-old, Chava's cheeks stick out. Her brown eyes have sunken into her head. Most of the elders have died or left so that those who are younger could have some small chance of living.

Meeker begins shaking Chava's skinny arm back and forth, then takes his other hand and swats at the berries she holds. Her whole body falls forward, but she keeps hold of my granddaughter Kam. Chava is so fragile. "No! Please, let me keep it!" she begs, tears flowing from her eyes, trying to pull her arm from Meeker's grasp. But the berries fall to the ground. Meeker pulls her toward him, raising her arm up as he does and spitting: "I saw you go into the woods and have waited here for your return… *YOU KNOW* you're *NOT ALLOWED* to *GO* into *THE WOODS,*" he says sing song, as if he's talking to a small child. He takes a breath but holds Chava tightly. "You, my dear, serve me absolutely no purpose. Do you understand?" he asks. He pulls her up almost to eye level with him. She nods yes, though I'm sure she doesn't understand.

Then Meeker releases Chava, and she stumbles backward. Kaib rushes to catch her and Kam. Meeker then kicks the small pile of berries Chava gathered, scattering them in the dirt. "For your own good!" Meeker says. "Once the farm starts producing like it should, you won't need to go into the woods to gather food anymore," he patronizes. Then, he turns on his heels and leaves us.

***

The morning after Meeker knocks the berries from Chava's hand, I find myself working alone in one of the fields. Though Meeker showed us how to plant seeds and till the land— just as he promised—none of the men has bothered to work. Just as I finish setting down a row of seeds, Mrs. Meeker comes by on her horse. She often takes her horse for rides through the woods, but today she walks him closer to where I work. Turning him expertly she comes right next to me. I stand and smile at her, sure she is going to make polite conversation. She stares down at me, then leans over conspiratorially "Savages, all of you!" she hisses. "I'd like to see you all wearing good, stout rope neckties!"

Just as quickly as she came up to me, she clucks and kicks her horse in the barrel. She leaves me shaking, my knees knocking together.

***

My encounter with Mrs. Meeker requires a few minutes of calmness before I can continue working. So, I hop onto Nublada, who stands not far from where I work. I steer her into the forest, where it's cool. We weave between pine trees, stopping when the trees get too thick to walk between. I hop down and sit, legs sprawled in front of me, my back against the thick trunk of a sturdy pine.

Sighing, I turn to scratch at the tree bark, then inhale the perfume it creates. Kit once told me the bark smells of vanilla, though I can't be sure. The thought of Kit has me thinking I can hear his deep, gravelly voice: "Don't tell them…" I hear.

Huh? That's when I realize—I'm not alone.

Still sitting on the forest floor, I slowly reach for Nublada's reins. She and I make eye contact, and I know she hears them too. Why is Kit here? And who is he talking to? They must be just on the other side of the clump of trees from where I am resting. The horses' telltale snorts make it seem as if they are very close. If Kit is riding Taos, I hope he won't nicker to Nublada.

"It's four million acres," Kit says. "You're just going to waltz in there and demand they give it to you?"

"They have plenty of land." It's a voice I can't place. A man's voice, for sure. The voice is nasally and high pitched.

"Obviously, you don't understand their culture. They are hunters. The Uncompahgre is a rich source of food for them. Without it, they might leave the reservation completely and start hunting in eastern Colorado again," Kit argues.

"That's preposterous. They are farmers now. At least that's what I've been told. Just let me do the talking."

"Fine—"

Just then Nublada paws at the ground, shuffling some pine needles. Not enough for most to hear, but enough for Kit.

The two are silent for a moment. I *know* Kit heard us.

"Let's go and get this over with," the other man says. "I'd like to be back to my wife before the week is out."

Kit doesn't answer. I'm sure he's looking this way even as the other man seems oblivious. Although I can't figure out exactly what these two men are up to, it seems important. I've got to get back to camp to warn Ahwatt. Still, I keep Nublada where she is longer than necessary, just waiting until I can't hear their horses' clip-clop any longer. Then, I hop onto Nublada and kick her flanks harder than necessary with the nerves I feel. I've got to find Ahwatt.

***

The man tips his hat to Ahwatt and a small group of our Ute men. I spot Kaib among them…but I'm too late. Kit and this other man have already found my brother at the far side of the reservation. Nublada and I get to the group just as the strange man is introducing himself.

"Dr. Felix Brunot, at your service...."

Brunot's long light-colored hair curls around his head. His dark eyebrows nearly encircle his eyes. Where they end, deep half-moons sit upside down under his brown eyes. Although most merikac of the day keep facial hair, this man has none. He has the look of a man on a mission, someone who usually gets what he asks for, no matter what.

Ahwatt doesn't bother to extend his hand this time.

Kit is here too, standing next to Brunot. But he doesn't say a word.

After telling us his people have found gold in the Uncompahgre, Brunot informs us we will have to return that land to the merikac. Four million acres due south. A high plateau overlooking meadows of green dotted with aspens. The dirty, red water of the Uncompahgre and the green grasses mean good hunting grounds.

"It's in your best interest. In return, we give you the sum of five hundred dollars American," he tells Ahwatt and the other men.

"You can't have that land," Ahwatt says. "I don't care how much gold you've found; the Uncompahgre is part of the land you gave us. *We* are keeping it."

The man stands only up to Ahwatt's chest; few can rival my brother's height. He uses it to his advantage whenever possible, but this man will not be swayed.

"What are you going to do, hunt there?" Brunot asks. He seems defiant, goading my brother into using hunting as a reason not to give up the land.

Of course, we hunt. Our men sneak off then bring the kill to a designated place, where the women butcher it and cook it. All out of sight of Father Meeker and any other agents who might be here. Otherwise, we will watch each other starve to death.

"You signed a treaty, that is *our* land," Ahwatt replies. "We haven't seen any of the merikac money you've promised in the past. Whether we hunt or not isn't important," Ahwatt says, hoping to end the conversation.

"The cows and sheep we give you every year should comprise an entire herd by now," Brunot continues. "Where are they? Shouldn't they be grazing with your ponies?"

Although we are weak, we still find comfort in racing our ponies. We've made a small racing area that is flat, where the ground is solid. In the evenings, we take turns racing one another while the Meeker family dines in their cabin up on the hill. Surprisingly, the ponies have fared far better than any of us. They continue to feed on the wild grasses that grow abundantly across the land. So much so, I've taken to using more and more quantities of grass for our everyday meals. Usually, it's the only thing to eat.

"Cows and sheep?" my brother asks. He shakes his hands angrily at Dr. Brunot. "We've only received *one* shipment of cows and sheep. That was almost ten years ago, when we first came here. All females," Ahwatt says. "How do you make a herd with only females?"

Brunot shakes his head. "No, that's not what happened," he says, waving away history as if he can change it with his words. Not bothering to ask further questions.

"As for the money," Ahwatt adds, "I'm sure we'll see just as much of it as we've seen for the past ten years." He is referring to money the government owes us.

"How much have you seen?" asks Kit. It's the first words he's spoken. I used to think he was checking on us to keep us safe because he cared. Now I think he's just been checking to see if we're alive. Probably, he's been hoping we're dead. Then he'll bring homesteaders onto the land so fast the merikac's heads will spin.

"None," says Ahwatt.

Kit smirks at the response. *Does he know?* I wonder.

"Well, I don't see a whole lot of farming going on," Dr. Brunot says. "I believe you were to farm in order to get your annuity. The government isn't in arrears as long as you wait to till the land."

Kit nods his agreement. Then Dr. Brunot spreads his arms wide. "This is good country," he says. "You should be able to grow anything you wish."

The soil here gets whipped up by strong winds, carrying it away. No rain falls here. Only huge amounts of snow in winter. The spring thaw rushes south quickly.

Half-turning to Kit and whispering under his breath, Dr. Brunot says, "The ungrateful trash should be wiped from the earth…."

The next moment, Dr. Brunot turns fully to Kit, this time asking him for all to hear why we are still living in teepees when wood is plentiful enough for us to build cabins.

Kit shakes his head in disgust. "I've told them year after year: A cabin makes a suitable dwelling. They refuse to listen." Then he makes eye contact with Ahwatt: "Do you remember when I told you the Ute would be killed if they didn't move here? The same is true with the Uncompahgre. Give it up or expect deaths. Loads of them," Kit threatens.

***

A different morning. Several weeks later. One of Meeker's workers, Fred Shepard, comes running toward me as I plant seeds — digging a little hole, dropping in a seed and then spreading fresh dirt overtop. The morning has been overcast, with dark clouds threatening from the west. I'm kneeling in the dirt, but when I see him out of the corner of my eye, I'm so startled I fall to the ground, spilling the seeds. I recall that he's been kind to us—but my only thought is to run. I pick myself up, hike up my elk skin skirt and try to escape.

He's too fast for me to outrun him. His hat has long since fallen off so that his thick white hair is waggling back and forth as he runs. But his long, thin legs keep charging toward me.

"Stop, please, stop!" he yells to me. "I need your help!"

I stop and wait for him to reach me. "I've tried talking with him, but he just won't listen..." the man tells me.

"Who? What are you talking about?"

"It's Meeker," Shepard says then stops short. Looking bashfully at the ground, he corrects himself. "Father Meeker, I mean. He's at the racing field. He's plowing it up," he tells me. "You've got to come quickly!"

I can't move. I simply look into his eyes for the longest time.

"Come!" he says, bringing me out of my fog.

As I start running alongside him, I see my daughter Chava ahead. She's just walking to the field to start her turn at planting. "Chava! Find Ahwatt! Tell him it's urgent! Tell him to come to the racing field and bring the other men!"

Before she can ask me why I'm off with the man Meeker's workers call Jack. My mind is racing…How can I possibly stop Meeker from plowing up the racing field?

When we get down the hill to the field, I see Meeker's horse hooked to the plow. Meeker is urging him on to till the land. The once tamped-down grasses and hard earth is being split in two by the plow's blade, revealing fresh, dark dirt. Meeker has finished plowing only a few rows, but it's enough that we won't be able to use the land anymore. The rest of the reservation is too hilly to accommodate a new field. *This* field is the one thing we had left.

Jack has stopped, probably fearful of going against his employer. So, I run ahead and set myself in front of the horse, reaching for its bridle. "Please, Father Meeker!" I yell. "Stop!"

Meeker is so surprised to see me that he indeed stops dead in his tracks. But he quickly revives himself and urges his horse onward. The blade of the plow moves forward even as I hold on to the horse and walk backward. "You don't understand what you're doing!"

Meeker ignores me. He continues moving forward. But then he looks up again in surprise: My brother is riding toward us. When he reaches the plow, he hops off the horse and grabs for the plow handle closest to him.

"Stop!" is all my brother says.

"Take your hands off me!" Meeker yells. "I'll report this assault to the army!" It's his usual ploy. When we do anything that upsets him, he sends off a telegram to the military. They are stationed hundreds of miles from here, but Meeker does it anyway.

The horse had stopped when Ahwatt arrived. I hold on to its bridle and unconsciously pet the end of his nose. *It's not your fault*, I think.

"Jack, Jack!" Meeker orders. "Come over here!"

Caught in the middle, Jack is slow to move.

"Keep plowing, Jack," Meeker says, "while I deal with my flock."

He steps from the plow so Jack can insert himself between the two handles. He and I make eye contact, but I don't immediately let go of the horse. It's awkward. I know he wants to help us, but he isn't in a position to be of much use.

"Ahwatt, you and your people need to plant those seeds!" Meeker is pleading with my brother as though talking to a naughty child. "I want to give you your money for a job well done, but so far there hasn't been any planting. Please, don't make me hold your food for another week."

"You can't keep taking from us," Ahwatt says, balling his fists. "You've gone too far."

Meeker moves closer. "Are you threatening me?" he says.

I think my brother must be in a state of shock. He's never been good at confrontation, choosing most often to walk away. I can tell this encounter has flustered him more than previous outbursts with Meeker. When the others find out we have lost our racing field, there will be a lot of anger.

Turning to look me in the eyes, Ahwatt shakes his head. "Chaska, we can't do this any longer. I hope you understand," he says.

Then, he walks away.

I look at Jack one more time. Then I release the horse so he can continue plowing.

Chapter 18

Kit's dilemma, No. 2
(Fall, 1878)

"There wasn't any other land you could have plowed besides that field?" Kit asks after arriving at Meeker's cabin.

Meeker eyes him suspiciously. "Don't tell me you're on their side," he says.

"No," Kit replies. "You're doing the best you can to civilize these folks. I understand that. But egging them on by plowing over that field might have gone too far. Out here on your own with them, I don't want to see you and your family in any danger."

Kit stares at Meeker.

When he arrived at the Ute reservation, Kit had headed straight to the agent's home. He hadn't had confidence in his newest agent from the first time they met. Still, Meeker was a hard-headed do-gooder. Unlike all of his previous agents, he was so convinced of his abilities he had decided to live among the Utes. *Probably get himself killed,* Kit had thought. Now he's convinced Meeker's action might cause war.

"I assure you I can keep my family safe," Meeker returns, obviously resenting Kit's suggestions. "But I have concluded that the only way to make these Indians obey me is to obliterate their ponies. Horse ownership doesn't bring anything of value to these people," he continues. "And, I'll have you know, I've been in constant correspondence with Captain Thornburg, who I thought would be ready to bring troops here immediately to quell the Utahs' fury.

"As for doing my best with these savages," Meeker now explains, "I *need* this to work." Kit stares at him, waiting to hear more. "It's my wife. She's —"

"Unhappy. Of course, she is. That doesn't mean you've got to appease her," Kit offers.

"No, there's more. I don't want to let her down again."

Kit isn't getting the feeling this isn't going to be good. He hasn't had the urge to tug at his ear for many years, but he reaches and tugs at his right ear to prepare himself for what he's about to hear.

"You see, I owe a bit of money."

"How much?"

"Oh, a good chunk of what you're paying me…several years ought to do it."

"God, man! What happened? You a gambler?"

"No! Nothing like that. I may have put the town of Greeley into a small conundrum with the bank. The people there…" Meeker takes a moment to shift his weight and look up to the sky. "Now don't get me wrong, those folks, they love me." Again, he shifts his weight and grabs for the bridge of his nose. "It's just, well…I can't go back there if I don't pay them back."

"I see," says Kit. He really doesn't understand how this is such a bad turn of events. The man made a mistake and is paying it back honestly. What's the problem?

"My wife's family lost a good bit of money, so it's them that I'm paying back. Once my debt is paid, she'll forgive me, and we can leave this God-forsaken place behind."

Kit sighs. He had purposely made a quiet entrance onto the reservation this morning, because whenever the Ute realize Kit is in the vicinity, they crowd him, hurling complaints louder than he's heard before. Today, to make matters worse, Ahwatt was nowhere to be found. *Which is odd,* Kit thinks. But in truth, a small part of him understands the Utes' getting upset: Their racing field had been plowed over. He recalled the times he'd seen the tribe racing ponies. Young and old, all of them riding fast, laughing, at each other's shortcomings—a boy falls off his pony, trying too hard to cross the finish line first, or when a man can't coerce his pony to the starting line. *These people revere their ponies,* he had thought at the time. On the other hand, and more importantly, they needed to change.

Kit reminds Meeker he had lived among the Ute early in his career. "Sir, after having spent the better part of my time in the West with the very people you describe to me, may I remind you that your job with the agency is to build good relationships with these Indians. Eventually, this may allow us to safely bring in settlers." He can't blame Meeker. These folks just don't want to change. And just like that his mind pivots. "They just ain't interested in making a culture for themselves. Rather lallygag in the woods," he asserts.

"My family deserves to be in a place where there is only goodness," Meeker says.

"You ain't found goodness here, my friend. These injuns, they hate us for taking care of them—ungrateful louts! I've tried for years to get them to be more like us. And what's the thanks I get? They accuse me of spreading disease and killing their men!"

"Why, pray tell, won't they entertain more gentlemanly pursuits such as farming?"

Before waiting for Kit to answer, Meeker leans in conspiratorially. "Tell me something, Kit. I've heard these Utahs have been starting fires. Big ones. All across Colorado, they've been setting fire to homesteaders' cabins. I heard a man lost his life. Lived up along the Platte there outside Fairplay. Truth?"

"Who knows," Kit tells him.

In all honesty, Kit doesn't believe the rumors. *No initiative,* he thinks. "I've heard stories myself but can't verify anything. Military tells me they've been trouble all up and down the Rocky Mountains. All I can tell you is that I'm done with trying to help them. Chaska took me in long ago, but now, all I feel for this tribe of hers is resentment."

At the mention of Chaska, Meeker asks, "The woman? She's been testing my patience ever since I got here."

Yep, Kit thinks. *That sounds about right.*

"Why must I deal with *her*?" Meeker says.

Kit knows the man has his hands full. But he also wonders whether Meeker is the man for the job. The Utes could give him a run for his money.

Meeker isn't willing to talk any more about the racing field. It seems he has his mind made up—the ponies must go. He changes the subject, seemingly to convince Kit of the work he's accomplished thus far. "We started their training by digging ditches. I've shown them time and again how to hook the horses to the plow. They just won't help. The Utah men say they aren't 'supposed' to be in camp. They tell me they are embarrassed for their wives to see them like this. 'Like what?' I ask them. 'Working?' Then, when I asked them to clear the field, they refused! So, I did it for them."

Kit knows the Ute men would very rarely remain in camp. Instead, they were out hunting, fishing, or keeping the camp secure, patrolling on horseback or on foot, for the Americans had asked them to do so. He realizes he had failed to recognize that their traditional roles would be upset once they were forced to stay in camp.

"When I explain their role is changing now, they shake their heads at me. I can't figure why," Meeker says.

Kit stays quiet.

Changing subjects again, Meeker says, "Speaking of their ponies. Let me tell you. I've had my hands full with them too. Stubborn things. And mean! I've been bitten pulling them into the plow *many* times. No horse from the east would bite someone like that; they're much more docile. *These* animals are wild, just like their owners.

"When I beat on the ponies for not working," Meeker continues, "the man named Kaib gets angry with me. 'That's not how we train our ponies,' he told me. 'Well, that's how they *will* be treated from here on in,' I told him."

Kit chuckles at Meeker's tirade. He also had to learn the hard way that the Ute ponies aren't like the horses back east. They're feisty and demand respect. Hell, his horse, Taos, kept him safe more times than he can count—but that animal also demanded regard in return.

Meeker continues talking, but Kit is thinking back on the Ute, drawing on his experience with them. Now that Colorado is officially a state in the union, the Utes are eligible to become citizens, although Kit can't imagine why the country would want to have these folks as upstanding citizens of the nation. He simply wondered whether granting citizenship to the Utes might move them along the path for them to becoming civilized residents of the country.

"Once the field was finally plowed, no thanks to most of the Utah men, I expected them to plant the seeds we've given them," Meeker says. "You would have thought I asked them to commit murder. They've been huddling together, talking, singing at night. Who knows what they're up to," he observes. "Seeds are still sitting right where I put them. I tell you, when those men come up to my door, I'm scared. 'Course, I don't tell my wife, but they honest-to-goodness scare me."

"What did you tell Thornburg?" Kit asks, knowing the military man is fanatical about killing Indians. Has been ever since he came to the West. Keeps a scrapbook of his killing. For what, Kit can only imagine....He doesn't like the Indians either—but to keep a scrapbook? That's obsessive.

"I've got my copy of the letter here," Meeker says, pulling it from an interior coat pocket. He reads the contents of his correspondence: "'The Utahs under my care are consistently disobedient. One of them, the chief, assaulted me as I was teaching him to plow, injuring me badly. I need your aid posthaste.'"

"And did the good captain respond?"

Meeker nods. "The military is on their way as we speak."

"Do the Utes know of your correspondence?" Kit asks.

Meeker shakes his head. No.

Kit has heard enough. This man is not going to be successful, he believes. When he offers to speak with Ahwatt, Meeker says, "Oh, he's gone."

"Gone?"

Meeker seems surprised. "Doesn't matter," he replies. "Talk with any of them and you get the same response."

When Kit presses further, Meeker finally informs him that Ahwatt and a few others had gone north to hunt.

"Up north? Why go there?"

"I don't know, and frankly, I don't care," Meeker says.

He shows Kit to the door.

"How about Chaska? I didn't see her when I arrived," Kit says.

"The woman?" Meeker asks. "Don't lower yourself to such a standard, son. She's worthless."

Kit holds his tongue, knowing nothing he can say will put Chaska on Meeker's good side. He wonders himself if Meeker might be right. Was Chaska worthless? As much as Kit has come to despise the Ute, he would always have a soft spot for Chaska. Although that soft spot was dwindling in size.

***

"Meeker says the military is on its way now," Chaska tells Kit.

"Kaib and Ahwatt are not here on the reservation just now, but you are welcome to sit with me as a brother."

"They out in Rawlins these days?" Kit asks, but Chaska raises her shoulders, saying she doesn't know. "Did Ahwatt go to talk with the captain?" Kit asks as nonchalantly as possible.

Chaska looks up at him, quickly meeting his eyes. *She doesn't realize their intent,* Kit thinks. They've gone off to war and left her in the dark to keep her safe. "You know they can't leave to hunt," Kit says quietly.

"Look at me," Chaska replies. "Although I'm an old woman now, I'm skin and bones. We have nothing to eat. All last winter Father Meeker limited our food supply, saying we were ungrateful; he wouldn't cow tow to us as the other agents had. We can't take much more," she adds.

Kit stares at her. "What does that mean, Chaska? Is that a threat?"

"We don't know what to do, Kit! Many of our babies have died from malnutrition. Most of the other elders allowed themselves to die this past winter. If something doesn't change this winter…I'm next."

Chapter 19

Battle at White River,
(September, 1879)

I miss the quiet of the forest. The tall pine trees have been like family to me: secure, safe, grounded. All I used to hear was the *swish* of the treetops in the wind. No more. Now, the lodge pole pines that used to grow prominently around our camp is just open field. No matter what I did, the merikac were going to come. They were going to take it away.

Ahwatt drags me from my thoughts. He's riding toward me, Luksi in a fast trot. The horse's eyes are wild…I can feel the urgency radiating from him. When Ahwatt pulls up, he says, "I've been to talk with Thornburg. They are camped within the reservation."

"But they know that's not allowed! Merikac cannot be here…."

"He knows. He told me there isn't any water running outside the boundary, so he told me 'Mind your tribe, and I'll mind my men.' Prepare for war, Chaska," he says.

He kicks Luksi gently in his barrel. I turn and run as fast as my legs will go, heading to camp while he gathers the men. I reach Chava's teepee just as her husband is heading out to prepare for the war Ahwatt has assured us is coming. His face is determined. With a brief glance my way, he tells me all I need to know: He and the other men are capable of winning this fight.

I open the flap of Chava's teepee and lock eyes with my daughter. She is cradling little Kam in her arms.

"Is it bad?" she asks.

"Yes, this is it, Chava," I say. "Help me to move the women and elders to a safe location…Be careful not to raise Meeker's suspicions!"

"Hmph," she snorts. "That shouldn't be a problem. If we aren't digging ditches, he couldn't care less about us."

"Leave the teepees. Tell the women to bring what they can carry. We'll head south until the fight is over."

I watch as she heads out, carrying Kam easily in one arm. Turning in the other direction, I see Fred Shepherd heading to the fields. I must remain calm. Keep my face neutral. Just another day.

"Hello, Fred…" I say calmly, waving an arm over my head back and forth. Fred never enters the circle of our camp. He's as respectful of us as he possibly can be while working around us. He waves and continues past me. I wonder if later tonight he will notice we are camping in another location. Hopefully, if he does, he won't alert Father Meeker.

***

The next morning, I wake to quiet.

I could hear the men chanting all night long, a sure sign they intend to defend us and our land to the end. Preparing in this way for battle, the men asked the Creator, Shin-Ob, for help: May this battle bring us the peace we so deserve, may it bring us safety and health, may it make our ancestors proud. The Colorado morning has a slight chill to it. It's early morning. The cold is nothing we can't handle, even in our starved state. My husband Kaib has been with the men all night. I'm curious to see what's happening, but women aren't allowed as they prepare for war. Instead, I grab the musket from my teepee and keep it with me just as Ahwatt has taught me. Walking through the tall grasses I breath in their stale odor as they slowly brown while the seasons change. The Falling Leaf moon shines high above me. It's the travelling moon, but we won't be making a trek this year. Far off, I see Ahwatt on foot, walking to the ridge that overlooks the White River valley; he is followed by our other men. None ride their horses: Our ponies have been stabled, safe from the skirmish.

I know I shouldn't be here, but my legs keep heading in the direction of the battle. Call it guilt, call it anger; I realize I fully intend to fight side by side with my brother. He hasn't seen me, and I won't interrupt him as he leads the battle. He waves his hands on either side of him, indicating to the men that they should fan out along the top of a high ravine. Once positioned, they stand perfectly still, waiting. I keep myself back from them, hoping I don't attract their attention. I've never done this before, but they are well versed in keeping trespassers from our land.

I can't see into the long ravine that leads to the river where the merikac army is apparently advancing, but I see our men become more alert. From my position, I hear Ahwatt speak. "Let us see if they have come to talk," he cautions. Thornton should know we don't appreciate a full military company advancing in our direction. It can only mean war. Then again, from what Kit has told me, this man lives to kill us.

"Aim for the horses as they come into view," Ahwatt tells the men.

I gasp. What? No! How can they shoot the horses? To save them from being injured?

I wish I could run to Ahwatt, but he knows what he's doing....I know, as the men know; we have tried everything possible to find peace with the Americans. Again, our treaty has been broken, as have all the others. They have invaded our sovereign nation by disobeying our requests that they camp some place other than on our land.

“I see them,” says Ahwatt calmly. “Wait for more horses to come into view!” he commands.

I start counting our numbers. Nearly a hundred of our men stand atop the precipice. When Ahwatt had gone to talk with Thornburg, he said more than two hundred military men had camped along the White River.

I sense the men’s restlessness stationed above the ravine, ready to battle. I’m shaking with fear, or maybe anger at what we need to do. Why can’t the merikac follow their own treaties? What will it cost us?

A single gunshot rings out, echoing down into the valley, shattering the morning stillness. Thornburg’s troops. From my vantage point, I did not see any of our men raise their weapon. Ahwatt and the others look from one to the next; I take the opportunity to scramble into a small stand of Gambel oak trees near our men. A sudden barrage of gunshots slice through the once silent morning. Our men stand at the edge of the precipice, apparently in full view of the enemy, calmly shooting down into the canyon. The uproar of gunfire is earsplitting. Where once there was a nervous, energy and foreboding silence, now there is only upheaval.

My heart beats hard; so hard it feels as though I'm being pushed up from my position where I lie on the ground. I can feel it beating, my head pulsing. I've never been this close to battle! I can take only rapid, frantic breaths, my hands gripping oak roots and dirt and the musket....

Our men begin falling. Up and down the line. No! This can't be! I see one after another lose the battle they are fighting. But the Americans trespassed on our land! *They* made the mistake of breaking the treaty. Why are *we* dying from it?

Out of the corner of my eye, I glimpse military wagons travelling up a distant hill to the west of the canyon. Before I can wonder why the men in the ravine didn't use this incline to their advantage, I look to Ahwatt. He's in his element: He too has seen the wagons and has collected several men closest to him to fend them off. Kaib is with them. I suck in my breath. *Please, be careful*. I could go with them. Instead, I crouch low and make my way to the edge of the precipice that overlooks the ravine.

Several of our men are running toward the fighting from the direction of our camp. Why hadn't they been here, at the ravine, fighting to keep our land? Blood streaks their hands and faces. They run right up to Ahwatt, saying, "Meeker and his men are dead."

Meeker…dead? I can't believe what I've heard. How will killing an Indian Agent help us? I grow dizzy with terror. Surely, Ahwatt didn't give an order to kill Meeker and all his men. The slaughter must have been a singular act of aggression…of uncontrollable anger! Still, I can't lie. I've wanted to hurt Meeker too. Many times.

I hadn't realized, but bullets are flying past me. My surprise creeps up from my knees. The darkness approaches my eyes. With knees weak, I fall to the ground.

***

I must have passed out. When I come to, I see my brother, gun sighted. He fires downward. Then something strange happens. His body lurches backward. The rifle he holds lowers to his side. Then my brother stands doubled over at his waist, his free hand moving toward his chest. Staggering backward, his heel catches on a stump. His large body falls backward, his back smashing to the ground, his head striking the ground then bouncing sharply upward at the force of the fall.

"Ahwatt!" I scream, lifting myself up and running to him.

My brother eyes me through pupils that aren't looking straight on. His mouth is open, he huffs out hot, heavy breath. My eyes go to his chest, redness oozing from a hole, growing discolored and red on his bare chest. Blood mixes with the paint, drawing rivulets through the pigmentation and dripping down to the ground.

I reach for his hand. Ahwatt holds my eyes. "We'll win, Chaska. Don't worry." He holds my eyes until his hand goes limp.

I jump up to run and grab my musket. I reach the edge of the ravine to survey the progress. Military horses lie on the ground, men too. A few army soldiers are climbing hand over fist; our men pick them off one by one. A man is yelling orders to those still alive below us. Thornburg. He's not far from me.

I aim and shoot.

It's hard to tell whether my bullet fells him. But the commander mimics my brother's death dance, his eyes seemingly surprised, his body stumbling backward, his hand holding his stomach.

I feel it in my heart. This time, it's over for us.

Epilogue

Where Do I Go from Here? (1880)

Through a blizzard of snow and ice, I can barely make out one Indian from another, but all carry a sadness through the frigid temperatures. The last of the Utes walk single file by my vantage point along the ridge where they once killed our Army. Their clothes are in tatters. It's been weeks since any sort of annuity has come their way after what they've done. All walk to their new home. Utah. My intention was to kill these people off, but now I'm questioning my actions. They aren't the horrible savages' others say they are. Instead, for the first time in a long time, I'm seeing them as people, families.

Chaska was under the impression that she and I could work out a plan for peace. I truly believe that. The hope she showed in 1868 when we signed the treaty! I remember her anxiety—but there also was hope. Now, I don't see it on her face. She looks blankly out of dead eyes, defeated. Her daughters walk beside her; one on either side, looking just as haggard, just as lost. Kaib has already passed me, riding with his head held high, stoic. I know he saw me but refused to look my direction.

And why should she be hopeful? The American military trespassed on the Utes' sovereign, independent nation—and the Ute fought back. Isn't that what any nation would do to gain the respect of their enemy? One nation should understand the autonomy of another nation. Right?

But we Americans have forgotten from whence we came. Our forefathers left their homelands amidst religious persecution, seeking to be seen for themselves, to be allowed to practice their ways. Even now, homesteaders carry relics of their culture with them—pianos to play the hymns of their fathers. Cookware. Stoves to maintain their cultural meals. Decor to observe their holidays. How are we so different from Chaska's tribe?

I don't know if these native people can ever practice their culture again. It may be lost wholly when they move to their new reservation. No roaming, no hunting, no materials with which to practice the traditions of their heritage—basket weaving, beading, tanning hides. The nation's culture may be gone, and no one seems to care. These women and men who were once friends of mine, who let me survive when I should have died. Chaska kneeled by my side while I was suffering, she helped me unconditionally.

Even their walking sounds hopeless. Shuffling, none of them picking up their feet. None of them actually taking a *step*.

What is America's destiny anyway? A mindset we've created in a self-centered expectation. Entitled to it, are we? But what if it hurts as we move further along? Should the destiny of this country and countrymen be a priority over another people's destiny? And, even more importantly, at least to me: What have I done to cause this suffering passing before my eyes?

All any of us wants is to raise our family in peace. And yet my need to kill has removed an entire culture of people who also had a destiny. Why did ours come before theirs?

Why couldn't we both get what we wanted rather than one nation obliterating the other?

As I watch the last of the Utes leave this place, I fall down on one knee. Chaska looks to me, her eyes are soft, not angry.

Acknowledgements

There are so many people who have helped to create this book. I am indebted to them for the support and their knowledge. Editor William Oppenheimer has provided so many wonderful edits and called me out when I was telling and not showing. Thank you.

Laura Dent, my writing coach extraordinaire, truly guided me in creating the character of Kit Carson when I couldn't figure out how to tell the American side of the story. This book would not be what it is today without your amazing and patient guidance.

My wonderful friend Tookumseetch Kochampanasken to whom I sought help that she shared along the way. I am honored that you would share the wonderful stories and photos of your family.

My family, especially my children and husband allowed me to sit at the kitchen table and write.

My sisters Kelly Libolt and Susan Schaeffer have supported in this endeavor.

To my friend Chanda Chatham who has been cheering me from the sidelines the whole time. And to Lisa Hatfield, my fellow debut book writer, who has been on this journey with me while taking her own.

Casey BradleyGent, Snowshoe Studios for the lovely photos she took including the author dustcover photo.

Finally, my beautiful mother Geraldine Bernadette. I miss you so much every day, but I cherish all the time we got with you.

Afterword

The American government signed then proceeded to ignore treaty upon treaty with the Ute Nation. Thankfully, their culture did not die. Instead, there are bands of the Ute nation living on and off three main reservations in the west.

According to the Ute Indian Tribe, (http://utetribe.com), "The Utes have a tribal membership of 2,970 and over half of its membership lives on the Reservation. They operate their own tribal government and oversee approximately 1.3 million acres of trust land." In the Northern Utah region of Fort Duchesne. Three bands of Ute make up the tribe including the Whiteriver, Uncompaghre and Uintah.

The Ute Mountain Ute Tribe lives in the southwest corner of Colorado with 575,000 contiguous acres the tribe boasts 2,134 enrolled members who live on and off the reservation.

The Southern Ute Indian Tribe owns 307,838 acres and with 1,510 enrolled members is located south and east of Durango.

To learn more, consider reading and visiting the following:

The Southern Ute Drum newspaper, www.sudrum.com.

Southern Ute Cultural Center and Museum, southernutemusuem.org, museum@southernute-nsn.gov.

Ute Indian Museum, 17253 Chipeta Rd., Montrose, CO, Ute Indian Museum | History Colorado

Home » Tribalradio.org

Whether you love him, hate him, or are just learning the nuances of the man named Kit Carson, one thing is clear: he was complicit in subjugating the Utes.

To learn more about Kit Carson consider the following:

Kit Carson Home and Museum - Taos, NM (kitcarsonmuseum.org).

Fort Garland Museum & Cultural Center | History Colorado,
History Colorado Center | History Colorado

A full bibliography for this book may be found on my website, AlliCarterClose.com. Below are a few of the books and authors that made this journey so educational, providing stories and facts that made me feel as though I could really know….

These include An indigenous people's history of the United States by Dunbar-Ortiz, The history of the Southern Ute Indian by Hafen, Mayfield and Smith, Bayou Salade: The story of South Park by Simmons, Indian sign language by Tompkins, A short dictionary of the Southern Ute Language by Goss, The Writer's guide to horses: The author's essential illustrated reference to all thing equine by Kincaid, How Indian Relay works by the Independent Lens, and Kit Carson's autobiography by Carson and Quaife.

About the author

Alli Carter Close lives in the shadow of Pikes Peak in Colorado with her husband, two children, and four dogs. This is her first novel.

Made in the USA
Middletown, DE
10 January 2022